Just
One
Summer

Lynn Stevens

For Bean

CHAPTER ONE

Nobody sane should ever be up at eight on a Saturday morning. Especially not when said person stayed up until three a.m. for a horror movie marathon with her best friends Ivy and Nena. So totally worth it though.

What a waste of a Saturday. I could be sleeping, or bungee jumping, or sleeping, or ziplining, or sleeping instead of starting a job I didn't want in the first place.

I bit back a yawn as I smoothed the wrinkled turquoise polo, the required uniform for Mountain View Resort employees. Taking a deep breath to steady the waves in my stomach, I knocked on the door to room four-oh-two three times, as instructed, and squeezed my clipboard against my chest.

What had my father been thinking bringing this guy to Branson? For the last few years, I'd overheard Dad lamenting to my brother about how the shows didn't make enough money and the profits from the resort disappeared into the theater. If Dad wanted to revive that dump, he'd need someone to sell out every performance. I had serious doubts about his choice. Another reason I was in the doghouse.

I lifted my fist to hammer the door a second time when it flew open.

A wet torso greeted me, and a hint of the hotel's jasmine soap drifted from the room. My gaze followed water dripping down tanned pecs and over the only real six-pack I'd ever seen as it disappeared into the thick hotel towel wrapped around his waist. *Wow.* My face burned hotter than the coffee I'd slammed earlier, and I forced my head up to meet the gaze of The Gracin Ford, celebrity bad boy and former member of Accentuate, a one-hit wonder boy band.

Gracin's manscaped eyebrows arched as bright blue eyes took a circuit over my body. My skin tingled all over in response to his gaze.

Sadly, he had to open his mouth. "Not my type, but thanks."

Then he slammed the door in my face.

What? That... that... that son of a bitch! I punched the door three times, fully prepared to give this egotistical asshole a piece of my mind. Meanwhile, my father's lecture from half an hour ago echoed between my ears: "If you want to go to U of N in the fall, you work for me this summer to pay me back for the damage to the Mercedes. Don't, and you can go to Southern Community like your brother did." I counted to thirty, trying and failing to calm myself while I waited for his highness.

The door swung in. At least this time, he'd had the decency to put on a pair of khaki shorts and a t-shirt. His gaze shifted over me once more, and I tried not to squirm, but blue eyes gave me the creeps. And brought back memories I'd rather pretend didn't exist.

"What now?" he asked. If he was even slightly miffed, he didn't show it. The cool nonchalance in his voice didn't stop my temper from shooting toward the atmosphere.

I dug my nails into the back of the clipboard and smiled my best smile. "Hi, Mr. Ford. I'm Carly Reynolds, your ... personal assistant. Your father provided us with a detailed itinerary of your day-to-day–"

"Let me see it," he said, leaning his shoulder against the door jam.

I handed it over, keeping the tremor in my hands at bay. Personal assistant my ass, more like his errand bitch. If he hadn't fired his previous P.A., I could be lounging by the pool as a lifeguard or cleaning rooms or checking guests at the front desk. Instead, I had to spend my summer following every whim of a twenty-year-old has-been. As he took the itinerary, his eyebrows furrowed at something else. Before my hand could drop back to my side, he snatched it and tugged at the tie holding the leather cuff covering my wrist.

His eyebrows lifted again and amusement danced across his full lips. "Nice tat. Why hide it?"

"Who says I'm hiding it?" He let go of my hand, and I quickly retied the cuff over the small trinity knot tattoo on my wrist. It had only been two weeks since I'd gotten inked, but Mom and Dad hadn't noticed. Yet. I crossed my arms and bit the inside of my upper lip. As much as I didn't want to be here, I also didn't want to go to Southern Community. Keeping my mouth shut was kind of required if I wanted to go to Nashville in the fall.

Gracin nodded and refocused on the itinerary. He flipped the paper, shaking his head. "According to this, you're supposed to take me to breakfast every morning at eight so we can discuss the day's schedule." He handed the clipboard back to me. "I'm assuming that's why you're here now."

"Yep."

He sighed. "Let me get my shoes. No doubt the big kahuna will be expecting me." He moved into the room and I reached out to hold the door open. "I'll get a more realistic schedule to you."

"Realistic?" I asked as he slipped on a pair of boat shoes and a Rolex that could pay for half a semester at U of N or the entire two years at Southern Community.

"Yeah, that's clearly the schedule Dad wants me to keep. Not even close to reality." Gracin stepped into the hallway, patting his pocket. He groaned and turned to stop the door from shutting completely, but it was too late. He fell forward, letting his forehead thunk against the thick wood. "You wouldn't happen to have a key to my room, would you?"

"No, but we can get one from the front desk after breakfast. You're moving into one of the cabins today anyway." I shrugged because it wasn't that big of a deal. "No worries."

Gracin laughed, but there wasn't any humor to it. "Do me a favor. Keep this key thing between us, okay? The last thing I need is to hear how irresponsible I am. Again."

I held back the scoff and the sarcastic comment that would normally shoot from my mouth in record speed. Especially since I'd heard the same lecture more times than

I could count. "Yeah, okay. But we have to go now, or you're going to have to hear how irresponsible *I* am."

"Well, I won't say anything about the tat in that case." Gracin's smile showed his Hollywood white teeth.

We were half way between his room and the elevator when his cell rang. I tried to ignore his half of the conversation, but when you're alone with someone, it's hard not to listen.

"Hey, babe." Pause. "Yeah, I had a great time too."

Another pause. Gracin laughed, clutching his hand against his chest.

"Probably best they didn't catch us. Photographic evidence and all."

Another pause when we got to the elevator. Gracin's face turned from California tan to the shade of a bruised red pepper.

"You didn't? Please tell me you didn't."

I wanted to lean closer to hear what the person on the other end had done. Celebrity drama and all. I didn't seek it out, but that didn't stop me from reading the headlines when they popped up on my computer.

After I pushed the button for the elevator, we stood side by side. Gracin's fingers tightened around the phone. I could hear a female voice coming from his speaker but not what she said. Gracin slapped the mirrored doors.

Housekeeping'll love that.

The doors dinged open as Gracin's fist soared toward them, and he threw himself into the elevator. He managed not to fall, but it was so hard not to laugh.

"Next time you talk to that jackass, tell him you were just another one-night stand."

Wow. I'd somehow managed to keep my expression neutral when he fell into the elevator, but my mortification couldn't be hidden.

He stared at me in the mirror. "There goes hiding my lack of responsibility today," he said in a calm voice that didn't match the fury from a moment ago.

I kept my mouth shut despite the thoughts running through my head and held his mirrored gaze. Both took supreme battles of will. I thought only one thing: U of N. Nothing was going to keep me from going to Nashville.

Gracin tilted his head. His eyebrows sagged as he opened his mouth. A beep sounded from his phone, distracting him from whatever he was about to say. He shook his head at the screen and then handed it to me. "Here. Fair warning before Hurricane Albert leashes his wrath on me."

I wasn't interested in getting caught up in his drama, but curiosity got the best of me and I glanced at the image on the screen. It wasn't anything major. A beautiful girl with bright brown eyes and obviously dyed red hair kissed a smiling Gracin on the cheek. It was pretty clear they were in a bar when this was taken. Several empty beer bottles sat on the table in front of them.

"A hot chick took a photo of you guys in a bar?" I handed the phone back. "Big deal."

"The 'deal' is she sold it to a tabloid." Gracin shoved the phone into his pocket. He didn't spare me a glimpse, even in the mirror. "I can see the headlines already: 'Gracin Ford

Falls Off the Wagon.'" Finally, he faced me. "Except I didn't. I've been sober for almost a year. None of those empties were mine. Not that anybody will believe me. Especially King Albert."

"Oh."

"Yeah, 'oh.'"

I didn't say anything, but the heat burning the tips of my ears was enough.

The elevator opened to the lobby. Gracin motioned me out first and followed me to the private dining room. Dad sat at the head of the table in the middle of the room. My mother sat to his right, and a gray-haired man with a stringy comb-over sat on his left. His extensive lack of hair didn't stop Albert Ford from trying. My older brother, Luke, sat next to three empty seats for me, Gracin, and my little sister, Miranda. Quite the family affair.

"Carly, I'm glad you made it," Dad said, adding a fake laugh at the end. To anyone else, it might've appeared teasing. I knew better. Dad was not happy we were a minute late. Of course, when it came to me, he wouldn't have been happy had I been two minutes early either. My father was the consummate politician around here. He ruled more like a dictator, but was JFK when guests were around. "I thought you were going to be late."

"That's my fault, Mr. Reynolds," Gracin said. He threw out a hundred-watt smile.

I fought to roll my eyes. *At least he's taking the hit for me.*

"Carly rushed me out the door, then let it close before I remembered to grab my key."

And under the bus I go. Thanks, asshat.

Dad stared through me with his laser pointer green eyes. "Well, Carly, I suggest you head to the front desk and get another. While you're there, make sure housekeeping stays out of his room until this evening when the cabin is ready."

"Yes, sir." I let my head drop in good girl compliance, catching the laughing eyes of my brother. We both inherited Dad's light brown hair, but Luke lucked out getting Dad's eyes. Unfortunately, he used them to taunt me at every turn, which only served to remind me who was the chosen one in the Reynolds family. Hint, his name began with an L.

Gracin made his way toward the buffet spread. He piled fresh fruit on his plate, winking at me. I shuddered as I freed myself from the room. Guys who winked were just plain creepy.

My last summer before heading off to college was going to be the worst one of my life. All because of a little dent in a Mercedes. Smashing.

∞ ∞ ∞

Mountain View Resort had been in the family for four generations. My great-grandfather added a nearby lakefront property and built ten cabins along the water to lure anglers and gamesmen to the resort. When the boom hit Branson, my grandfather rehabbed the entire hotel and added ten more cabins, modernizing them as family getaways. Before he handed the reins over to my father, he bought a theater on the main drag away from the lakefront resort. Dad should've sold it years ago, but he held on even though the theater ran in the red every season. Pop star Gracin Ford's show was a last-ditch effort to keep from putting the theater on the market. Dad hoped a younger performer would draw in the younger, not country crowd. So far, it seemed to work. The first three weeks of Gracin's show had been sold out by the second week of May.

"Hi, Carly." Miranda bounced toward me wearing too much makeup for a fourteen-year-old. "So, what's he like?"

"Who?" I asked even though I knew. I just wanted to see her squirm. She'd been one of the more vocal people about the pop star's impending arrival. Along with my mother anyway. Bringing in someone who graced the cover of Teeny Boopers magazine made Mom act like she stepped up a rung on the Branson's finest ladder.

"Duh, Gracin Ford!" She smiled with that dreamy expression girls get around celebrities. I didn't get it, but whatever. "I used to love Accentuate. I still know every word to *Surrender 2 Me*."

"God, Meerkat, you were like seven when it came out." I shuddered at the image of my younger sister swooning over Gracin Ford when she was little.

"I was nine," Miranda sighed, her dreamy expression not wiped away by my words. "I had that song on repeat for a month straight."

"So did Luke, not that he'd let anyone know." I snickered, remembering the time I walked into his room as he danced and sang into Miranda's toy microphone.

"You never did answer me. What's he really like?"

"He's a class A jerk. Don't expect him to be anything

more or you'll be disappointed." I picked at the chip on the corner of my nail. "And he's a dumbass. He locked his key in his room." I glanced over Miranda's shoulder to the desk clerk of the month. "Hailey, can you get me another one?"

Hailey's eyes widened before dropping her gaze and typing on the computer.

Great. Either Gracin was behind me or my father was. Regardless, I was totally screwed.

I turned around and stepped back into the oak counter, an original at Mountain View. Albert Ford glared at me beneath a scowl rivaling any Principal Gibbons had thrown my way. And that was saying something. Gracin's father crossed his arms and sneered as he gave me the once over.

"Mr. Ford, is there something I can help you with?" I asked with added fake enthusiasm. If there was one thing my father had taught me, it was never let them see you sweat. No matter how cliché that advice was, it had merit. Miranda skirted around me in a wide arc, avoiding Albert's death stare. Traitor couldn't take the heat.

"Yes, Ms. Reynolds. You could not refer to my son as a dumbass," he snapped. He smiled suddenly and dropped his arms. "No matter how accurate that assessment may be."

Hailey snorted behind me while I matched his grin. "No problem."

"If you don't mind, could you get a cab ready? I have a flight to catch back to L.A." He bobbed his head back and forth. "In a roundabout way, at least."

"Sure." I reached over the counter and dialed the best cab company in town. "What time do you need them here?"

"An hour. That will give me plenty of time." Albert nodded before retreating toward the dining room.

Hailey sighed in relief as soon as I hung up with the cab company. "I thought you were done for when I saw him standing there."

I smirked. I'd been in a lot of trouble over the years, and getting out of it was one of my specialties. My father only knew a third of the things I'd done. Thank God. My 4.0 GPA helped.

"I had a huge crush on Jay," Hailey said, her eyes glazing over as she mentioned Accentuate's golden boy. Jay Edison was the son of the band's original manager, and the entire purpose of its existence. Once he left for a failed solo career, the band was done after three years, and the rest of the guys were left on their own. Gracin was the only one who stayed in the business, albeit on a course worse than Jay's.

My phone vibrated against my leg. I dug it out from beneath my keys, lip balm, and wallet. The annoying tiny blue light flashed a text message. I typed in my password wrong twice before getting it right and opened the text. It wasn't a number in my contact list, but it didn't take long before I figured out who'd sent it.

Take my set clothes to the cleaners. They are in a trunk in my dressing room. I'll text you more information later and email you an updated and accurate itinerary. ~G

Great, Gracin had my number. For once, I looked forward to Monday morning and school. Even if it was the last week. Even if it was only three measly days. Oh, how the mighty have fallen.

CHAPTER TWO

The best part about the rest of my weekend: no Gracin Ford. At least, not in the flesh. The worst part: he spent every minute texting me useless orders. Sunday night after I'd already left the theater, he sent a text reminding me to lock the door to his dressing room.

I responded, *Forgot. Your fangirls waited outside. I told them to go on in.*

Great, they'll just steal my wardrobe. Not like I need clothes onstage, he texted a second later.

Unfortunately, I made a really dumb mistake in my response. *Guess I shouldn't sell your undies on eBay then?*

Who says I wear any?

I didn't send anything back. It was just an invitation to say something stupid I was sure Gracin would tell or, worse, show my father. Maybe Dad was right, being Gracin's P.A. would teach me something, like keeping my mouth shut. Not sure I liked this plan. Changing my digits crossed my mind more than once.

Monday morning, Mom shuffled around the kitchen

turning her nasty brew into an even nastier latte. I ate my toast slathered in butter and blackberry jam, ignoring the vibrating phone beside me.

"Carly, could you please tell Ivy and Nena to stop texting you so early." Mom pressed the back of her hand to her forehead. "It's giving me a headache."

"Then tell Dad not to give my number out, 'cause it's not them. It's Gracin." Jam fell onto my pinky. I lifted my hand to lick it off, but I didn't catch it before it hit the leather band on my wrist.

"Honey, you should really call him Mr. Ford out of respect. He's our guest." She slammed her mug on the table and shrieked. "What is *that*?"

I followed her finger to the tat on my wrist. *Shit.*

"Please tell me you were just doodling? Or that it's temporary."

"Um…" Looking Mom in the eye, totally not an option.

"How could you deface yourself, Carly? Your body's a temple not a canvas!" She fell into the chair beside me and took my hand, tracing her finger over the trinity knot. "What did I do to fail you this way? Did I not teach you anything?"

Sure, Mom. It's okay to get a nose job and face lift, but God forbid I get a tattoo that means something. Three knots linked represented my two best friends and me. They were always teasing me about being such as sap. In a way, they were right. The tat represented something I wanted to hold onto forever. In hindsight, I should've gotten it in a less conspicuous location.

Mom stood abruptly, mumbling under her breath how she needed to lie down. Nena honked outside, and I put my plate in the sink, grabbing my bag on my way out the door. As usual, I'd disappointed my mother.

∞ ∞ ∞

I started my final three days at Branson North High. Hallelujah. High school wasn't bad, but it wasn't great either. I did enough to pad my college application and get into U of N.

The day I got the acceptance, I rubbed it in Luke's face. Unfortunately, Dad didn't react like I'd hoped. U of N had been his dream school, but he didn't get in. Neither did Luke. I applied on a whim just to see what would happen, and voila. Sure, Dad said he was proud of me and all, but it didn't *feel* like he was. It was more like he couldn't believe admission passed over his perfect son for his less-than-perfect daughter. Problem was I had no clue what to major in, although business was most likely. If Luke refused to take over the resort, I'd be expected to. Actually, I kind of wanted to run the place. I loved the old resort and the cabins, but I didn't want to deal with the theater. That place was a money pit with red velvet seats that were as faded as the so-called stars who performed on the stage.

I strolled into the building, enjoying the smell of impending freedom, when my phone vibrated in my pocket. I pulled it out, not at all surprised to see a text from Gracin.

I'm out of grapefruit. Bring some over.

No "please." No "would you be so kind." No nothing. I

started to shove the phone back into my pocket when it buzzed again.

Carly, I know you're awake. Don't ignore me.

What an asshole. I hurried to the nearest restroom and called his number.

"Where's my grapefruit?" he answered. His voice had that just woke up huskiness to it. Even someone immune to his charms and his good looks would swoon at that sound.

"Probably in produce showing the tangerines size does matter."

The sexy huskiness disappeared. "And how long will it take you to go to the store? I need more than coffee in the morning. If this stuff you bought even qualifies as coffee."

I ignored the jab at the local roasting company. "About seven to eight hours."

Gracin's tone stayed even. "Why is that?"

"I'm not home. Last week of high school and all. Kinda don't want to miss it." I drummed my fingers against the metal towel dispenser. "I'm not skipping to get grapefruit."

"Wait a minute. You're still in high school?" His shock reverberated down my spine.

A smile slipped onto my face. "Yes, your highness, for three whole days."

"Oh." Crickets couldn't fill the silence, although that would've made me grin even more.

"That's all you've got?" I asked when he still hadn't said anything. The warning bell rang in the hallways, echoing into the empty restroom.

"I'll text you if I need anything else." Then he was gone.

True to his word, whenever I checked my phone between classes, there were one or two texts. All of them had to do with stocking his pantry or getting better towels. Like there was anything wrong with our towels. Dad didn't skimp on stuff like that. He wanted our guests to have quality stays so they'd come back to us and not one of the corporate-owned resorts taking over the area.

By lunchtime though, I was fed up.

"What're you complaining about, Carly?" Nena dipped her fry into enough ranch dressing to cover two salads. She raised her over-plucked eyebrows at me, widening those dark brown eyes until she resembled a lovesick puppy. "You get to spend all summer doing whatever Gracin Ford wants."

"Yeah, we know what you'd be doing in her place, Nee," Ivy said. She pushed Nena's shoulder hard enough for Nena to drop her fry.

Ivy, Nena, and I had been best friends since sixth grade. We fit together like Legos. Each of us fell into a stereotype, and none of us totally suited them. Nena was the hot one. She played a good game, but the truth was she held onto her virginity like it was the Holy Grail. It seemed unorthodox in this day and age, but I loved her even more for it. No matter how many guys claimed they'd gotten down with her, Nena would simply smile and leave it a mystery. The truth was enough for her.

"More like you, Ivy. Ride 'em like a bronco." Nena pushed back. They started laughing like cartoon hyenas.

On the other side of the coin was Ivy. Her quiet demeanor fooled most people, but she loved to drink and she loved guys. Her big hazel eyes and strawberry blonde hair combined with her innocence made her the most unlikely sex-fiend on the planet. Ivy was picky, but once she set her sights on a guy, she let her mojo work. If she ever wrote a book of her conquests, it'd be longer than *War and Peace*.

"Seriously, Carly, you should loosen up. It's not Golf-A-Round, but it's still a job." Ivy popped a chicken nugget into her mouth and grinned.

I was the typical bad girl. Up until Friday, my purple hair, my black-lined eyes, and studded leather anything was the norm. Basically, everything that would irritate my father. Yet, out of the three of us, I pulled down straight A's and ranked third in our class. Just because I liked to look outrageous, and sometimes be outrageous, didn't mean I was stupid or lazy. Nope, it meant I was a little bit crazy. I liked crazy. Things were more fun when crazy was involved.

"Yeah, a job I will make no money at." I crossed my arms and leaned against the back of my chair.

"And whose fault is that?" Nena matched my pose. "I told you to designate a driver."

I held back the snort. And it wasn't easy. My gaze slid toward Ivy who glanced away quicker than a prairie dog into his hole. Nena was clueless about what had really happened. Had I been drinking? Yep, I was toasted. Was I driving? Nope, my designated driver was. I was just too drunk to realize Ivy had crossed the line of sobriety into inebriation.

"Anyway—" I'd avoided telling anyone what had really happened Prom night, and I wasn't about to start spilling the beans. I'd taken the heat, and, once again, Dad managed to bail me out. It helped that his head of security had pull with the sheriff's department. "—we've worked at Golf-A-Round every summer together. This was supposed to be our swan song."

"You're so sentimental. We'll have time together." Ivy reached out and put her hand on my arm. "Come the end of August, we won't even have that."

"I know," I muttered. Nena was headed to a small Christian college in Kansas, while Ivy was going to Southeast Missouri State. "I just wanted our last summer to be fun. Memorable even."

"It will be. We have to make the best of it, that's all." Nena squeezed my arm and let go as my phone vibrated again.

It buzzed four more times before I could read the first text.

I need my dressing room stocked with bottled water, not the water cooler. Somebody could slip something inside a water cooler.

When you get the grapefruit, get me two cases of water.

Make it three cases. And don't get generic, backwoods water. Don't forget the receipt.

Add a loaf of nine-grain bread. Do they have that here?

If they have Perrier, get that too.

I read each text twice, growing angrier after each word. Who did this guy think he was?

Nena waved her hand in front of my face. "Carly, are you okay?"

"Yeah, it looks like you lost your place at U of N or something," Ivy added.

Nena scoffed, "That's probably the one thing that would piss her off this bad."

"Well, or her dad." Ivy nibbled on another nugget.

The mention of my father almost stopped me. Almost. I'd dealt with his screaming, his anger, his absolute disappointment in me enough over the years. I could deal with it again. Even if Gracin fired me. I slammed my thumb into the touch screen to dial Gracin's number.

"Hel-"

"Who the hell do you think you are?" I asked, my voice rising enough that the tables around us stopped to listen. "No, don't answer that. I'll tell you. You think Branson is some hick town with no class and no taste. You think you're doing us a favor by simply being here. Well, let me tell you something, buddy, you need us as much as we need you. So stop with the ridiculous condescending demands and get over yourself." I didn't take a single breath during my tirade so, by the end, it sounded soft and less mean. My teeth ground against one another as I waited for his response. Gracin could've hung up for all I knew, but something told me that wasn't his style. "Well?"

"Are you done?" he asked, calmer than he should be after being waylaid by my verbal tidal wave.

"I'm sure I could come up with a few more things, but I'm in school," I said. The list of his transgressions grew in my head.

"What's it like?" he asked softly.

Talk about a slap in the face. That was one question I never expected. "What?"

After a couple of downbeats, he sighed heavily into the

speaker. "Never mind. Forget I said anything. I promise to do my best not to text you the rest of the day, okay?"

"Okay?" I said it more as a question. Something felt off about this whole exchange. I expected a fight from the male diva, not a quick agreement. "I will call you when I'm leaving to see if you need anything else."

"I'll make a list."

The line went dead. I looked up at Nena and Ivy. They shrugged in unison, a very bad habit they'd developed over the years and one I would miss. The noise around me picked back up as someone tapped my shoulder with more force than required. I glanced over my shoulder to see Principal Gibbons glaring at me.

"You're well aware of the rule about cell phones, Miss Reynolds." He held out his hand and waited for me to drop my precious phone into his palm. When I didn't give in, he wiggled his fingers.

The argumentative side of me kicked in. "Mr. Gibbons, the cell phone rule applies to the time during class periods. If I remember correctly, the student handbook clearly states cell phone usage is prohibited during each educational class period, but students are allowed to utilize cell phones between classes. As this is not an educational period, cell phone usage is not prohibited."

Mr. Gibbons stared at me for a full ten seconds, and for about two of those, I thought he'd let me keep my phone. He wiggled his fingers again.

"My logic is sound," I said as I dropped the phone into his hand.

"Yes, it is, but policy is policy. One day I hope you use your powers for good and not evil." He smiled and leaned down closer. "Take a serious look at pre-law, Miss Reynolds. You would do well on the right side of it for a change. You may stop by my office after school and retrieve your phone. After all, you know where I keep them."

Mr. Gibbons nodded to my friends. Turning on his heel, he strode toward a table full of freshmen who were all huddled over someone's tablet. They were being too obvious.

"He's never going to let you live that down, is he?" Ivy wiped her hands on the wet wipe she always had with her. Germs freaked her out.

"Well, he's only got two more days to remind me about it."

Nena laughed and snorted at the same time. "Carly Reynolds, genius and criminal. You totally cemented your legacy at B North. Even the freshmen have heard about your daring break-in sophomore year. Too bad you got caught."

"It's not much of a break-in when the door to the office isn't locked," I reminded them.

The bell rang, signaling the end of our last Monday lunch period. It felt liberating and sad at the same time. I was glad the year was almost over, but it meant changes I didn't want to make. Like losing Ivy and Nena. We'd always be friends, but we all knew our lives were changing for good. We'd lose touch, eventually just being friends on whatever social media site ruled the internet ten years from now.

We strolled through the halls toward our next class, which we all had together. Wisely, Mr. Anderson had separated us at the beginning of the semester so we'd actually study during study hall. Since it was the last week of school, he didn't care where anybody sat. Senior privileges and all that jazz.

We took over the desks by the windows. While Nena and Ivy reminisced about a party from our freshman year, which coincided with Luke's senior year, I tried not to listen. Nena had gotten us invited by flirting with Todd Higgins, quarterback of the football team. Back then, she'd only started perfecting her skill, but it was already devastating for unsuspecting guys. I didn't want to tag along on their trip down memory lane. That party was the one thing from high school I'd like to believe never happened. The suspension, the detentions, all of those I would triple if I could forget that night. Unfortunately, it was burned into my brain and my heart forever, like a brand announcing my stupidity, my carelessness. If only I could find a genie in a bottle to wish it away, but my wishes never come true.

CHAPTER THREE

The photo hit the tabloids Wednesday. The ten-sentence blurb accompanying it made page twelve, and it was enough to bring some paparazzi to town. They staked out the theater, and I had to turn into a jungle adventurer to get through the bodies. If only I had a machete.

"Hey, do you work here?" one guy asked, shoving a microphone in my face.

I pushed it away only to have it replaced with another one. By the time I got to the door, they hovered around me like starving vultures. The security guards held them back.

"Have you seen Gracin Ford drunk?" another guy shouted over the din.

I should've kept my mouth shut. I should've kept on walking. Shoulda, coulda, woulda.

Spinning around, I shoved between the two security guards and held up my hands. The paparazzi stopped, holding their breath for the scoop.

"The only thing I've seen Gracin Ford drink is water."

Their cameras dropped at once.

"How do we know you're not lying?" a woman asked.

I shrugged. "Guess you don't. But the only thing you're going off of is a photo some vindictive ex-girlfriend took three months ago."

"Are you the new girlfriend?"

I laughed hard enough to clutch my side. "Not even close."

My father pulled into the parking lot, distracting the crowd. I made my getaway into the theater and turned the corner toward the stairs, slamming into Gracin. He grabbed my arms to keep me from falling. My forehead rested on his shoulder too long to be polite. Or impolite since I'd run into him. He dropped his hands and took a step back.

"I overheard what you said." His voice cracked, and he swallowed hard. He closed his eyes and inhaled slowly, opening them as he exhaled the same way. Honestly, boredom started to set in while I waited for whatever thoughts circulated in his mind. "Thank you."

"What?" My throat closed around the word, cutting off the T.

"You heard me, Carly." He stared over my shoulder toward the still open door. We stood far enough inside nobody would see us. "They'll go away in a day or two, once they realize there isn't a story here. You may have helped make it faster."

I glanced back at the crowd. Dad stood center stage, and I had no doubt he was telling the paparazzi the same thing.

"They feed off other people's misery." Gracin settled his gaze back to me. There was a sadness about him I'd not seen. "Sometimes I wonder if I'll ever get ..."

"Get what?"

He shook his head and turned around. I stared at his retreating back, waiting for the answer I'd probably never get.

∞ ∞ ∞

Graduation had seemed so far away when I was a freshman. Saturday morning, it loomed over my head like a gray cloud that may or may not rain at any given moment. Gracin had texted the night before reminding me to be at the show by six for the opening night sell-out. Like I'd forget.

Dad had an emergency at the resort, and Mom scheduled an all-important mani-pedi, which I conveniently bowed out of. Miranda volunteered to take my place much to Mom's delight. Luke sucked up and went in to help Dad even though he was supposed to work the theater later. Talk about a brownnoser. Even though they'd all be at the stadium for the ceremony, it hurt that we wouldn't go together.

Thank God Nena's dad let her pick me up. When Nena honked the horn of her fifteen-year-old Cavalier, I ran out the door carrying my black slingbacks and wearing the forbidden flip-flops. Gibbons had announced Monday that any student who showed up to graduation in flip-flops would not be allowed to participate. I thought it was stupid, but then again most of the rules the school came up with these days were stupid.

We crowded into the locker rooms behind the bleachers, draping our gowns over our arms. Once we put them on, it'd be final. No turning back. It was a terrifying thought. I wanted to get to Nashville, but I didn't want to leave my friends.

After an hour of organizing us, reorganizing us, and then yelling at us to get back in line, the teachers stopped once the band started playing, their notes wafting in the warm spring air, signaling the beginning of the end. Then Pomp and Circumstance began. One by one, we made our way to the folding chairs lined up on the track by the football field. Less than a hundred kids in my class, one of the smallest to ever graduate here, sat and pretended to listen to the boring speeches. The only common theme was "you're leaving this life behind." Tears rimmed my eyes.

Nena and Ivy were right. I was a sentimental fool.

Finally, Mr. Gibbons announced Nena's father as the speaker. This would be quick. We begged him to keep his speech to less than three minutes. Reverend Brand laughed, but he agreed.

"This is a bittersweet day for me," he began.

My phone buzzed in the pocket of my skirt. I closed my eyes, fighting off the frustration filling me. This was my day. He wouldn't do this, would he? It could only be Gracin. Everyone else was here. I slipped my hand under by gown and tugged the phone free. A few of my classmates gave me the stink-eye and I mouthed "Sorry" at them. Guilt filled me from the pit of my stomach to my esophagus, and I thought it would spew from my mouth.

I unlocked the screen as discretely as possible. Thank God, I was toward the back and at the far end of my row. If

Gibbons saw this, he'd blow a head gasket without caring who witnessed it. I tried to be stealthy, but several people around me heard the slight gasp escaping my lips after I read the text.

Congrats. ~ G

My head shot up and I turned around, searching the stands like an idiot. No way he'd show up at my graduation. My dad's balding head stood out near the middle of the bleachers. Mom sat beside him, dabbing her eyes with a hanky. She loved going all Scarlett O'Hara at times like this. Luke and Miranda sat beside her. My gaze drifted back toward Dad and the guy sitting next to him. A dirty Dodgers hat hid his golden locks, but there was no doubt it was Gracin. He cocked his head to the left and raised his hand. I nodded as a smile spread over my face.

There wasn't a reason for him to show up. He hardly knew me. In the week since I'd been his P.A., we'd probably spent a total of two hours together tops. Even then, we'd been doing a million things at once with Gracin barking orders at me in rapid-fire succession. But I appreciated his presence.

Reverend Brand kept his promise of less than three minutes. He wrapped up his speech and the senior class applauded as if he'd just won the Nobel. Nena beamed at her father and wiped the tears from beneath her eyes. Ivy squeezed her shoulder. Not for the first time in my life, I wished my last name began with a B.

Mr. Gibbons called each name. Nena walked across the stage like a runway model as she accepted her diploma. After

Ivy had hers, she bounced off the stage and waved toward her family. It felt like an eternity until he got to the R's. I smiled widely at him as we did the practiced handoff. Gibbons leaned down and squeezed my hand tight.

"One day, you'll put that phone away, Carly," he whispered.

I laughed as I made my way back to my seat. When I glanced back at the stage, Gibbons smirked and shook his head. This time he couldn't bust me for using my phone, and we both knew it.

∞ ∞ ∞

Gracin leaned back in his dressing room chair with his eyes closed and his feet crossed at the ankles a half hour before the show. His hair curled up like a flame reaching for the sky. It didn't look right on him, but this was his stage look, or so I'd been told.

"Carly, you ready for this?" he asked without opening his eyes.

I brushed the lint off the velvet jacket he would wear during a ballad. It looked more like something you'd see in Vegas than Branson. "Why wouldn't I be?"

"Everything's going to happen pretty fast. Just making sure you're ready, that's all. You don't need to bite my head off."

"I didn't bite your head off, Gracin. I asked a question." I shook the coat, causing it to snap like a towel in a locker room. "And you might as well get used to it. I ask a lot of questions."

"I'll try to remember that," he replied.

"Good. Then why'd you show up to graduation?" I hung the velvet jacket back into the wardrobe so I couldn't see his face. Honestly, I wasn't sure I wanted to not see him or for him to not see me.

A long sigh slid through his lips. "I … I would've graduated this year, but never went to school so I didn't. Got my GED on the road when I was sixteen. After that, I never had a reason to go to one."

What about friends? What about dances and parties and football games? I kept those questions to myself. He probably didn't want to hear them. I couldn't imagine never being in school. My hands covered my face before sliding through my hair. Then I actually heard what he said and I spun faster than a Tilt-A-Whirl. "Wait, you're twenty."

Gracin met my gaze. "No, I'm not." He pressed his hands into the vinyl covering the armrests. "King Albert lied about my age to get me into the group. They wanted a fourteen-year-old and I was only twelve. Nobody ever figured it out or questioned it." He shrugged and leaned back into his seat. "Just one of the many cover-ups by Albert Ford. There are three people in this world who remember the truth."

"Just three? Somehow I doubt that."

"Last year, my aunt gave me a card that said Happy 20th and my uncle signed it. I've been faking it for so long, people believe it. Even my family. So yeah, three people. Me, my father, and now you. Welcome to the ever-spinning web of lies."

"Oh." My mind whipped around this information, barely able to grasp what I'd just heard. Pretending to be older just to get into a singing group. But continuing to lie about it. Why?

"You remember the set list? Which jacket goes with which song? When the wardrobe changes are? It's going to happen pretty fast —"

"Yes, I know." I straightened and inhaled sharply. Despite his confession, he didn't need to be such a dick. "You've already said this today, and yesterday. Maybe even the day before. I didn't miss a beat during rehearsals. Or did you forget?"

Gracin stretched his arms above his head, finally opening his eyes. He sat up suddenly, causing me to take a step back into the wardrobe. "People expect certain things from me onstage. I have to be charming, witty, and sing like an angel. They want me to dance until my legs fall off. They want me to stare into their eyes and sing only to them." He sighed and collapsed back into his chair, entangling his fingers across his taut abs. "They want me to be everything they desire. That's my job. Your job is to make sure it goes smoothly."

I rolled my eyes. Talk about stating the obvious.

"Don't screw this up for me, Carly." Gracin stood and closed the gap between us. He stared down, capturing my gaze. The intense heat radiating through his eyes caused my stomach to tighten and toes to curl. "This may just be a job for you, but this is my life."

Holy hell. If he used that intensity on stage, soccer moms

would swoon alongside their teenage daughters. Gracin smiled and stepped back. He knew he'd gotten to me, and I hated him for it.

A rap on the door prevented me from opening my mouth and saying something that probably would've sounded stupid. My knees knocked together as I moved around him. Dad smiled when I opened the door, and Gracin's dad stood beside him.

"You two ready for the big night?" Dad crowed. He stepped into the room as if he owned it. Technically, he did, but he never understood boundaries. When I was fourteen, I put a padlock on the inside of my bedroom door to keep him out. He broke the lock with bolt cutters. At least he had the courtesy to knock on Gracin's door before barging in.

"Gracin, are you prepared?" Albert asked. I detected a hint of disgust in his voice. A quick glance at Gracin told me I wasn't the only one. "The show's sold out. Mr. Reynolds even opened some standing room only tickets earlier in the week. They sold in under an hour."

"It'll be fine," Gracin said. The playful tone in his voice had disappeared the moment his father came into the room.

"Good to hear, son." Dad slapped Gracin's shoulder and turned to me. "Everything good?" He raised an eyebrow with an unasked question.

"Yep, all dandy." I smiled widely without it being obviously fake. "Just discussing the wardrobe changes with Mr. Ford. Again."

Gracin mouthed, "Mr. Ford?" toward me. I hadn't called him that since the day we met. I shrugged. It didn't hurt if my father thought I was still being respectful.

"Glad you stepped in to help with wardrobe after Ree quit." Dad beamed at me. "I knew you'd be a good fit for this job, bug."

Oh my God, Dad, I thought. *And if Gracin or his father knew exactly how I landed this job, I doubt they'd agree.*

"Time to get ready," Albert said. "You've got less than ten minutes to showtime. Unlike L.A., the people around here expect you to start on time and not when you decide to climb on stage."

The brief surprise on Dad's face dissipated back into cool professionalism before either Ford noticed. But I caught on. Dad glanced at me out of the corner of his eye before following Gracin's father into the hall.

Once the door clicked closed, Gracin collapsed into his dressing room chair, burying his head in his hands. The tension between father and son wasn't direct hatred, but it wasn't subtle either. Albert's digs at Gracin were meant to sting. Maybe he earned the anger from his father, but something told me there was more to the story.

Everyone knew of Gracin Ford's antics a little over a year ago when he hadn't even bothered to show up for two concerts, and one had started an hour late because he'd been too drunk to go onstage. The tabloids had willingly reported his alcoholism and his stint in rehab. By camping outside the stage door for the last few days, it was clear they didn't believe Gracin had cleaned up his act. Hell, even I expected him to chug a bottle of vodka at any minute. But didn't Gracin deserve a second chance?

"Okay, get the leather jacket," Gracin said as he stood.

I hurried to the wardrobe, trying to think of something to make him smile before he went out there. As I tugged the leather jacket off the hanger, I realized the best thing to say was nothing. It wasn't any of my business.

"Thanks, bug," he whispered as I slipped the jacket over his shoulders.

I cringed. "Please don't call me that. It's not… The story behind it's funny to my family, but not to me."

He held my gaze in the mirror, a flash of understanding in his eyes before he nodded once.

The show went by without a hitch, but I couldn't help feeling something about it wasn't right. The music sucked. I mean, big time sucked. Not that the crowd cared. Gracin did two encore performances, all planned of course. Sweat covered his face after the last note left the stage. I followed him dutifully to his dressing room.

"Well?" he asked between breaths. He bent over and inhaled deeply. The encore, a fast-paced rap-style song, sent him all over the stage at a sprint.

"It was good," I answered, hanging his discarded denim vest back in the wardrobe. *Febreeze that tomorrow.*

"Good? Only good?" His eyebrows furrowed and his lips pressed into a thin line.

I hated lying, so I usually made a practice of telling the truth no matter how much it got me into trouble. This was the perfect time to change things up, so naturally I didn't. "Honestly, it's not my type of music."

"You're saying it sucked?" Gracin kicked his shoes off

with more force than necessary.

"I'm not saying that." *Yes, I am.* "It's not my thing." I waited for a reaction. My legs burned, and I wanted this to be over so I could head to the last few hours of the final big senior class party. I had no idea being behind the scenes would be so exhausting. "You were great, though," I added sincerely.

"Little late for that." He turned, staring me down much like he did before, but without the sexiness of it. "What would you change?"

I blanched when I realized my mind used the word "sexy" alongside an image of Gracin.

"Well?" he prodded. The intensity of his gaze, the sincerity in his eyes, and the sheer closeness of him turned me into a puddle of goo. I couldn't let him get to me, not like this. Gracin Ford was a self-entitled jackass, not a guy to swoon over. Besides, I don't swoon over guys. Not my thing. "I see," he said when I failed to respond. He backed away and returned to his chair. "You'll criticize, but you won't back it up with any real thought."

That knocked the still-forming dirty thoughts out of my head. "Whoa, whoa, whoa. Hold on, cowboy. I can back it up."

"Really? I doubt it." He crossed his ankles, relaxing back in his throne.

My calves tightened from all the running I'd done during the show, but I stood strong. "Fine, the sound is too techno. It was all vibrations and screeching. There wasn't any real music going on. The band looked bored, and irritated.

Nothing they did came out pure since it all sounded computerized. So, yeah, it sucked."

Gracin's expression didn't change. He just stared, waiting for me to go on.

So I did. "The dance numbers were predictable. The dancers fake-swooned over you and also looked bored, not like they care since they at least have a job, but there wasn't any heart in it." I took a breath and went on. "And I have no idea what you sound like. Even during the ballads, it was like you were too afraid to let people hear your voice. It's just not -"

"Okay, I get it," he snapped, holding up his hand. "You hated it."

"I didn't hate it, I just didn't like it that much."

"Let me ask you this, what did you like?" The tension in his jaw could slice through granite.

This was going to be hard to admit, but I hadn't lied yet, so some embarrassing truth was called for. "You." I was going to need some serious downtime after this. Preferably involving tequila. "You're graceful up there. You moved through the numbers and songs, even the silly between song banter, naturally. I could tell you enjoyed being in front of the crowd." All the truth telling weighed on me, adding to the exhaustion of the evening. I scooted toward the wall, using it to hold me up as I made myself as clear as possible. "Look, I'm not into techno-pop music. This isn't the kind of show I'd see willingly. Don't be offended, but you did ask for my opinion."

Gracin nodded and stared off toward the door. I couldn't

see his face and had no idea what might be going through his mind. Without looking at me, he asked, "What kind of music are you into?"

The laugh that shot out of my mouth was louder than intended. "That's not an easy question to answer."

"Try me," Gracin said. He turned toward me, his face still unreadable. "What do you like?"

This was not the time for an in-depth conversation about my musical tastes. It was nearing midnight, and I wanted to get my party on with my high school friends one last time. I slid down the wall until my ass hit the shag carpeting. He wasn't going to let this go, so I thought I'd just get it out of the way. "I like music that makes me feel alive."

A week before prom, Nena, Ivy, and I snuck into a bar in Kimberling City for an open mic night. There was a guy who got onstage with just his guitar and sang a few original songs about living in the Ozarks. He wasn't a very good guitar player, but his voice was like a vanilla latte warming me from the inside out.

"I like purity, unrestrained voices, simple guitar riffs. Songs with emotions reverberating through each chord, each lyric." Sighing, I tucked my feet under my thighs. "It could be jazz, metal, alternative, anything that makes me feel like the songs were written only for me or even about me."

"So anything but techno-pop?" Gracin leaned forward, resting his elbows on his knees.

I chuckled. "The problem with techno-pop is the techno side. Maybe if you stripped down the techno, I might like the real music behind it."

"But maybe not?" Gracin's small smile fought for freedom.

I returned it with a warmer one of my own. "Yeah, maybe not."

He nodded and pushed his hands off his knees to stand. "You're tired. Clean up tomorrow afternoon."

I glanced around the nearly spotless room. There wasn't much to clean up, which was part of the reason I was so exhausted. Not like I was going to let that stop me for the night. My phone buzzed in my pocket. I slid it out and unlocked the screen as Gracin pulled off his black t-shirt. The phone almost fell to the floor, but I caught it before it was too obvious. Seriously, this was not going to happen all summer. Just because I wanted to trace the lines of the muscles curving around his arms and chest, didn't mean I should.

I glanced at the text from Nena, *Where R U?*

Just as I started typing back, Gracin ruined the peace and quiet. "You can text your boyfriend tomorrow. Or at least wait until you're out of my dressing room."

My head snapped up before I finished typing the space after "I'm." Gracin sneered, the slight grin long gone. What a dick.

"Problem?" he asked.

The edge, yeah, I went over it. I was way too tired to deal with his bipolar bullshit. "Yeah, there's a few problems. One, I don't have a boyfriend. Two, I'm late for a party. Three, you're being a colossal asshole right now, and I'd rather you wouldn't. Is that enough or would you like more?"

"There's more? Please, enlighten me." He crossed his arms over his bare chest. "Although I have to admit, I'm not surprised you don't have a boyfriend. Scare them all off with your wonderful personality?"

"And we all know how your lovely personality handles the ladies," I shot back like a spitting cobra. It was a strike below the belt, and I knew it, but this guy was so freaking arrogant and self-assured and just a jackass overall.

He laughed, and I hated him even more. "If you're referring to Sheila, you're so far off the mark you can't see the target, sweet cheeks."

"I wasn't referring to Sheila," I said. The tabloids were pretty sure Gracin's fall from grace had to do with his famous girlfriend dumping him by cheating in plain sight. She was seen at a film festival with her arms wrapped around pop music's latest bad boy. Apparently, she hadn't bothered to tell Gracin it was over between them.

He closed the gap between us, breathing heavy as he bent so we were nose to nose. "You can't believe everything you see on TV, Carly," he whispered.

"What about what I read, Gracin? Or is everything that's been written about you just a bunch of fairytales?" Me and my big mouth. I should've let it go, but I wouldn't be me if I let him, or anybody else for that matter, have the last word. Well, that and arguing with someone who fought back was kind of a turn on. This was so not good.

"You don't shut up, do you?" His lips were parted slightly. All it would take was a tilt of the head and an inch to close that distance.

And I waited for that to happen, wondering what his lips would taste like.

Gracin stepped back, breaking the hold his stare had on me and knocking reality back in. God, what was I thinking?

He shook his head and grabbed a white t-shirt as he strolled toward the door. "Lock up on your way out."

I flinched when the thick wood connected against the frame behind him. Rage built inside me, resulting in a very childish scream and foot-stomping incident. Worse, I threw the only thing I had available. My precious cell phone shattered against the door like glass against concrete.

So much for screen protectors.

Why did August twenty-seventh have to be so far away?

CHAPTER FOUR

Ugh, the hangover to end all hangovers. I glanced around to make sure I was, in fact, in my own room and not waking up in someplace I'd regret. The dark purple comforter half covering my body slid to the floor. Black dresser with white drawers near the window, lamp with black shade on the nightstand, and a bookcase with rocks, leaves, and various colored carabiners filled each shelf. I smiled at my trophies, each taken or left over from a climb or jump or whatever adventure I had survived. Yep, made it home.

I closed my eyes to block out the sunlight breaking through the blinds. The night before flicked in and out like a blurry slideshow on my eyelids. After breaking my cell, I had pushed through the fans and photographers outside the theater and climbed on my scooter. The graduation party had been in a hidden cove south of town. The bonfire had licked the sky, and the alcohol had flowed like water. Things had gotten fuzzy really fast. I vaguely remembered midnight skiing, Jell-O shots, and a fire jump. Wait, had I tried to jump through the bonfire? I grabbed my hair and smoothed my hands over the strands. No damage. That was a massive relief. Then another question hit me. How had I gotten home?

The pounding on my bedroom door only intensified the pounding in my head. It was like a crew of miners were trapped inside my skull, and they were using every tool at their disposal to get out. Maybe that last round of quarters had been a bad idea after all.

"Carly May Reynolds, get your ass out here right now!" Dad didn't need to yell so loud.

I rolled off the bed, tangling myself in the sheets and comforter. At least I'd had the forethought to change into my usual sleepwear – a tank and boxers.

"Yeah?" I asked after I yanked the door open. "What'd I do this time?"

If Dad's face turned any redder, he could be mistaken for jolly. Although that was highly unlikely at the moment.

"Do you know what time it is, young lady?"

"No idea, Pops. I was dead asleep." My sarcasm wouldn't be suppressed by a mere hangover.

He pointed to his watch like I could see it. I'd left my contacts in all night so everything looked dry. After blinking several times, he finally came into focus.

"It's one in the afternoon, Carly." He rubbed his hand over his extended forehead. "Albert Ford called and said you hadn't shown up yet."

I waited for more, because with my father there was always a long pause before the indictments came. He stared me in the eye. I did my best not to flinch or look away. Chalk it up to another failure on my part, because I couldn't handle the unsaid accusations. Especially since I was totally guilty on all charges.

"Just get dressed, Carly. I'll drop you off at the theater." He turned around, and I kept waiting for the ball to drop. "I'm sure you'll find a ride home after the show tonight."

Dad walked down the hallway, stomped down the steps, and didn't say another word. Never in my life had I gotten off so easy. Never in my life had I felt worse, either. I showered in record time and didn't even bother with makeup. Nobody to impress anyway.

The ride to the theater was silent, but the tension tasted like unrealized expectations on my tongue. Dad parked in the loading zone by the stage door. The car idled while I tried to come up with a feasible explanation. I hated lying. Usually twisting the truth to my family was a necessary evil, but I couldn't come up with anything that would make sense. Maybe it was time I apologized for being such a selfish dolt.

"Dad –"

"I don't want to hear it, Carly." His hands tightened on the steering wheel. "We've been doing this for years, and it doesn't matter what you say anymore. I'm tired of bailing you out. It's time you learn that your actions have consequences." He turned and stared at me, searching my face for something. Maybe the little girl he'd lost long ago. His shoulders dropped, and he sounded tired. "Just get to work."

Swallowing the lump of guilt in my throat, I nodded and

got out of the car. The door had barely closed before he backed away. I watched my father drive off. Not once did he even glance back in the rearview mirror.

Nobody said a word as I shuffled toward Gracin's dressing room. This was the last place I wanted to be. Outside the door, I heard the distinct sound of an argument. At least someone else's problems would be a distraction from my own. I pressed my ear to get a better idea of what was going on. It helped that hangovers amplified all sound.

"That's final. How many times do I have to tell you this?" Albert Ford's distinct timbre enunciated each word. "Stick with the set list. Don't even think about deviating from it."

"I just wanted –"

"It doesn't matter what you want, boy. When will you get that through your thick head?" Albert paused before a heartless chuckle left his lips. "It matters what the crowd wants. Your opinion means shit."

I opened the door without knocking. Gracin may be a dick, but his father shouldn't talk to him like that.

"Oh, sorry." It was pretty clear I wasn't. "I guess I should've knocked first, but I'm running late –"

Albert turned on me. "Don't be late again, Miss Reynolds. I won't tolerate such behavior from my employees."

"It's a good thing I don't work for you then, Mr. Ford," I snapped and pointed to the white embroidery on my turquoise polo.

That seemed to piss him off to the point he didn't know what to say. It was a gift I didn't mind bearing. Albert slammed the door behind him, rattling Gracin's mirror, and sending a few of his assorted hats tumbling to the floor. I closed my eyes as the vibrations ricocheted around my head at lightspeed.

"Well, then," I said, turning toward Gracin with a smile. It disappeared when I saw the anger building in his blue eyes. I'd be lying if I said it didn't scare me a little. His gaze intensified, reminding me of something I'd not like to relive in his dressing room. So, I tried and failed to diffuse it. "I'm here."

Gracin came at me like a tornado in a trailer park. He ripped the sunglasses off my face and grabbed my chin.

"Hey, unnecessary roughness," I whimpered. My legs weakened as his fingers burned into my skin. Memories swirled, raising bile in my throat. I pushed them back down with a heavy gulp.

"A little hungover, Carly?" Gracin cocked his head to the side. "Too much tequila?"

"Back off." I tried to shake off his grip, but wooziness hit me wave after wave. He wasn't holding me that hard either. His thumb rubbed over my jaw. My emotions joined the hangover dizziness. I closed my eyes, actually enjoying the softness of his skin. Then he opened his mouth, ruining everything.

"As long as you're my personal assistant, you won't drink. You won't even look at alcohol the rest of the summer. If you fuck this up, I will tell your father and he will fire you. And if I understand the deal you made with him, you won't go to U of N this fall." Gracin let go of my chin and stepped back. "Now go home. I don't need you today."

I felt like a petulant child, and I didn't like it one bit. And damn him for knowing the deal. "I'm fine."

"Carly…" The way he let my name roll off his tongue sent shivers down my spine.

"I'm not leaving. It's not the first time I've had to work with a massive hangover."

"Make it the last."

We stared at one another for a moment before I understood he wanted me to agree with him. Finally, I nodded.

"Good." Gracin strode to the door with the grace of a gazelle. "Meet me at my cabin at six tomorrow morning. You're going to start running with me."

It took a minute to register, but when it did, my heart skipped a beat. "Excuse me?"

"You're exhausted because you're out of shape, and you need a different hobby. I run three to five miles every morning." He glanced at me over his shoulder. "You'll run with me. It'll help."

The door clicked behind him, but it might as well have slammed. Ow.

Not too many people can make me speechless. Gracin Ford seemed to be one. Out of shape my ass. I ran cross-country in the fall and track in the spring. I'd done it to pad my college applications but had no desire to become a professional marathon runner. I reached for my phone to text Gracin to go to hell before I remembered why it wasn't in my pocket.

Dad's voice rang in my head. "Give him whatever he

wants, Carly. Make this the best place he's ever played. We want a happy singer, not a pissy one."

Dad wanted Gracin happy, which would make Dad happy. I'd have to do whatever it took to make my father proud of me again. Besides, there were worse things I could do than run with Gracin Ford. Running was actually fairly harmless. It also gave me a chance to show this guy what I was made of. Gracin thought I was some lazy alcoholic. Time to prove him wrong.

I loved a challenge, and Gracin Ford was going to find out how much.

CHAPTER FIVE

I stared at the coffee slowly dripping into the pot. Talk about torture. Five a.m. was too early for anyone under the age of thirty.

"Carly?" Dad shuffled into the kitchen in a Led Zepplin t-shirt and shorts. What was left of his hair stood at awkward angles, making him look like a mad scientist. If I wasn't so tired, I would've laughed. "What're you doing up at this hour?"

"Apparently, running." I turned back to the coffee pot. Just one more cup to brew.

"Ah, that explains the clothes," Dad said.

I glanced down at my neon green racerback tank and black running shorts and shrugged.

He slid onto a stool and leaned his elbows onto the island. "Pour me a cup when it's ready. Any reason why you're running?"

I reached into the cabinet and took out Dad's favorite mug, setting it beside mine on the white granite counter. "Gracin runs every morning at six. He wants me to run with him. After …," I didn't want to remind him of yesterday's issue. He wasn't quite awake yet either, so it would only ruin the moment. "Anyway, he said I need to get into shape if I'm going to survive the summer."

Dad chuckled as the coffee beeped. Finally, I poured the liquid gold into the mugs, setting Dad's in front of him as I moved toward the fridge for the cinnamon creamer.

"That's a little outside your job." Dad sipped and let out an exaggerated "ah."

We sipped in silence. The coffee woke me to coherency. "Well, you did tell me to give him everything he wants. I'm just following orders."

Dad cocked his head to the side, his brows furrowing. I could almost see the cogs churning in his brain. When his eyes widened, I wondered what his mind suddenly focused on. "There are … limitations to …."

I almost choked on the last of my sweetened coffee. "Dad!"

"I just want you to understand –"

"Oh my God!" He couldn't possibly imagine I'd … No, even imagining it made it too real. I'd never sleep with Gracin just to keep my job. For crying out loud, I had some standards. I rushed out of the kitchen, my face burning from anger. How little my father thought of me.

"Carly," Dad yelled.

I kept going down the hall, grabbing my keys and wallet from the small table in the foyer without stopping. Dad yelled after me again, but I slammed the front door behind me before I heard anything other than my name. It didn't matter anyway. Nothing he said could take back the implications, the idea I'd do something like *that*. It would be a step below prostitution. I'd done some stupid stuff in my life, but nothing warranted this kind of reaction. I tugged my helmet on, rushing to get away before Dad could come outside and make matters worse. The scooter started with a kitten's roar. As I pulled onto the street, I glanced at my mirror. Dad stood in the front yard, watching me drive away. His head dropped to his chest.

Good. I deserved a bit more credit.

∞ ∞ ∞

Gracin opened his door. His smile disappeared as fast as a blink.

"You okay?" he asked.

"Fine. Let's get this over with." I tossed my wallet and keys on the loveseat just inside the door, stepping back before they fell with a clunk onto the hardwood floor.

"Okay," Gracin said. He closed the door behind him and locked it, shoving the key card under a potted plant. There wasn't any other place for him to put it. His tight black shorts and blue tank didn't have pockets. Obviously. Not that I checked out how his butt looked beneath the thin material, but it was a great momentary distraction.

Dad's unsaid allegation snapped me back to reality. Even if I found Gracin attractive – which hello, what living, breathing female wouldn't – I wouldn't have sex with him out of any sort of obligation to my father or my job. That's what pissed me off more than anything.

Gracin stretched and instructed me to do the same. My body listened, but I fumed as I replayed the conversation again. And again. It made me angrier each time. We started to jog, Gracin talking non-stop. I heard nothing but the lull of his voice. He was so self-assured, he probably thought any woman would jump into the sack with him with a flutter of his too-sexy eyelashes. What an ass. After a few minutes, I lost it.

"Do you ever shut up?" I snapped. Our shoes slapped on the pavement, echoing off the buildings. Gracin had chosen to run along the road leading away from the lake and toward the heart of Branson. The slight incline forced me to run harder than I wanted to at the moment.

Gracin didn't break stride, but he stopped talking. We ran in silence, my breath growing heavy. The incline changed to flat ground, and I picked up the pace. Every time my foot hit the pavement, I saw my father's eyes widen. My run turned into a sprint. Sweat mixed with the tears flowing down my cheeks. I ran out my anger until I had to stop to catch my breath. Sobs racked through my body, and snot oozed from my nose. God, I was a mess.

Gracin stopped beside me, his breath blowing hot air into my space. "What's going on?"

"Nothing." I put my hands on my hips and stretched, arching my back and staring at the lightening blue sky. The orange tint from the sunrise faded before my eyes.

The last time I'd seen the sunrise was a week before prom when my then boyfriend had dumped me. The break-up hadn't been as upsetting as the timing. Tyler and I had only gone out for a couple of months. He had been smarter than most guys I dated, and his runner's build was sexy without being overly athletic. While I had liked him well enough, I wasn't in love with him. I had wanted to be though. I had wanted to know what it felt like to love someone. No, the fact he dumped me only hours after we'd had sex for the first time had raised my inner bitch. Hell, I hadn't even cared it was a week before prom. We were lying on his dad's bass boat, half naked, when he'd said it wasn't working. Let's just say one of us had ended up taking a swim. I'd run to my favorite hiding place, a parking lot overlooking the lake. I'd sat there for hours, staring at the water and wondering why I'd let it get as far as it had with Tyler. I'd been trying to control every aspect of my life. The truth was it had been spinning out of control for so long, I'd forgotten what it was like not to spin.

"Are you —"

"I said I'm fine. Drop it." I turned toward Gracin and grimaced. He wasn't trying to be a jackass.

"Then stop crying like a girl, and let's run."

"I *am* a girl, jackhole. In case you didn't notice." My jaw tightened, grinding my teeth together.

He shook his head as he took off at a brisk pace down the street. I had to hurry to catch up. When I did, he slowed down enough for us to match a pace. We ran the rest of the way back to his cabin without saying a word to one another. My legs felt like ground hamburger when we finally stopped. Gracin retrieved his key card and held the door open for me. The smell of freshly brewed coffee pulled me inside.

I loved the cabins. During the winter months, Dad would let Nena and Ivy come over and spend the night in an empty one. Very rarely did that happen, but it was a treat when it did. As we got older, it happened less and less. I called him out on it the summer after my freshman year when I saw an open one on a Monday night. Dad's excuse had been stupid. He'd claimed the cabin needed to be sprayed for bugs. They had all been sprayed a month before, and I knew a lie when I saw it. A lot of things changed during my freshman year. Most of all me.

Gracin's cabin was a two-bedroom loft, one of the smaller ones on the resort. The front of the house split between an open living room and a kitchen with vaulted ceilings. The stone fireplace took up the wall opposite the kitchen sink. The ladder leaned against the short wall of the kitchen, leading toward the tiny loft. Down a hallway were the doors to a full-size bath complete with Jacuzzi tub and separate shower and a large bedroom. To make the guests' experiences unique, Dad had decorated each cabin differently and given them individual names. This one was the Fisherman's Deluxe. The small deck off the back had an excellent view of the lake and a path to the nearest dock.

Gracin had clearly made this place his own. Three acoustic guitars stood in front of the fireplace, one appearing to be older than both of us combined. My surprise must have registered on my face.

"That used to be my grandfather's." He picked up to the old guitar and showed me the front of it. Etched into the body and fading with age was a cowboy with a guitar riding on a horse. His head was down and a corn tassel hung from his mouth. It was very country for a techno-pop singer. "He taught me to play on it."

"You play?" I asked, the disbelief seeping into my voice.

Gracin laughed and gently placed the guitar back on the stand. "Yeah, I can play a lot of instruments." He brushed by me as he moved toward the kitchen, motioning me to take a seat at the table. "Breakfast?"

"Don't tell me you cook too? I might not survive all this shocking information." I pulled out a chair and sat down, not once taking my eyes off him.

He laughed again, as I'd hoped he would. "Afraid all your preconceptions might be shattered?"

"Something like that."

"Well, don't get too excited. I'm just getting some *sizable* grapefruit." He set a plate in front of me with half the fruit and a spoon before turning toward the coffee pot.

"You do this a lot?" I asked as he moved with the same grace he had onstage.

"You mean have girls over for breakfast?" He didn't turn around, but I noticed how the muscles in his shoulders tightened. "Not as much as you think."

It was my turn to laugh, partly because that's exactly what I'd meant and partly because that was the answer I'd expected.

He didn't say anything else. I kept waiting for a smartass comment or argument, but he kept his mouth shut as he poured the coffee and placed the creamer and sugar on the table. Finally, he sat down across from me. When he lifted his head and smiled, something was off about him.

"What?" he asked, raising his eyebrows.

That's when I noticed it. His eyes were a different color. I leaned over the table to make sure I wasn't imagining things. "I thought you had blue eyes."

"Contacts."

I sat back, a little disappointed by this development. Not that his eye color was important or anything, but it was like hiding a bit of himself from the world. He didn't need to do that. His soft hazel eyes were far more beautiful than the too-blue-to-be real ones.

"What's the difference between my contacts and your purple hair?" Gracin said out of nowhere.

"Whoa, whoa, whoa, how did you know about my hair?" I asked a little shocked. "And what are you implying?"

Gracin shrugged and dug into his grapefruit. I waited for an answer, which took a few minutes.

"Your little sister is full of information."

I closed my eyes. Miranda would not see her freshman year if I had my way.

"I like the dark brown though. It suits you. But you didn't answer my question." Gracin smirked around his coffee mug.

"My hair was a personal expression." He stared back at me, waiting for more. "I liked it." Still more staring, so naturally I went on the defensive. "So, what's up with the blue eyes?"

"Personal expression," he deadpanned. I threw a napkin at him, knowing his answer was just a way to mock me.

Gracin ducked with a chuckle. The napkin landed on the floor, and Gracin bent to pick it up. "Okay," he said, setting the napkin back on the table. "The real reason is worse. The original manager of Accentuate wanted someone with blue eyes. Dad told him I'd wear contacts. So, there you go. Your turn. Why purple?"

"Why not ditch them now?" I asked. "You've got beautiful eyes. Why keep hiding them?"

Gracin's gaze was far more intense without the fake color. The heat of summer took over the small room. Finally, he looked away. "It's who they think I am."

A million smartass replies whipped through my brain like icing. Each one was funny, but this moment didn't need funny. Gracin opened up, so why not do the same? "I … It wasn't always purple. I started with hot pink my freshman year. It stayed that way, well, with the exception of a brief lime green period, until my junior year when I dyed it red. Last summer, I decided purple was the way to go." I shrugged and sipped my coffee. I'd never been so open, so exposed.

"But why?" he asked.

God, why can't I lie to him? It would make this so much easier. I forced the words out in a strong, confident voice. Not at all how I felt. "Because I needed to be somebody else for a while."

Gracin nodded, and the sudden need to throw up overwhelmed me. Why had I told him? It wasn't something I'd ever shared with anyone. Nobody even knew why … I couldn't focus on that now. I needed to get out of this cabin.

The walls closed in on me, and the air made it hard to breathe. I stood, my knees shaking from both running and hovering so close to the truth. Without a word, I moved toward the door.

"Carly?" Gracin asked. The concern lacing through those two little syllables was just too much.

I didn't say anything as I rushed out, letting the door click shut behind me. Halfway home, I pulled off the road and threw up what little breakfast I'd eaten. The memories pushed into my head, and I pushed back. I'd fought for too long to let them get the best of me now.

∞ ∞ ∞

Ignoring Gracin wasn't easy, but I managed to keep our interactions to a minimum for the next several days. Running with him in the mornings made it difficult, but he stopped trying to make conversation when I refused to participate. I hid in Luke's tiny office during the day to make a million phone calls. Gracin's hair had started to lose its blond surfer look, and he needed to get it highlighted. Plus there were interviews to schedule with the media. Gracin's reviews from the local papers poured in, and they were all great. More than one paper called him "fresh" and "exciting." My personal favorite was from a reviewer who panned our shows for years. He wrote:

Mountain View Theater finally gets it right by bringing in a fresh young performer in Gracin Ford. Not only is Ford's performance exciting, but it gives the younger generation a show they can sink their teeth into. Michael Reynolds, owner of Mountain View Resort and Theater, has something that Branson theater has needed for some time: youth.

It was nice to see Dad getting some credit. He worked his butt off all the time. My chest tightened as I recalled the last several days. Things had avalanched between us, and it was up to me to make it right. How to do that was a whole other problem.

Church bells rang from my pocket. I still hadn't changed the ringtone on my new phone. Even worse, my SIM card had been damaged when I broke the other phone so I had no idea who was calling me.

"Hello?" I answered after wiggling it free of my pocket. Phones kept getting bigger. At this rate, I'd have to actually start carrying a purse.

"Where have you been?" screeched Nena. "I've been calling you forever. Why haven't you answered?"

A much-needed laugh erupted from my throat. "Thanks, Nen. I needed that."

"Okay," she said, dragging the word out so each letter created its own syllable. "Seriously, though. Why haven't you called me back?"

"Oh, my phone sort of … died the other night. I just got a new one this afternoon." I tapped my pen against the datebook. "What's up?"

"Not much. Enjoying my last summer of juvenile delinquency."

"Yeah, right."

"Okay, okay, point taken. You're the juvenile delinquent of the bunch. But that's not why I'm calling. I know you're off Monday, so come over for a barbeque. We can get our tan on." Nena started to sing my least favorite song with her own lyrics, which was always good for a laugh. "It'll be fun. Ivy's coming. And I'm sure Janey'll invite some peeps."

"My brother included." That almost put the kibosh on the entire scheme.

"Yeah, your brother will be here, but, seriously, Janey will keep him ... occupied."

"Ew. That's not something I ... Just ew." The idea almost made me throw up in my mouth.

"Say you'll come?" Nena begged.

I pretended to think about it, but let her off the hook. "Okay, I'll be there." A knock on the door brought me back to reality. I turned to see my father sneak in. "Nena, I have to go. I'll talk to you later."

"Hey, Carly," Dad said as soon as the phone was off my ear. "Can we talk?"

I didn't like this. Normally Dad's requests for conversation meant things weren't going to be good for me. He tugged on his turquoise button-down shirt with the Mountain View Resort logo, looking as uncomfortable as I expected to be in a few minutes.

"I just wanted to apologize for our misunderstanding ..." His nervous tick took over as he yanked on his right ear. It was always the right, never the left. Dad was not an equal opportunity ear tugger. "I spoke with Gracin –"

"Oh, God," I moaned, dropping my head into my hands. How could he bring this up to Gracin? Even worse, how could I look at him without thinking of him talking to my father? My life kept spiraling downhill. Every time I thought I'd hit rock bottom, it was only a ledge on my descent.

"Wait, it's not what you think. I know I had some concerns about … Anyway, it was unfounded and uncalled for." He sighed, tugged his ear, and sighed again. "I should've said Gracin came to me. We talked about the morning runs and what he expects for the rest of the summer." Another ear tug. This would make a great drinking game. "He asked about you moving to the hotel for the rest of the season."

Words stuck on the edge of my lips, turning me into a blubbering mess. "What?"

"I agreed."

"What?" That time it was louder to the point of shouting.

Confusion covered Dad's face. "I thought you'd like this. You've been bugging me for years to let you spend more time at the hotel. We aren't sold out, and one room won't mean much financially –"

"Did you ever consider asking me or am I just expected to do whatever you and Gracin decide?" Rage replaced the shock. I stood and pushed by him into the hall. Then another thought hit me like a cartoon anvil and I turned to face him. "Are you in that big of a hurry to get rid of me?"

Dad gaped like I'd just slapped him. In a way, I had.

I held up my hand. "Never mind. Don't answer that. I

don't … I just don't want to know."

A few of the grips witnessed the last bit of our conversation. They moved out of my way as I passed by. Each step brought another tear from my eye. I didn't dare wipe them away in case he saw me crying. Was I so bad he didn't want me around?

Gracin sat in his dressing room throne when I walked in twenty minutes to showtime. The rage from earlier had twisted to pain, but it was now back to full-on rage. He glanced up at me with his fake blue eyes. I hated those contacts right then, because he could hide behind them.

"Where've you been?" he asked.

I shook my head as I strode across the room and hung up his dry cleaning from last night's show. I didn't say a single word as I went about my job, ignoring his questions until he stood in front of me, blocking me.

"Stop, Carly." He reached out as if he was going to put his hands on my shoulders, but let them drop at the last second. "What?"

"Oh, I'm allowed to speak. Sorry, wasn't aware." I pushed by him toward the dresser that housed his abundant collection of scarves he threw into the crowd each night. Fresh my ass.

"You're going to have to explain, because I have no clue what you're talking about." Gracin stood in the middle of the room so he was never out of my sight or out of my way.

"Hmmm, let me see." I tapped my chin. "Sleep in my own room with my own stuff or move into the hotel for the summer. What would I choose? Oh wait." I held up my finger and widened my eyes. "I don't get to choose."

Gracin ran his hand over the tips of his perfectly sculpted hair. "Can I explain or would you rather go off the handle more?"

"Since this seems to be my only choice, I choose the handle." I spun toward the door and grabbed the knob, yanking it out of the shoddy wood. Shaking my head, I threw the cheap thing on the carpet and used my fingers to pry open the door. Before it shut behind me, I leaned back into the room. "You may be used to controlling other people's lives, Gracin, but you don't control mine."

I waited in the wings for Gracin to head toward the stage. He strode past me without a glance. I had three songs until the first quick change, so I listened for the opening number. Gracin ran onto stage with his usual vigor, but once the song started, the charisma disappeared. It felt flat and lifeless, like his heart wasn't in it. Well, that wasn't my problem. I hurried to the dressing room and grabbed the next few changes and some scarves. When I got back to my post, the third song was just ending.

Gracin stopped in front of me but didn't shed his fake leather jacket. "I'm sorry," he said. "It was selfish, I admit, but I had my reasons."

I stared at him as the band switched into the opening frame of his next song, but Gracin didn't budge.

"I thought it would be better if you were closer. The nights are tough. Having you stay at the hotel would make it easier than seeing you cross town on that scooter, which I'm fairly sure isn't all that safe. Plus, you've been getting up early to run with me the last few days, so that's cutting into your sleep as much as the late nights. And …" He inhaled and closed his eyes. On the long exhale, he opened them and the bright glint of the light reflected off the blue of his fake eyes. "And I wanted you closer. Is that so bad?" He reached out this time and put his hands on my shoulders, bending his head down to stare me right in the eye. One of the stage managers shouted that Gracin needed to get back on stage, but he wasn't paying a damned bit of attention. He kept his focus on me. "Forgive me?"

My head bobbed before what he said registered. I mean, I'd heard him well enough, but it took a minute to sink into my brain. He smiled and switched from his leather jacket to the denim vest on the run back to the stage.

What the hell had just happened?

CHAPTER SIX

When my alarm went off at five the next morning, I regretted not agreeing to the move. I could've slept for another forty-five minutes. I stretched my arms over my head as I strolled to the kitchen, the tiles cold against my feet. Most people hated cold tile against warm feet, but I didn't mind. Mainly because they woke my sorry butt up. I couldn't remember pouring the water into the coffee maker or putting the coffee into the basket, but I must have because the smell of black gold wafted to my nose. That's the best aroma in the morning.

My groggy head almost missed the sound of vibrating metal dancing across the granite countertop. I stared at the text for a minute, wondering if this was a dream or not. The phone vibrated again.

Come to the front door.

Carly, I know you're awake. Come to the door. It's important.

At this time in the morning, it better be important. When I got to the door and opened it, I realized my first mistake. Gracin's eyes widened at the sight of me, then dropped slowly as he took in every inch of my exposed body. It wasn't like I was naked, but the white chemise and black satin boxers weren't exactly appropriate with a guy standing at the front door. So I wore it with attitude. I slammed my hands on my hips and winced when my phone crushed against the bone.

"What?" I kept my voice at a barely contained whisper.

Gracin shook his head, like he'd just remembered why he showed up at my house unannounced. "Nice hair." He pointed at my wild locks. Static refused to let my strands lay flat in the morning. It was like my hair wanted to escape my head. "And nice clothes."

I clenched my jaw and dug my fingers into my boxers. "Why are you here, Gracin?"

Instead of answering, he held out his cell phone to an open email. My mind wasn't really focusing on the words. "Shipment" and "six a.m." were the only ones making a lick of sense.

"Let's go," he said, slipping his phone out of my hand before turning on his heel.

"Wait a sec." I pinched the bridge of my nose. "You may not get this, but I'm still waking up. Just tell me what's going on."

Gracin strolled back toward the door. "We need to get to the train depot to pick up my truck."

"Okay, I'm totally confused. How did you get here?" I dropped my hand and stared at him.

"I took a cab." He moved his hands in front of my face. I swatted them away.

"Why didn't you just take a cab to the train depot?"

"Isn't that obvious?" I shook my head. "Carly, I don't know how to get back to my cabin from the train depot. Duh."

I wanted to laugh at the use of duh, but his logic baffled me. Wouldn't it have been just as easy if I met him at the train depot? "Wait, don't you have GPS?"

"Don't use it." He leaned in closer and whispered, "You'd be surprised how many people can tack you using *your* GPS."

"Paranoid much?"

"Call it cautious." His eyes dropped to my barely covered chest for a moment. "Oh, and get dressed. I don't really think you should go out like that."

My response was to slam the door in his face. Unfortunately, I woke up half of the house in the process. Luke ran out of his room wielding a miniature baseball bat with Dad fast on his heels. Mom and Miranda huddled together behind them.

"Carly! What the hell?" Dad yelled, fear making his voice quiver. "We heard a loud bang and the windows rattling."

"That," I emphasized, "was Gracin Ford pissing me off before I had my coffee."

I stalked past them and headed toward my room. My phone buzzed in my hand.

Well?

I WILL BE THERE IN A MINUTE!!!!!! I responded.

K.

This guy was going to send me to an early grave. I

changed quickly, glad my family left me alone. For all I knew, Dad was chewing Gracin a new one. Instead, when I came out of my room, fully clothed and still pissed, Gracin sat at the counter with a mug of coffee. Dad beamed beside him. I took Gracin's mug and slammed the too hot liquid. The bitter brew slid down my throat like lava. Of course, he hadn't sweetened it.

"Better?" Gracin arched his eyebrow.

"Not even close. Let's go." I put the mug in the sink and grabbed my keys.

Gracin said goodbye to my father and followed me to the garage. I hit the button to open the garage door, revealing the three vehicles parked inside. He headed for Dad's Mercedes, and I walked toward the scooter. While I would've preferred the SUV, the scooter was all I had left in terms of transportation. Besides, Dad would never let me touch the Mercedes ever again. He'd made that perfectly clear after I put a dent in it. Okay, it was more like a crater in the back passenger panel and the removal of the rear bumper and it technically wasn't my fault, but that wasn't the point. The Mercedes was off-limits. It was the scooter or bust.

"I'm not getting on that thing." Gracin pointed as I climbed on and started the engine. "It can't possibly be safe."

I tossed him the extra helmet, which was a glorified bicycle helmet, but it would do. The train depot wasn't too far. Gracin caught it with both hands and held it in front of him like it was a bomb.

"I'm not kidding, Carly. There is no way I'm riding on that thing."

Smiling, I pushed forward and the kickstand popped up. Gracin watched me pull slowly out into the driveway. I revved the tiny one-hundred-fifty cc engine, not bothering to glance over my shoulder. If Gracin wanted his truck, he had two choices: call another cab and go solo or get on my scooter. I heard the huff before I felt his weight behind me.

"If I die, I'm haunting you," Gracin said just before I gunned it.

The scooter took off like a rocket when I opened the throttle. It couldn't quite hit sixty miles per hour, but it had a surge of power if you gassed it. Gracin must have been surprised, because his arms wrapped around my waist like a straitjacket. His hands clenching the fabric of my shirt and the heat radiating off his chest as it pressed into my back almost caused me to career off the road and into the neighbor's yard.

The drive to the train depot usually took all of ten minutes, but the way Gracin kept tightening his grip during the corners prompted me to take a longer route.

I pulled into the lot and parked by the entrance to the offices. Dad and I had come here a few times over the last year and a half to sign off on equipment he'd had shipped in from New York. It had been cheaper to ship the theater's new marquee by train than by truck.

Gracin climbed off the scooter and gave me the helmet with shaky hands. "Never again."

I snorted back the laugh.

"Seriously, Carly. No wonder you wrecked your dad's car." He spun on his heel and sauntered to the office.

How much does he really know? I wondered as I waited outside. There wasn't any reason for me to go in, so I sat on my scooter with his helmet pressed to my chest. He seemed to know all my secrets that weren't really secrets. More like information I didn't share with most people. What really bothered me was the way he stared at me, like he could look right through me. No matter what bullshit I tossed at him, he knew there was more to me than what I let him see. I hadn't lied to him once, but everybody has bits of their lives they keep to themselves. Mine just happened to be less like bits, and more like entire pieces.

Gracin came out with a slip of paper after a few minutes. He disappeared around a crate at the other end of the lot and drove out in a black Nissan Titan. The diesel engine idled as the truck rolled toward me. After parking it, Gracin jumped out of the driver's side with a huge grin on his face. Without saying a word, he reached out and helped me off the scooter. Not that I resisted. His happiness was normally an apparition, but it was so palpable at the moment that I didn't want to be the one to take it away from him. He pushed the scooter toward the back of the truck and dropped the tailgate.

"What're you doing?" I asked, putting my hands over his on handles. His fingers tightened beneath mine. "You can follow me back."

"Don't be absurd. We're going the same direction."

"Need some help?" a guy asked. He strolled out of the office, wiping his hands on a dirty towel. The guy was huge, nearly six-five with arms the size of Gracin's chest. "I doubt you and your girl can lift it alone."

Gracin pulled his hands from underneath mine. "Yeah, that'd be great."

My face burned like embers in a dying fire, just under the surface and barely visible. Turned out the guy didn't even need Gracin's help. He lifted the scooter by himself and leapt into the bed, pushing the scooter all the way to the cab.

I just stood there, staring at both men. It was a sight to behold. They struck up a brief conversation about trucks as if they'd known each other all their lives. How did men do that? And where did prissy Gracin Ford learn how?

"You and your girl have a nice day," the older man said as he shook Gracin's hand again. He strolled back toward the office, tossing the dirty towel over his shoulder.

Gracin turned away from him and draped his arm around my shoulders. "Come on, my girl. Let's go." He opened the passenger door and helped me into the cab.

This entire episode had me dumbstruck. Well, that and I actually liked it when the guy called me Gracin's girl. Oh, shit. This wasn't good. No, not at all. I couldn't get involved with Gracin Ford. He was arrogant, self-centered, and not even slightly interested in me. Not in the least. No, no, no.

Then again, he did want me to move into the hotel to be closer to him. But was that professional or personal? It was so hard to tell.

Gracin jumped into the cab, bouncing on the leather like a toddler with a new car seat. I glanced around the light gray interior. The fully loaded truck probably cost more than two years of college. Leather seats with butt warmers, a high tech albeit disabled GPS, Bluetooth, and when Gracin turned up the radio, one of the best sound systems I'd ever heard.

What surprised me more than anything was the voice of Hank Williams crooning from the speakers. I reached over and turned the music down.

"Seriously?" I pointed to the satellite radio station labeled "Classic Country."

"Who doesn't like Hank?" Gracin grinned as he reached for the dial.

I smacked his hand away before he could turn it up. An idea sprung into my head. It was five-thirty and the sun was about to break the horizon. When was the last time Gracin had sat and watched the sun?

"Let me drive," I said, lifting my leg over the console.

It was Gracin's turn to smack my leg away. "Not a chance in hell, Carly. I want to live."

There wasn't enough time to pout, but I still crossed my arms to sulk. "Fine, but we need to hurry."

"Where?"

"Just drive and I'll tell you as we go."

Gracin put the truck in gear and followed my instructions. Ten minutes later, we parked on top of a bluff overlooking the lake. Technically, the sun was already up, but it hadn't hit the top of the mountains yet. The pinks and oranges crossed over the sky, entangling with the lightening blue of daylight and the darkness of night. Sunsets were pretty, but nothing beat a sunrise over the Ozarks. They were so much more important. A sunset meant another day was over, a sunrise brought on a new day and new possibilities. Plus, almost everyone saw the sunset. Very few took the time to notice a sunrise.

Neither one of us spoke, but we didn't need to. Gracin didn't start the truck right away. I waited patiently for several minutes before enabling the GPS and programming mine and the resort's addresses.

After a few more minutes, he started the engine and followed the GPS's directions back to my house. He pulled into the driveway and jumped out. I waited a beat before climbing down. Gracin had dropped the tailgate and pushed the scooter toward the edge. Together we lifted it down with ease and rolled it out of his way.

We stood facing each other, still not saying a word. In that moment, I wanted to slide my hand around the back of his neck and pull him toward me. I wanted it so much I could almost feel his lips against mine. But wants were what usually got me into trouble, so I kept myself in check.

"Carly," Gracin said. I waited for more, but he didn't say anything.

"Yeah?"

He inhaled deeply, closing his eyes as if he needed the added strength. After a long exhale, he responded, "Thank you."

Before a word popped from my mouth, he was back in his truck. He glanced at me through the windshield and waved.

I lifted my hand and waved back, feeling like something significant had just happened between us.

What, I had no idea.

CHAPTER SEVEN

Ten straight days of shows. All sold out. All energetic, nonstop craziness. Why Gracin agreed to do so many back-to-back shows was beyond me. Beside the money. Money was always a factor. Fortunately, we finally had Mondays and Tuesdays off.

Gracin and I fell into a pattern. Every morning started with a run, then we'd head back to our respective homes to rest and clean up. I'd bring over lunch and we'd go over the day's schedule. Usually that consisted of Gracin rehearsing while I ran errands, but there was always the occasional crisis I had to avert, like finding a seamstress when his favorite leather jacket ripped on the day our regular costume repair lady was in the hospital. Most nights, we'd have a light dinner in his dressing room before show time. When it was over, I'd head home and crash. Rinse and repeat.

It worked, but I needed a break. Even though we'd stopped fighting, I needed to spend some time having a life. All I had was the show. Quite frankly, the show could suck it.

At the top of my list of things to do on my two days off: sleeping in—which meant it was a surprise when Mom roused me at six-thirty. I had a visitor. Mom's eyes glazed over in that still sleep-induced state as she headed down the hall to her bedroom. I rubbed my eyes, too tired to work up any anger. It didn't matter. I already knew it was Gracin. Nobody else would knock on my door before ten in the morning.

He stood in the hallway, dressed for a run.

Oh no.

"What happened?" He cocked his head to the right, staring at me like I was a science experiment gone wrong. I probably looked like one. "I was … Why didn't you show up?"

An eye-watering yawn slipped free as I said, "It's my day off."

"Oh," he glanced toward the door. I had to admit it impressed me how much he understood. His head snapped back around, and I saw the hurt in his eyes. "I thought you enjoyed our runs."

Oh, crap. Another moment I wished I could lie to him. "I do, but …," another yawn interrupted my sentence. I smacked my lips together and squeezed my eyes shut. I was so not a morning person. "Sorry. I do enjoy running with you, but I'm tired. We've been going nonstop and I need a break."

He nodded. I waited while he stared at his too expensive sneakers and traced the seams between tiles. His hands were behind his back, and his shoulders tensed with each of his breaths. I could see his mouth tightened into a thin line. He really wanted to run this morning, and he really wanted me to go with.

After another minute, I broke. "Fine. Let me change."

"Only if you want," he said, the tension easing from his body.

I rolled my eyes. "It won't kill me, but we need to discuss boundaries, buddy. My time is precious, you know."

"May God forgive me for interrupting your unnecessary beauty sleep." He bowed gallantly.

I spun away as he chuckled. My mind focused on the word "unnecessary." Did that mean he thought I was beautiful or I was so far gone no amount of sleep would help? I shook the first thought out of my head immediately. It didn't matter. There were plenty of guys I thought were attractive, but it didn't mean I wanted them in any carnal way. A giggle slipped between my lips. Thinking of Gracin and carnal in the same sentence made me flush like a freshman. I grabbed the clothes I ran in yesterday. They reeked, but I threw them on anyway. Since I hadn't planned on running this morning, I hadn't washed them. This was a reason to go shopping. Like I needed a reason. Maybe I could sneak some outlet time in while I shot from place to place taking care of errands for Gracin.

"Ready?" I asked as I strolled back down the hall. Gracin wasn't by the door where I'd left him. He'd moved into the living room, where he stared at the family photos on the bookshelf that didn't hold books. Mom was a firm believer of showing off her family, so there were pictures all over the place. They all brought back great memories, even if some were slightly embarrassing.

Gracin pointed to one of me and Luke in ugly yellow lifejackets. Our arms were around each other's shoulders, and the laughter we'd shared hadn't left our faces. Miranda took it after we'd done our first tandem ski the summer before my freshman year. But Gracin wasn't pointing to me or Luke. His finger hovered over the edge of the picture by the world's ugliest elbow.

"Was that cut off for some reason?" he asked, cocking his head to the left to get a better angle. Not like that would help him see the person the elbow belonged to.

Yes, there was a damned good reason. I shuddered and tried to contain it. The photo had been taken two weeks before … well, just before. I swallowed the lump in my throat and fake smiled. "Miranda took it. She just sucks at photography."

I consoled myself that I hadn't really lied. Miranda had taken the photo and she did suck at photography. But I'd cut the person out of the photo. If I didn't actually answer the question, it wasn't a lie, right?

Gracin motioned in a circle at the photos. "This is pretty cool, Carly."

The wistfulness in his voice was hard to miss.

"Your family cares about you," he added. When he turned toward me, he smiled. "I wish I had a sister or brother sometimes. You're lucky."

I snorted at that. "It's not all it's cracked up to be, Gracin. My brother's tortured me my entire life, and my little sister steals my shit. I found half my wardrobe just by walking into her room."

He laughed and glanced back at the photos. "Still lucky."

It wasn't my idea, I swear it wasn't. My hand developed a mind of its own as it reached toward him and trailed down his upper arm to his elbow, stopping there. Gracin's eyes immediately went to where my fingers burned into his skin. The electric current between us was almost visible. Imagine if I kissed him.

Whoa, whoa, whoa. Get that thought out of your head, Carly.

Gracin stepped back, letting my hand fall limp back to me.

"Ready?" he asked in a strained voice.

I gulped, knowing my disappointment showed on my face like a zit on prom night. "Yeah."

He nodded and took a wide berth around me to get to the door. I followed at a three-step distance outside. We stretched in silence, and at opposite ends of the driveway. The awkwardness extended to our run. Normally, we'd run side by side matching each other's pace, but I hung back and Gracin sped up. After a mile of this crap, I matched his pace.

"What's your problem?" I asked between breaths.

Gracin glanced at me out of the corner of his eye, but he didn't respond.

I shook my head, stepping up my pace a bit. "You're such a child, you know that?"

"How so?" Gracin lengthened his stride to match mine.

"How do you think?"

"I'm not the one trying to outpace his running partner." He grinned and slowed down to our usual speed. The smile disappeared after two steps when his eyebrows battled for position above his nose. I'd quickly learned this look meant he was having an internal debate, and it was best to wait it out. Several times, he opened his mouth, only to snap it shut again. It took us another mile before Gracin finally said what he wanted. "You … surprised me."

Totally not what I expected. "Never touch me again" would've made more sense. I posed the same question he'd asked me moments before, as innocently as I could of course. "How so?"

Gracin didn't crack a smile. "I wasn't expecting … that."

It didn't take a genius to realize he was trying to be honest without giving anything away. I knew what had thrown him off; I just didn't understand why. If I asked, he might not answer in the way I wanted. So I didn't ask.

I cleared my throat. "What're you planning on doing today?"

Gracin shrugged, his mind clearly somewhere else. Was it back in my living room? All I had done was touch his arm for the span of ten seconds. Ten incredibly intense seconds.

"It'll be nice to get away from the theater," I said. The awkward conversation turned even more awkward by the step.

"Yeah, maybe." He paused and glanced at me before continuing. "What about you?"

My plans made me grin. I couldn't wait to spend the day in the sun with my friends, lounging on the dock and relaxing. Nothing exciting for us, which wasn't par for the course. "Just hanging with my friends at the lake. We're barbecuing."

"Sounds like fun," he said. His head dropped an inch. Gracin normally ran with the confidence of a marathoner, head high and form loose. Even deviating from the norm was disturbing to me

That's when it hit me. The run, spending every waking moment together, even his request that I move into the hotel all made sense. Gracin Ford, singing sensation, was lonely. It would've made me laugh if it wasn't so sad. So I did the least logical thing in the world.

"Why don't you come along?" I asked, fighting to keep the nervous quiver out of my voice. *What if I'm wrong?*

Gracin stopped and stared down at me. I stared back, but he didn't answer as his eyebrows fought it out on his forehead.

"Come on," I prodded. "It'll be fun."

"Are you sure you don't mind?" He shifted foot to foot and glanced at his shoes. I wanted to reach out and comfort him, but I kept myself in check. Gracin nervous wasn't normal.

I craned my neck to look him in the eye, smiling with encouragement. "Like I said, it'll be fun."

He found his swagger and straightened. "What barbecue wouldn't be fun with Gracin Ford there?"

"There's my cocky friend," I said.

He tilted his head to the right. "You mean that?"

I wasn't sure what he meant, and I was sure it showed on my face.

"That we're friends?" he clarified.

I didn't hesitate. "Well, yeah. Aren't we?"

Gracin smiled, and it was the most beautiful thing I'd seen. He'd always been attractive, even when he was an ass, but seeing him smile like he was actually happy made him so much more so… interesting.

"Yeah, we are."

We stared at one another, and I didn't care my face burned more than it usually did during our runs. And I thought his looked the same, but I wasn't about to point it out to him. We turned toward the street, both of us running with an extra bounce in our steps.

∞ ∞ ∞

After our run, I went back to sleep for a couple of hours. So, I didn't get to sleep in, but I got some much needed z's in anyway. I took a little extra time getting ready, until I realized why I was doing it. The only reason I spent so much time in front of a mirror was when I was heading out to find a quick hookup. Most of the time, I'd find a guy and we'd make out for a while. Very rarely did it lead to anything more.

Which naturally brought Gracin and an imaginary hookup movie playing in my head. Yeah, it was not PG-13.

At eleven, Gracin knocked on the door. Dad was at work, and thankfully, Miranda was at her friend's house. Mom's social calendar showed a luncheon with some other resort owner wives today. No doubt Luke drove her before heading to Nena's. When I opened the door, I almost dropped the cooler I'd packed. A dirty Dodgers cap hid his floppy, unstyled hair, and yellow tinted wraparound sunglasses covered his eyes, not to mention half his face.

"Expecting some paparazzi?" I cocked my hip and gave him my best glare.

"Maybe." He flashed a grin and reached for the cooler. "Who brings a cooler to a barbecue?"

"How many vegans go to a barbecue unprepared?" I asked.

Gracin's lower lip stuck out, and oh my God did I want to suck on it. I shook my head and turned around before he could see the pure want covering my face. This wasn't good, not at all. I needed to shake this lust pronto, because it so wasn't happening. Fortunately, he didn't notice or he didn't comment. Either way, I was glad.

I punched the address into his GPS and sat back to listen to some Johnny Cash. Gracin didn't shy away from cranking his stereo. "Jackson" came on and we both ended up singing along. Gracin smiled, letting his country side roll. He sounded great, and I could totally see how he ended up in the music business. Somehow, though, I still didn't believe I'd heard the real Gracin Ford sing. I wasn't sure what it was, but the notion nagged at me. Gracin was an enigma. One minute he was a cocky jackass, the next a sweet boy-next-door, then he could turn into a ranting diva.

He slipped the truck into low as we turned down the private road toward the Brand's house. Nena's family had lived in the Ozarks for a century, and they'd owned this land for almost as long. Some long-lost relative came upon a massive amount of money and bought as much of the lakeside property as he could get his hands on. Over the years, the parcel's gotten smaller, but the Brand family has held on to more than half of it.

I'd always envied Nena's life. She was gorgeous, flirtatious, but she stuck to her convictions. Her parents loved her no matter what kind of trouble I got her in. Over the last four years, that had been a lot. But she had one thing I wished I had in my life: a sibling who cared about her. I could jump off a bridge and Luke would just shrug.

Gracin parked the truck behind Nena's Cavalier and turned off the engine. I reached for the handle when I heard him exhale. Glancing over my shoulder, I stared at his profile. His eyes were closed and his fingers drummed on the bottom of the steering wheel. A count of twenty later, he opened his eyes and climbed out of the truck. I did the same and led the way toward the front door, opening it without even ringing the doorbell.

"Hey, Carly," Janey called. She leaned back in the kitchen to stare down the hallway. "Nena's down by the dock with Ivy. The boys are out back by the grill, arguing over every ..." Her eyes widened, and she stepped into the hallway to meet us halfway. "Hi, I'm Janey," she said, adding half an octave to her tenor voice. "I don't believe we've met."

Here we go. I rolled my eyes, but Janey didn't notice.

Gracin offered his hand and smiled. "Jonathan. I'm working with Carly at the theater this summer."

I raised my eyebrow but didn't correct him.

"Nice to meet you," Janey said. She flashed her eyes to me before turning the charm back toward Gracin.

He moved a step closer to me. "You too."

Janey's smile turned plastic as she spun back toward the kitchen. "You can put your cooler on the deck, Carly."

"Thanks," I said, leading Gracin out the sliding glass doors to the wraparound deck overlooking the lake. It didn't matter how many times I'd been here, the view always made me stop for a minute and take it all in. It was nature at its finest. The water lapped the edges and gently rocked the dock. Since we were in a small cove, most of the boat traffic didn't affect the peaceful surroundings.

Gracin's sharp intake of breath meant one of two things: the view did the same to him as it did to me, or he'd noticed Ivy in her red bikini. I didn't want to know which.

After depositing the cooler in the shade, I hurried down the steps toward the dock. Ivy and Nena spotted us, waving like they hadn't seen me in a year. Their flagrant waves slowed and stopped at the same time. I knew it was because of who walked behind me.

"Hey, Carlsbad, you didn't tell us you were bringing dessert?" Nena smiled like Gracin was covered in chocolate. The thought made me sweat, and I had to shake it out of my head. Fortunately, they thought I was shaking my head no. "Not in the mood to share? Too bad."

God, Nena had the vixen card down. I hated to think what would happen once she got to college. Who knew? Maybe she'd change her ways and start acting like the person she pretended to be.

"Nena, you're terrible," Ivy giggled. She slipped her sunglasses to the edge of her nose and checked out every inch of Gracin as if she was using her tongue to taste him.

His breath caressed my ear before I heard him. "I'm feeling a little objectified, Carlsbad."

Giggling was not my thing, but damned if I didn't then. Nena and Ivy heard me and raised their eyebrows, but they didn't call me out. Both turned their attentions toward Gracin as they introduced themselves.

"Nice to meet you. I'm Jonathan." Gracin flashed his million-dollar smile.

"Well, come on down. We've got a full cooler and the boat's ready to go." Nena turned toward the lake with Ivy matching her move for move.

I stared at Gracin and mouthed, "Jonathan?"

He shrugged, but a real smile brightened his features as he leaned closer to me. "It's my first name. Now tell me why they call you Carlsbad?"

I laughed so hard I almost peed myself. "That's a much longer story."

"Can't wait to hear it," he said.

I turned toward my friends, keeping my smile to myself. The idea he might want to hear the story touched something inside me I couldn't recognize. I wasn't sure if it was good or bad. It was definitely different.

Nena's father wasn't much on luxury, but he did love to spend time on the water. Reverend Brand had bought the powerboat when we were in seventh grade. He enjoyed the speed and skiing, a hobby Nena had picked up on as easily as a fish to water. She was prepping the boat for a quick ride before lunch.

Gracin and I were halfway to the dock when Luke called my name. I turned to wave to my older brother and stopped when I saw who stood behind him. My blood turned to ice.

It was an apparition. It had to be, because there was no way that Derrick Russo was here. There was no way he would show his face after all these years.

Willing him not to exist hadn't worked four years ago, and it wasn't working now.

"What's the matter, sis?" Luke asked as he strolled toward us, Derrick hot on his heels. "Drink too much last night?"

I shook my head, my mouth too dry to form a single word.

"Who're you?" Luke's eyes shot to Gracin.

Gracin offered up his hand. "Jonathan."

"Have we met before?" Luke tried to place him, but he wasn't quite catching on. My brother wasn't the brightest bulb in the pack.

"Yeah, I'm one of the grips at the theater. Your dad hired me for the summer." Gracin's voice took on a bit of an accent, not quite Ozark enough but definitely not his usual California suave.

Luke snapped his fingers and pointed. "That's it. I knew you looked familiar."

Gracin smiled, stepping closer to me like he did with Janey in the kitchen. "Your sister's been kind enough to let me tag along since my family's out of town this week."

"That's our Carly," Derrick said. My skin crawled at the sound of his voice, a sound I'd ignored even in my nightmares. That was nothing compared to how he stared at me. His ocean blue eyes shot icicles into my chest. "Oh, I'm Derrick, by the way. I'll be starting at the theater tomorrow."

Thank God that Gracin moved closer to me, because I

needed his strength. My knees buckled, and I fell back. His arm wrapped around my waist, squeezing me against him. Ice may have invaded my body, but it melted the minute Gracin touched me. It didn't matter, though. The security I got from Gracin couldn't change the past, and it wouldn't change how I reacted around Derrick Russo.

"Carly, you don't look so hot." Luke reached out to touch my forehead, but I leaned further back before he could touch me. Gracin's arm tightened as he let me push into him.

"I'm fine," I whispered. Turning half around, I hurried toward the dock with one eye on Derrick. Gracin's arm slipped away from my waist in the rush, and the chill easily ate away the warmth of his touch.

Once we got to the dock and I was sure Derrick didn't follow, I jumped on the boat and reached in the cooler for the nearest drink. Gracin climbed in behind me, eyeing the beer in my hand. He shook his head, but that wasn't going to stop me as I popped the top.

His fingers closed around mine, forceful and gentle. I didn't try to fight him.

"You don't need this, Carly," he whispered, prying the beer from my hand. "Talk to me."

I laughed harshly. "Look at you, Gracin Ford, trying to play sponsor. Well, I don't need one and I don't need to talk. Especially to you." I turned to the front of the boat where Nena and Ivy watched us. "Hit the water, Nena. We've got a party to start."

Ivy whoo-hooed.

Nena grinned and pumped her fist. "There's our Carlsbad. Ain't a party until somebody gets hurt. Let's hit it, girls." She paused and cocked her head to the right. "And boy."

I took off my tee and shimmied out of my shorts so all that was left was my black bikini. The engine roared to life and the smell of diesel filled the air. I stumbled into Gracin as Nena gunned the gas. Speed, that's what I needed. Gracin's hands landed on the bare skin of my waist. The hard calluses on his fingertips scratched a little, and I leaned against him for more. My body pressed along the length of his. The icy chill left by Derrick's presence disappeared. Until Gracin shoved me onto the seat beside him. Still, talk about seven seconds of heaven.

The wind whipped through my hair. I pushed myself to my feet and held onto the back of Nena's seat. I squeezed the seat tighter, digging my nails into the white leather. The memories I'd held back for four years rushed through me. The dryness of my throat as I'd begged him to stop. The spit spray as he'd laughed at my pleas. The way his blue eyes had closed and his mouth had opened with pleasure while I'd screamed in pain.

My body tensed as the entire scene flashed in my mind. I'd managed to block it out of my conscience. This was the first time he'd come back to Branson since he had left for college. Just seeing him made everything fresh in my memory.

I needed to focus on something else, something less painful. Scanning the shoreline, I spotted a potential diversion. Someone had tied a rope from an overhanging branch and people lined up to take a swinging drop into the lake.

"Nena!" I shouted, pointing at the same time. She'd already started turning toward the swing.

Ivy grinned over her shoulder at me. "How high can you go?"

"We'll find out!"

Nena slowed, but I didn't wait for her to stop before I dove into the water. Before I went under, I swore I heard Gracin calling my name. He'd probably disapprove of the swing, but he had no say in what I did. Besides, he'd done far worse with alcohol and drugs. Maybe if he'd been an adrenaline junky instead, he'd be a lot more fun. These days, Gracin Ford lived a clean life.

That shit wasn't for me.

The guys managing the rope had graduated last year. They let me jump the line, much to the boos of a few other girls.

"Hold the rope," I ordered Jeff or maybe it was Randy. Funny, I should've remembered his name since we went out once. He smiled, his eyes crawling up and down my body to places he never got to visit. I moved as far away as the brush would allow before turning back toward the rope. My water shoes weren't made for running in the woods, but they'd protect my feet. I dug in to get better traction and waited a breath, imagining the rush.

Then I ran.

Leaping up and grabbing the rope as soon as I was

airborne, my body weight and speed powered me out across the lake. For a split second, I was free. It was like flying and all I wanted to do was keep going higher and higher, but Derrick's breath echoed in my head and the memories didn't disappear.

So I let go.

Gravity took over, and I plunged toward the water. I'd done this a hundred times, so I knew how to hit the water safely, but my memories were too distracting and my body didn't cooperate. My left foot wasn't in line, and the pressure of the entrance pushed it farther away from my body, sending me sideways into the drink instead of straight down.

It felt like a giant hand slapping me with the G-force of an F-14. My lungs burned after the blunt trauma freed them off all their oxygen. Instinct took over, and I managed to push myself to the surface. My chest stung with the sharp intake of air.

What a freaking rush.

I glanced toward the boat where Nena and Ivy cheered. Gracin stood on the edge, ready to jump in. I experienced a different rush as I stared at him, partly wishing he would jump in. Seriously, I needed to let it go. The pain in my leg pulsed as I swam toward the boat. The rush faded, but the pain increased. When Gracin and Ivy helped me back into the boat, the throbbing focused on my left ankle.

"Nice fly, Carly, but shitty landing," Ivy said. She lifted my ankle onto her leg to inspect it. With three younger sisters and an older brother all athletically gifted, Ivy had become the medic of her family. Her skills were legendary enough that she'd been the manager for the football and basketball teams the last two years.

"Are you okay?" Gracin asked. He knelt beside me, just out of Ivy's way.

"Yeah, I've had worse." I smiled, but Ivy turned my ankle too fast and the pain shot up my spine. "Way worse," I added through gritted teeth.

Ivy didn't lift her head as she inspected my ankle. "Sad but true. Haven't you noticed the thin scar running from her left shoulder to her butt? At least that didn't need stitches. One time she –"

"Shut up, Ivy." I groaned again. This was worse than I thought.

She raised her eyebrows, but didn't say another word about my past adventures. "It's not broken. I'm sure you just sprained it. When we get back to the house, I'll put an icepack on it and wrap it tight."

"Shouldn't she see a doctor?" Gracin lips pressed into a rigid line.

Ivy and Nena both laughed, but this time Nena answered. "And risk her father finding out? Yeah, that's not going to happen. "

"Remember when –" Ivy started. I didn't have to stop her this time; a fit of giggles did.

"I don't think Carly wants us to talk about this in front of …." Nena nodded toward Gracin, who watched the three of us from his side of the boat. "Let's get out of here. I'm sure Luke and Derrick have the pork steaks ready by now."

At the mention of Derrick, the rush was gone. A hollow

emptiness settled into my stomach. Ivy and Nena didn't notice, but Gracin did. He moved closer as my friends climbed into the front of the boat.

"I know it hurts, but how bad?" he asked.

I snorted and rolled my eyes. "Have you ever felt like your body was going to split in two, but snaps back together? Kinda like that only worse."

"Sounds like a hangover I had on the Sunset Strip." His attempt at a joke failed in its delivery.

Any further conversation was cut off by the roar of the engine. I leaned back, resting my head on the leather and staring at the sky as we zipped down the lake. Nena and Ivy sat in the front laughing about the swing incident. Honestly, they'd seen me do crazier stuff, but nothing insanely crazy. I stayed mostly tame around them. My other adventures were just stories they may or may not have believed. This time was different. I'd always been one for an adrenaline. Skydiving, yep. Bungee jumping, multiple times. Whitewater rafting, what a rush. I'd done it all. It's amazing what can be accomplished in Missouri.

Like I said, this time was different.

I did it to push back the memories overtaking me.

Nena expertly pulled the boat alongside the dock, and Ivy jumped out to tie up. Gracin climbed out and offered his hand. I stared at it for a moment, but I slid my fingers along his and let him help me from the boat. My ankle barely held my weight. It almost gave out as I hobbled toward the blankets laid across the wood. I eased myself down, stretching my legs before me.

"Aren't you coming to the house to eat?" Nena asked from the edge of the dock.

I shook my head. "I just want to sit here for a while."

"What about you, Jonathan?" Ivy's voice had an added dose of sultry.

"Nah, thanks." He knelt beside me, completely ignoring Ivy's vocal attempts at seduction. Loud enough for my ears only, Gracin whispered, "I'll get the cooler. Don't move, okay?"

"Smartass," I whispered back.

Gracin smiled and disappeared. I propped myself up my elbows and watched the water lap against the hull of the boat. The sound brought the memories back again, and I tried to fight them off. After so long, I couldn't believe they felt so raw. The tears fell first, then my body racked with sobs. I pulled my good leg to my chest and buried my forehead into my knee. How could he have done that to me? I was just a kid.

A shadow blocked the sun. When I glanced up, Gracin stood beside me with the cooler in his hand. I wiped the tears away and faked a smile. For all he knew, the tears were for the earlier incident with the rope swing. His eyebrows furrowed, and I held up my hand to stop him.

"I'm fine, really."

That only made his eyebrows start World War III with each other. Still, he didn't say a word as he sat beside me on the blanket and opened the cooler. I waited while he shuffled through it. He pulled out two bottles of water and turned to me with a confused expression. "You packed my favorite foods."

"Yeah, I figured you'd want to stick to your diet and all that." His stare made me more self-conscious than when he'd caught me crying a moment ago. He didn't say anything, and my discomfort grew taller than the Ozarks. "What's wrong with that?"

"Nothing," he whispered. "It's just …" He glanced out toward the water and didn't look back at me as he finished his thought. "It's just that nobody's … The only people who even think about doing something, anything, considerate like this are on my payroll."

"Technically, I work with you," I pointed out.

He laughed harshly and turned toward me. "Yeah, but you know what I mean. Besides, you fight with me, tell me my show sucks, and don't hold back your opinion at every turn." He paused, his eyes dropping to my lips. His voice turned husky. "I've never met anyone like you, Carly."

We sat like that, staring at one another until the water bottles stopped sweating. I leaned closer to him, to do what, I had no idea, but I felt the pull to be in his personal space. Kissing seemed like a good option though. Unfortunately, someone rudely interrupted any chance of that happening.

"Hey, sis," Luke said as he strolled onto the dock, making more noise than a gaggle of fleeing geese. "Aren't you coming up to eat? Got pork steak, ribs, and brats."

I smiled warmly at my brother, without real warmth. A skill I'd learned well. "Nah, I want to hang in the sun."

"What about you, Jonathan?" Luke turned his attention to Gracin. "What do you want?"

Gracin's eyes flicked to me before he answered. "I'm good. Thanks."

"Whatever. Hey, Carly, can you get to the theater early tomorrow? Derrick starts as a security guard, and I need someone to show him around."

Each word was a pinprick puncture wound draining the blood from my body. The breeze off the lake suddenly chilled my bones as the heat of the sun disappeared. I must've looked like a finely carved ice sculpture. Luke didn't seem to notice as he stared at me expecting an answer.

"She can't," Gracin answered. I turned toward him, our eyes locking. He didn't break his stare as he explained. "I overheard Gracin tell her there was a smell in his dressing room and he wanted it out by showtime tomorrow."

"Why not call in the exterminators or something?" Luke asked.

"Oh, you know Carly. She'll try to prove Gracin wrong first, just to make a point. The guy's a bit of a diva." Gracin raised an eyebrow, and I would've smiled if tomorrow didn't loom over me like an asteroid.

Luke laughed. "Yeah, he can be a dick. Don't worry about it, Carly. I'll get someone else to do it."

"Okay," I said.

Gracin smirked and pulled a salad from the cooler, setting it between us. Once Luke was out of earshot, he chuckled.

"So, I'm a dick, huh?" he asked, popping a cherry tomato into his mouth.

"If it quacks …" I tried to smile, but the image of Derrick

at the theater wouldn't let me. The shaking started in my hands, then crept up my arms. I wrapped myself in them to stop the tick.

"Carly," Gracin said my name gently, but I didn't face him. I couldn't. He put his hand on my arm. The shaking eased at the warmth of his touch, and I turned toward him. "You don't have to tell me what happened, but I promise you he won't be at the theater for long."

"I don't need you to fight my battles," I whispered as he lifted his sunglasses.

"No, you don't. But I'm in your corner." His eyes were the color of gold lamé, swirling with intensity. "It never hurts to … have someone to stand beside you, does it?"

"No," I said on breathe of air. "It doesn't."

CHAPTER EIGHT

Gracin demanded I go to rehearsal with him the next day. He didn't want me out of his sight while we were in the theater, but he had to get on stage to check the sound and make slight adjustments to the songs from the night before. It amazed me how he went through this before every show. I never detected any variation in the songs, tempo, or sound and lighting, and I hadn't been close to the stage during rehearsals to notice how things changed on a daily basis. Most of the time, I was either on the phone or running errands.

We stood together just off stage left a few minutes before rehearsal started. Luke strolled by with Derrick. My insides turned to oatmeal. Derrick leered at me, a smirk turning him uglier than usual. Luke didn't seem to notice how the tension stunk up the small area. He kept talking as if Derrick listened.

"Hey." Gracin snapped his fingers at Derrick. The air around him took on a superior edge. He stood at his full height and threw his shoulders back. "What's your problem?"

Luke glanced at his friend before turning toward Gracin. "Mr. Ford, this is Derrick Russo. As of today, he's on the security team."

Gracin didn't take his eyes off Derrick as he sneered. "I didn't ask you, Luke. I asked him what his problem was."

"I don't understand," Luke responded, glancing between the two.

If I could've only folded in on myself.

Gracin stepped closer, staring down at Derrick. There was only an inch between them, giving Gracin the edge, but it seemed so much more at that moment. Gracin stood over Derrick like a pissed-off giant looking for his magic beans.

"I ..." Derrick stuttered. It wasn't a lack of confidence, of that he had an abundance. Gracin had knocked Derrick down a notch with his stare.

"If you have a problem with me, then this isn't the place for you," Gracin said with a calm voice. "You should just go."

"Derrick doesn't have a problem with you, Mr. Ford." The quiver in Luke's voice was not only uncharacteristic, but it was unnerving. Seeing my brother so out of his depth didn't settle right in my gut. "Right, Carly?"

His eyes pleaded with me to back him up. I couldn't. Fortunately, Gracin gave me an out.

"Leave Carly out of this," Gracin snapped. His gaze shifted to Luke, and my brother started to wilt. "I don't like this guy. Get rid of him."

"You can't —"

"Get rid of him or I don't go on. Then explain to your

father why I'm not on the stage for a sold out show." Gracin crossed his arms over his chest, glaring down his nose at Luke. "Clear?"

Nobody said anything for several minutes as the epic show of masculinity continued. There was no way Gracin would lose this battle. Luke finally relented as soon as someone called Gracin to come to the stage. Gracin cocked an eyebrow at him, and Luke backed away, motioning for Derrick to follow him. I watched until they disappeared around a corner, then I exhaled a heavy breath.

Gracin's hand fell on my shoulder. "Better?"

I nodded since the baseball-sized lump in my throat expanded into a softball. This wasn't over, not by a long shot. Gracin couldn't really believe he'd handled Derrick like a valet, could he? This wasn't some Hollywood movie.

"Stay here during rehearsals, okay? Just stay here until I know he's out of the building for good."

Again, I nodded until common sense kicked in. "I can't. I have too much to do."

"It can wait."

"I need to get your dressing room ready. It's still a mess from Sunday night. "

"It. Can. Wait." Gracin bent down until he met my eyes. "Stay here. Please."

Someone called for him again, and he nodded once before spinning on his heel and heading out to the stage. As much as this fascinated me, I hadn't agreed to stand here like a groupie and wait for him. Anger welled inside me, melting away the remaining oatmeally sensation. There was no way

Derrick was going to stop me from doing my job.

Gracin waved at me. Once he turned around, I headed toward his dressing room. The memory of Derrick, of what he'd done to me, had haunted me long enough. For the last four years, I thought I'd taken control of my life, but all I'd done was hide behind the crazy girl image. It was time to let it go.

I hurried up the steps and down the hall, forcing myself to stay calm and not check over my shoulder. A shiver crept down my spine like fingers caressing a piano when I turned the corner toward Gracin's dressing room. Damn, why did the hall have to be so dark? Even in the middle of the afternoon, it felt like midnight.

Pulling the key from my pocket, I managed to slip it in the lock and turn it even as my hands shook. Gracin was right. I should've just stayed by the stage. But this was ridiculous. Luke would've kicked Derrick out of the theater by now. There was no way Luke would risk a performance for a friend. Losing Gracin, even for one night, would cost the theater too much money. Since this was Luke's first management gig, there's not a chance in hell that he'd let Gracin walk. Besides, he'd seen Dad's wrath enough times over the years.

I turned the doorknob. Remnants of Gracin's cologne filled my nose, calming me down. I loved the pepper, vetiver, and leatherwood scent. Inhaling deeply, I let it fill my senses.

Until a hand slammed into my back, pushing me into the dressing room and onto the floor. My face burned against the shag carpeting, taking my breath from my lungs.

This wasn't happening. A bubble swelled inside my chest, breaking when fingers closed around my swollen ankle. Panic froze my muscles as the attacker flipped me onto my back. I screamed and the sound choked me, but Derrick only laughed.

"Fucking the singer, Carly?" he asked, slamming the door behind him.

I crab crawled away from him until my back hit the unrelenting wall between the wardrobe and Gracin's dressing table. The cold hand of fear caressed every inch of my bare skin from my neck to my legs as Derrick's gaze roamed around with the hunger of a predator about to be fed. The rush of memories I'd suppressed overtook me. I couldn't stop them this time, and it felt like I was on the precipice of reliving them. The edge of my sanity loomed on the horizon and I ran toward it.

"You put him up to firing me? Huh? Is that what happened?" Derrick grinned as he unbuckled his belt. "I taught you a lesson once before. Maybe it's time you relearn it."

Oh, hell no. You aren't fucking touching me!

I waited, partially paralyzed by fear, but also feeding off of it. He wasn't going to win. Even if my body was trying to get away, my mind formed a simple plan. Derrick stood before me, sliding his jeans down past his hips. I slid farther down the wall until I was almost completely prone.

"Damn, Carly. You know you ruined me for most women. None of them felt as good as you did." He licked his lips and a sinister smile appeared. Those blue eyes blazing with intense heat. "Of course, they all begged for me willingly. You begged for me but pretended not to want it. I knew you wanted to, though. No matter how many times you said no, you wanted me as much as I wanted you."

He tipped his head back to laugh and I took my shot. My arms supported my weight as I slammed my boot-covered foot into his crotch. He wailed like a chick in a horror movie. I scrambled to my feet and limped past him toward the door.

Derrick's hand shot out, grabbing my bad ankle and dragging me back to the floor. I kicked out with my good boot and nailed him in the face. The crunch of his nose breaking echoed in my head. I cherished how his scream gurgled in this throat as I crawled away from him. The door wasn't far. Once I was out of his reach, I pulled myself to my feet and yanked open the door, smacking into Gracin as I tried to escape.

He pulled me against his chest for a moment, before moving around me. Luke pushed by me, totally unaware of what was going on. But Gracin knew. He'd figured it out the day before. I didn't pay much attention to what happened next. There was so much going on. I heard Gracin yelling at Luke. I saw security rushing into the room. I smelled *his* blood on my boots, and I tasted my own from a cut on my lip.

Then nothing. It was like a black hole swallowed me and took all of it away: the pain, the anger, the fear. The only thing that didn't disappear was sight. As I stared at the tips of my favorite boots, I noticed Derrick, still with his pants down, being hauled from the room by the head of security and three of his lackeys. More people had shown up than I realized while I sat there.

Someone touched my arm, and I yanked it away. I stared at the culprit and saw my mother. When had she gotten here? She reached toward me again, but I shrunk from her. Tears rimmed her eyes, but they didn't fall. Just like they hadn't fallen all those times Dad yelled at me for something that I hadn't really done. Even the reason I worked here this summer wasn't entirely my fault. Not that it mattered to my father.

Mom stood, and she motioned toward someone else. Dad was here too.

God, please don't let Miranda see me like this.

Luke and Dad played hand puppets with one another, gesturing wildly. My ears were stuffed with impenetrable cotton. A hand shot between Dad and Luke, pushing them apart. I watched as Gracin shoved his way between them. His eyes found mine, and his mouth dropped open. He knelt beside me, keeping his gaze locked with mine. A sudden rush overcame me as my senses woke.

"Carly?" he whispered.

It broke me. I fell into his chest, sobbing uncontrollably. I hadn't allowed myself to cry like this in four years, but I couldn't stop it. Derrick had stolen so much of my life from me, and I felt like I finally had it back. Gracin's arms wrapped around my shoulders. He rocked me, slowly and gently, as I cried. He didn't lie and say it was going to be okay. He didn't even speak, actually. Instead, he offered the one thing I needed more than words of comfort. He held me against his chest, making me feel safer than I'd felt in a long time.

When I finally pulled away from him, everyone else was gone.

"How long have we been sitting here?" I asked through my cracked voice. I hadn't screamed that much, had I?

"About an hour, I think. My butt went numb a while ago." He smiled, but it quickly turned into a frown. "I told you not to move."

Indignation rose in my chest. "So this is my fault?"

"God, no." Gracin sat up, taking my face gently between his hands and forcing me to meet his eyes. "None of this is your fault, Carly. Not a damn bit of it. You understand?"

I nodded and swallowed down the sour bile burning in my throat.

"You are amazing, you know that?" His face brightened. "Jonesy got his version, but we all figured out the truth. Derrick's in cuffs and on his way to the station. Jonesy said you'll have to go down and give a statement. Can you do that?"

Jonesy, head of Dad's security team and brother to the Chief of Police, was the reason my younger antics had never gotten me locked up in juvie. He'd take care of everything. He'd arrest Derrick and make sure the bastard never looked at another girl again.

Could I tell the cops what happened to me? Would they even believe me?

"You kicked him in the groin?" Gracin asked.

I nodded, and Gracin's smile widened.

"Then you kicked him in the face?"

I nodded again.

"You probably broke his fucking nose."

"God, I hope so."

My head dropped an inch, and Gracin's fingers massaged my temples. Any other day, I would've relished this moment for other reasons.

"He raped me. When I was fourteen." The words tumbled out of my mouth, finally free. I said it. I told someone. I'd read enough online about victims and moving on, but I never realized how it would feel to say it out loud. My head shot up. Gracin's grip slipped. "I've never ... I've never told anyone."

Gracin closed his eyes and his nostrils flared. Seconds later, his eyes opened. "I'll kill him."

"Gracin, it's over." I'd beaten him at his own game.

Finally, I won.

∞ ∞ ∞

The rest of the day flew by, and I found myself looking over my shoulder less and less. Once the show started, I was too busy to worry about Derrick or anything else for that matter. Plus my ankle throbbed to the beat of the bass. That was definitely distracting. Gracin's energy electrified the crowd more than ever. It was intense. I chalked it up to having a day off between shows.

After the final encore, he rushed off the stage and stopped in front of me. Gloria, one of the backup singers and dancers, slipped between us. Her eyes flicked up toward

Gracin as her hand slid across his bare abs. I wished he would put a damn shirt on.

"Coming by later?" she cooed. Seriously, who coos at a guy?

Gracin raised an eyebrow, but didn't answer. Her smile widened as if no answer meant yes. She kept walking, her hand only leaving his skin when he was out of reach.

I wanted to ask what the hell that was about, but it wasn't any of my business.

"Well?" Gracin asked.

"Well what?" The resentment crept into my voice.

He rolled his eyes. "How are you?"

"Irritated." I really needed to learn how to lie.

That seemed to catch him off guard. Good. I turned around and headed toward his dressing room to clean up for the night.

"Hey, Carly. Can you come in here for a minute?" Luke stood outside the small room Dad had designated as Luke's office. The real theater manager's office was located by the lobby and totally Dad's, but since he let Luke play manager over the summer, he had to give his golden son a place to put up his boots.

Technically, Luke was my boss, so I had to comply.

I wobbled toward Luke and through the office door he held open for me. Glancing over my shoulder, my gaze met Gracin's as he stood rooted to the spot. Luke closed the door, breaking our contact. It wasn't the slow door close seen in the movies either. Luke slammed it shut, rattling the three pictures he'd hung on his only wall space. One of those had

Derrick in it. I mentally willed it to fall to the floor and shatter. It didn't work.

Luke sat on the edge of his desk. I glanced around for a place to sit, but the only chair was behind Luke's makeshift desk. Instead, I leaned against the wall, clutching my ever-present clipboard and Gracin's purple satin shirt against my chest. The shirt smelled like his cologne and sweat. I inhaled, letting the scent calm me. I didn't know why this seemingly disgusting thing had such an effect on me, but it did. No sense fighting it.

"Carly, about earlier –"

"I don't want to talk about it, Luke. Not here and most definitely not with you." I reached behind me and grabbed the doorknob.

"Just let me finish, okay?" Luke shuddered, and I wondered if it was because of what had happened or because of what he was going to say next. Either way, I didn't really want to hear it.

"Finish what? You defend that piece of shit? He raped me, Luke!" Okay, so maybe I did want to talk about it. "Again. He tried to rape me again!" The anger deflated as I admitted what happened to me for the second time that day. "Don't you understand?"

Luke's face flushed, but he pressed on despite what I'd just told him. "He didn't mean –"

"Didn't you fucking hear me?" My voice tore through my throat.

"He said you came onto him –"

I laughed harshly. "Yes, I'm a female so therefore it's my

fault. Any girl's fair game in that case."

"Carly, I'm just trying to understand what happened?" The desperation in my brother's voice didn't go unnoticed, but neither did the lack of compassion.

"Wasn't it clear enough?" How could he not see the truth in front of his own eyes?

"I wanted to hear your side of the story."

"My side! You saw my side. My God, how can you be so blind? So stupid?" I didn't understand. What wasn't I saying that he didn't get? "He raped me once, Luke. Your friend forced me to … God, and you're defending him? You saw him with his pants down, and you still want to take his side over mine."

"When?" he whispered.

I never wanted to acknowledge that moment in my life, but now it was out there, I couldn't not talk about it anymore. "Two weeks before my freshman year started. At Janey and Nena's house."

Luke gulped, his face paler than I'd ever seen it before.

"Remember that party?"

He nodded but still didn't say a single word.

"Remember how I begged you to take me home early? How you refused?"

He nodded again. All the blood had disappeared from him face.

"And do you remember … do you remember how sick I was a few weeks later?" I didn't want to tell him this, but I couldn't stop. Now that the floodgates had opened, the truth wouldn't stop spilling out. I'd never lied about what happened, but I'd never told anyone either. Maybe not talking about it was just as bad as lying. Luke needed the entire truth, even if it meant breaking open wounds I thought had long since healed. "I … I miscarried. Ivy's mom –"

"No –"

"There was no way I could tell Mom, so I told Janice. She took me to a clinic." I inhaled, hurting my chest as I fought the sobs desperate to escape. "He fucking raped me and knocked me up when I was fourteen years old, Luke. Do you get it now? Do you understand what kind of person he really is?"

"He wouldn't –"

"He did!" I yanked the door open and hobbled out of the room, dropping Gracin's shirt and my clipboard along the way.

Once I broke free from the theater, the humid night air welcomed me. I inhaled, sucking in the air as if it would wash away everything else, as if it would clean the wound. My heart slammed around my chest, making every muscle ache. Pressure built in my abdomen until holding it back wasn't an option. A scream shot out of my mouth like Old Faithful, tearing up my throat along the way. A few people stopped and stared, but they didn't bother me as they got into their cars and drove off.

The relief started at the top of my head and eased down my body. I fell to my knees, tears spilling down my cheeks, and laughed. Nothing about this was funny, but the pressure I'd carried for so long was gone. I laughed at the freedom of having that weight disappear.

I'd spent the last four years trying so hard to forget what happened, trying so hard to hide those memories. After spilling every last detail to my brother, the peace I'd sought in hiding came forward. I couldn't hide any longer.

And I'd never hide from it again.

The truth does set you free, and damned if I was ever going to be a slave to my past again. It was over. With every detail exposed, I really felt like this was over.

Derrick would never hurt me again.

CHAPTER NINE

Nobody asked me how I was. Nobody talked about Derrick's release from jail. Nobody mentioned the increase in security around the theater. And I was glad. Avoiding all conversations suited me just fine. I kept my phone off, ignoring Nena and Ivy and anyone else who wasn't part of the show. My world was the theater and Gracin. It kept the nightmares at bay and my sanity intact.

Gracin's demands over the next few days didn't give me time to do anything other than work. Whether he upped his diva attitude or just wanted to keep my mind off what had happened, I had no clue. Three days after the whole Derrick thing had gone down, we prepared for a commercial at eight in the morning in his dressing room. Dad wanted to increase the advertising to sell out the rest of Gracin's summer run. Basically, I stood on the sidelines and waited for someone to tell me to get something. It was pretty boring.

My conversations with Gracin focused on scheduling and wardrobe. Hell, we weren't alone enough to talk lately. The morning runs were the only time Gracin and I had to ourselves. Even then, we only discussed business. I kind of missed him. It was weird. He ran alongside me, but it was like he was already on the other side of the country.

I stood in my usual spot while the film crew did their thing. Gracin shifted from foot to foot when the camera wasn't recording. More than one time I noticed his eyebrows battle it out. Toward the end of the two-hour shoot, Gracin had to fight to keep his hand from running through his hair. Not that it would've gotten very far with all the product in it.

Dad escorted the film crew out, leaving Gracin alone on stage. He stood under the middle light, with his hands on his hips and his head tilted up as if he was relishing the sun. Someone shut off the rest of the stage lights, leaving him basking in the spotlight.

A crackle echoed through the empty theater, and a static-filled voice followed it. "I'm shutting down, Mr. Ford. Will you be here much longer?"

"Yeah, Mitch," Gracin answered. "I'll get the light. Just leave a note by it so I hit the right one this time."

"Yes, Mr. Ford. Will do." Mitch, the lighting and technical director, turned off the remaining lights in the seats and along the rows, leaving that one light on Gracin and the emergency exit lights. Color me impressed. Mitch never let anyone into his control room alone.

Gracin disappeared into the shadows for several seconds and returned with his grandfather's acoustic guitar and the stool they'd used during the shoot. He half sat, half stood by the stool, and gently pulled the guitar strap over his shoulder. His face softened, and the boy inside the man appeared.

My breathing slowed as I tried to remain inconspicuous. He didn't know I stood offstage and I didn't want him to. My gut told me the real Gracin Ford was about to emerge, the one I'd only seen glimpses of on rare occasions.

His fingers moved over the strings, caressing the first chords from the instrument. The air filled with sorrowful notes reverberating through my chest. The intro fell away as Gracin's voice slipped into a deep tenor with a slight country twang. Each note wrapped itself around my chest, squeezing my insides into a ball of want.

No regrets, that's what she said
No promises, no goodbyes,
This is the moment for us,
Every second we melted
Every moment we seized,
By morning, she disappeared.

Amazed, intrigued, and totally needing more, I stepped onto the stage and cautiously made my way toward him. He was so lost in his music, he didn't see or hear me approach. As I limped closer, I realized he'd closed his eyes. The final strings sounded from the guitar, and his eyes opened. He jumped off the stool away from me, and I smiled gently.

"Jesus, Carly, don't sneak up on a guy." He clutched his chest with one hand and the neck of the guitar in the other.

"Sorry, I just ..." Why had I snuck up on him? Because I'd wanted him to keep singing. No, I *needed* him to keep singing. "Why don't you add that song to your show?"

Gracin laughed, but there wasn't anything funny about it. "You really think Albert would allow that?"

I watched his face, waiting for any kind of expression or emotion to take over the blank stare he'd adopted whenever he mentioned his father. "It's your show, Gracin. And that … That was amazing."

His lips quirked in a half-smile before falling into a frown. "It's not my show, Carly, you know that. But thank you. Knowing you don't think I totally suck means a lot."

My eyes widened, but he'd already dropped his gaze to the floor. Without even looking at me, Gracin strolled off the stage. My jaw locked as I tried to figure out what just happened. I never said he sucked, only the show. If he didn't consider it his show, whose was it?

Gracin's voice hollowed out a space in my chest and rooted itself there. The song went on replay in my head. I remembered every single word. Growing up around music, especially country music, I was incredibly picky about what I listened to. If a song didn't fill me with any kind of emotion the first time I heard it, I wouldn't listen to it again. Gracin's song did something so rare, so unusual. Every emotion imaginable had swelled as his voice caressed those lyrics—even now they did. I wanted and needed to know who, if anyone, inspired it.

My stomach rolled. I didn't want anyone to have inspired such a sad song, such a loving song, such a lonely song. I didn't want him to still be in love with her.

∞ ∞ ∞

I stood on the stage with those thoughts running through my mind until the light went out above me. My eyes adjusted as the emergency lights illuminated enough for me to find my way backstage. By the time I got to Gracin's dressing room, he was gone. A note taped to the wardrobe planned the rest of my afternoon. Most of the stuff didn't need to be done today, but it was pretty obvious he wanted to avoid me. Especially when the last line read, "See you at showtime."

The errands took me right up to dinner. Usually, we'd eat an hour before he went on, but he'd made it clear that wasn't happening tonight. Or did he? I read the note again to be sure. It didn't say anything about dinner, and we'd always eaten together. For some reason, an inkling in my brain told me he couldn't fend for himself. I hurried back to the theater and up to his dressing room with his favorite cucumber avocado rolls.

When I opened the door, he sat on the floor beside Gloria with a full spread of Gracin's favorite foods in front of them. My breath caught in my throat, followed closely by a lump the size of Texas.

"Can I help you?" Gloria's smile spread across her face with the glee of a child on Christmas morning.

"I ... uh ..." Words were no longer my friends. I met Gracin's stare. There wasn't anything behind his eyes. Over the last few weeks, I'd pretty much learned to read this guy. His emotions were always present in his eyes. They weren't always clear, but they were there. It was like staring at a blank movie screen waiting for the show to start.

"Did you need something?" Gloria asked again.

The stifling heat in the room overwhelmed my senses, but I somehow managed to recover enough of myself to answer. Smiling at Gloria, I said, "I'm sorry. I didn't realize Mr. Ford had dinner plans, so I brought him some food." I stepped farther into the room and slid the cucumber avocado rolls in front of him. Gloria clapped her hands and squealed. I didn't hide the eye roll. "I'll leave you be."

I spun on my heel, slamming the door behind me hard enough to rattle the lights above the stage. Hurrying down the hall, down the stairs, and out the side door, I fought back the tears filling my eyes. There wasn't any reason to be this upset. Gracin Ford was a job. Nothing more. Nothing less. Somewhere along the way, I'd forgotten that. I'd let a few moments of something more get in the way of reality.

A quick glimpse at the clock told me I had an hour to kill before work. I hopped on my scooter, wishing for the millionth time it was a Harley, and sped off for a little fun.

It only took me fifteen minutes to get to ZipLine tours. The line was out of control, but I had an in. I strolled over to Denny George and put on my best smile. He glanced up at me and grinned like a starving man seeing a steak. Denny had graduated two years ago and spent the summers working for his dad. We'd hooked up last summer after a link in my harness had slipped, making my body less protected than it should've been. Talk about a rush.

"Hey, Carly. Long time, no see." He didn't hide the fact he was checking out every inch of my body, which I knew he wished he'd explored completely. We'd gotten pretty close, but it took a lot before I'd sleep with a guy. Unless I trusted them, they didn't get laid. "Looking for a rush?"

I could tell by his expression what he actually meant. "Yeah, but I've got to get on quick. Help a girl out?"

"I dunno. What're you doing later?" His fingers danced over the black straps in his hands.

"Hmmm …" I tapped my finger against my chin. Hanging with Denny for a few hours wasn't a *terrible* idea. "Well, text me after ten. The show will be over by then and I'll know more." I smiled with parted lips for good measure. A little sultry never hurt. It was time to get back in the groove.

"Alright, darling, let's get you harnessed." Denny motioned toward the steps and led me past a couple who'd been next in line. They shot me dirty looks, but Denny held them off. "Sorry, folks. Ms. Reynolds had a reservation in advance. You'll be on the next line."

That seemed to pacify them.

Denny jabbered nonstop, but I stopped listening. My brain wouldn't shut down. The events from this past week wove through my mind like silk. It was almost surreal. The whole thing with Derrick shook me to the core, but fending off his attack was an ending more than anything else. He was outed for what he was. The guilt, the hatred, would always stay with me, but the secret didn't weigh me down. Even if I saw him tomorrow, I wouldn't be terrified anymore. Then there was Gracin. I liked him, and it bothered me. Obviously, he was a lonely guy looking to hang with anybody. Why else was he so interested in being around my friends? And the way he'd held me after Derrick attacked me. Gracin had been gentle, caring, almost loving. Something stirred inside me. I didn't know what it was, and I didn't want to either.

"Okay, you're good to go," Denny said, snapping me out of my thoughts.

My mouth was dry so I offered a thumbs-up.

Denny leaned close to my ear. "Don't forget about later. I'd like to finish what we started last summer, Carly. I regret we haven't had a chance until now."

I shuddered, and not in a good way. Even if he texted me later, I'd decline. His warm breath had been great last year, but it felt cold and unforgiving as he whispered. I just needed to clear my mind, get a rush, and then I'd be able to figure everything out.

"Go on three." Denny counted, and I pushed off the platform at the designated time.

The black straps dug into my butt as I slowly picked up speed. A few seconds in and all I could think of was the way my heart slammed in my chest, the way the air whipped through my hair, the feeling of flying through the air with nobody to stop me. No Luke. No Gracin. Nobody.

The answer hit me then.

Gracin had sung about it, and Denny mentioned it. The answer to my problems.

I never wanted to look back on any part of my life and regret any more decisions I'd make. Good or bad. I didn't want to look back and wonder "what if I didn't do x, y, or z." I wanted to be able to say "at least, I tried."

No regrets.

That was the answer to everything.

CHAPTER TEN

Gracin avoided me for the next few days, keeping everything between us strictly professional. It sucked, but I let him do what he felt was necessary. Even if it meant putting some distance between us. We still ran every morning. We still ate lunch and dinner together. Gloria continued to flirt with Gracin, but he smiled politely and didn't encourage her.

Nena and Ivy stopped asking me about Derrick. Things were getting back to normal between us. I'd avoided even texting them, but it wasn't their fault. They cared. They just didn't understand why I didn't want to talk about it. It was in the past, over. I wanted to leave it there and move on. Instead of talking, we shopped. Retail therapy helped. Mom was more than willing to give me her platinum card for "respectable clothes," as she put it. Of course, I bought some kick ass leather pants instead.

Saturday afternoon, I stopped by the theater to drop off some of Gracin's wardrobe for the night. After hanging everything in the right order, which made it easier for me to grab and go during the show, I headed toward the stage to catch a bit of rehearsal.

The voices echoed off the empty seats. I recognized Gracin's immediately, but the other one wasn't as familiar. I rushed toward the stage, peeking out to see what the hell was going on.

"When are you going to grow up, Gracin?" Albert Ford snapped. His hands were out of control, flapping in the air to his sides as he berated his son. "This isn't a game. This isn't just your life. Everything you do affects me and everyone associated with you. Face it, boy, you can't do this without me."

I'd never seen Gracin look so small. His confidence, his swagger was missing as his dad continued to scream.

"You're not a songwriter. Sing the damned songs we agreed on." He paced in a small circle before stopping in front of Gracin and shoving a finger in his face. "You try to pull this bullshit tonight, and we'll be out on our asses. Reynolds will say you've broken the contract. He hired a pop star, not some wannabe country singer. Branson's got enough of those. So get your head out of your ass and do what I tell you. That's the only way you'll survive this business."

I waited for Gracin to say something, anything, but he stood there with his head down while his dad kept on going. It tore me up to see this. The guy I knew wouldn't sit back and take this much crap from anyone.

"You're such a useless piece of shit," Albert added, and I lost it.

Nobody talked to my friends that way. I stormed onto the stage and let my freak flag fly.

"Don't call him that!" I jammed my finger into Albert

Ford's breastbone. It didn't matter that he was almost a foot taller; I wasn't backing down from him. "My father would relish anything Gracin brought to the stage, even his original songs. He wouldn't kick him out for breach of contract when the shows are already sold out for the rest of June, most of July, and several in August. So, don't threaten Gracin like that, Mr. Ford."

"You need to mind your own business, missy," Albert grunted between his teeth. "This has nothing to do with you."

"Maybe not, but it has a lot to do with my father." I raised myself on my tiptoes to appear as tall as possible. "And don't you ever call Gracin a piece of shit again. If you want to know what shit looks like, go stare at yourself in the mirror."

"Carly, that's enough," Gracin said with a sigh of resignation.

Albert's head snapped up as if he'd forgotten Gracin was in the same space as us. "You'll do what I tell you, boy. Remember who's managed your career for the last six years. I know the business. They want what you've been giving them, not some bullcrap love song."

Before I could open my mouth to start another verbal sparring match, Albert turned away from us and strolled off the stage like he owned it. My ass. I'd show him who owned this theater. I moved to go after him, but a hand tightened around my upper arm and I spun toward a very pissed off Gracin.

His eyes raged, and the frown would give him premature age lines if he kept it up. "Some things in this world aren't your business, Carly. So butt out."

"What?"

Shaking his head, he turned away from me and left the stage on the opposite side his father had a second ago. How many times was he going to leave me on this stage alone? That asshole was just as bad as his father. He won't stand up for himself but gets mad at me for doing it.

That was the final straw. I'd had enough crap happen to me in the last few weeks, and Gracin Ford had been smack dab in the middle of all of it. Time to show him what the hell he was doing to me.

With each step I took toward his dressing room, my anger grew. I felt six feet tall by the time I threw open the door to his room. Gracin paced with his chin in his hand. He stopped when I entered.

"What now, Carly?" He bit down each word.

"You really don't want to piss me off anymore, Gracin. I've had it up to here with your attitude." I raised my hand over my head so he'd get the point. "One minute, you're inviting yourself along to a barbecue and playing my protector, the next you're eating dinner with a wannabe showgirl. Are you off your meds or something?"

Gracin's head took on a sway as his anger at me increased. I was out of line with the meds comment, but sometimes my brain and mouth don't work together well.

"Seriously," I said, full steam ahead, "I don't understand you half the time. Everything you do is the exact opposite of what I see when we hang out. You perform music you don't like. You cater to your father's whims. You hold me one minute, then shut me out the next."

"Ah," Gracin's face lit like dawn. "Now I get it." He punctuated his realization with a harsh laugh.

"Get what?" He may have thought he understood what was going on, but I sure as hell didn't.

Gracin moved toward me, stopping toe-to-toe. He bent his head down to meet my gaze. "Admit it, you're jealous of Gloria. Just because we've developed something of a friendship doesn't mean there's anything else going on here, Carly. You should stop deluding yourself."

"Deluding myself? You really are crazy, you know that? You must be the one that's delusional to even think I'd be interested in anything with you." I'd inched closer to him without realizing it.

"Bullshit." His breath was hot against my lips. I wanted to close the gap.

"I'll prove it," I replied. Somewhere along the line, we'd stopped yelling and started whispering in frantic tones.

"How can you disprove a fact, Carly? You've got it bad for me, and nothing can happen here." His words slapped me across the face. Anyone else would've stormed out the door, but I saw it as a challenge.

"Then you prove it, Gracin. Kiss me, and you'll see we're in the same boat."

My heart stopped beating as I waited for him to call me out. He inched closer, and I thought he was closing the distance.

"You'd never recover," he said. His lips were a hair away from mine. The temptation was too great.

"Wanna bet?" I pressed my lips against his with hardly

enough pressure to really feel it. Just that tiny bit was enough to set my entire body on fire. Gracin's hands slid onto my waist, yanking me against his body as he kissed me back without any reservations. His mouth was the conductor and mine the orchestra, responding to every movement. When his tongue found mine, they danced in a slow, sensual ballet. My hands found their own way up his arms and around his neck.

God, this was more than I'd anticipated. I'd expected Gracin would be a good kisser, I just didn't realize he'd turn my entire being into the watery part of the jelly with barely a touch of his lips. I didn't want to stop there. I needed all of him.

Then he was on the other side of the room with his head pressed into his hands.

It took a minute for my eyes to adjust and my heart to calm down. Cooling my body off would take a cold shower and a few hours, or a few hours in a cold shower.

"This can't happen." He breathed heavy like he did after sprinting the final leg of our run. "We can't … I can't … It won't happen."

I kept my mouth shut. It wasn't like I'd been the only one doing the kissing here. He'd been just as involved, if not the real instigator. I'd only brushed my lips against his to prove him wrong. Which was funny when I thought about it. Still, I didn't say anything. Not when he told me no. Not when he said this heat between us wasn't going to grow. I let my gaze fall to the floor and walked toward the door slow enough for him to change his mind.

He didn't.

CHAPTER ELEVEN

"You can't be serious? You kissed Gracin Ford?" Nena's squeal almost knocked me off my feet. I yanked the phone away from my ear. "Wait, what about Jonathan?"

"Forget about Jonathan, Nena. Did you even hear what I said? He turned me down." I cringed as the words came out of my mouth.

"Did you ever think that maybe he did it for a reason? Maybe he didn't reject you but what you might represent."

"What's that supposed to mean?"

"Come on, Carly, face the truth. How many girls have thrown themselves at him over the years because of who he is?" I could practically hear the eye roll through the phone. "Maybe he's thinking you're doing the same thing."

"Psychoanalyze much?" Sarcasm was required here. "It doesn't matter why, it only matters what happened. And Gracin told me no."

"Do you regret it?"

"Hell, no. Totally worth it." I sighed and laid it all on the line for her. He'd kissed me back and, for about two minutes, everything had been perfect. "I would rather know he didn't want me than to look back on this summer and ask myself what if. It's better this way." A text beeped in my ear. "Hold on, Neens." A quick glance at the caller ID took a bit of pain from my sting. I put the phone back to my ear. "I have to go. Time to move on from the disaster that is Gracin Ford."

"Don't do anything stupid, Carly. I don't have enough money for bail."

I laughed but didn't let on that stupid was right up my alley at the moment.

A knock interrupted my response to Denny's text. He wanted to hook up after the show and go to a late movie. I was about to tell him yes, but Miranda waltzed into my room with a huge grin.

"What's up, Meerkat?" Her obsession with all things animal had brought about the nickname. My little sister was probably my best friend and worst enemy at the same time. She'd start her freshman year this fall, and I wished I would be here to stop anything bad from happening to her. Then again, Derrick wouldn't be coming anywhere near my family ever again. That was comforting.

"Did you really kiss Gracin?" Her eyes lit like first stars on a summer night. She had a framed photo of the two of them by her nightstand. He'd signed it, "To my best girl, Love, Gracin Ford." Miranda had declared her undying love for him at that point.

I fell back on my pillows. "I'm so not having this conversation with you." The red numbers on the clock on my nightstand reminded me it was time to face the music. Even after what had happened, I still had a job to do. And I was going to do it with more professionalism than Gracin had. In other words, no calling him a rat bastard to his face.

Miranda stood over my bed and stared at me. "You really like him."

I started to hide my head under my pillow, but stopped myself. Why not admit it to one person? "Yeah, Meerkat, I like him a lot. But it doesn't matter. He doesn't like me the same way."

Miranda nodded and clenched her jaw. "He's a jerk then."

I smiled at her defense of me and sat up. Taking both of her hands into mine, I thought I'd offer more truth. "No, he's not. He's just being honest about it. If he doesn't want to be with me, then he shouldn't. You know how I always try to tell the truth?"

"Except with Dad," Miranda pointed out.

I really laughed that time. "Yeah, well there are some things Dad should never know. This is one of them. Keep it between us, okay?"

Miranda nodded.

"Okay, I've got to go or I'll be late." I pushed myself off my bed. Miranda wrapped her arms around me in a hug.

"I miss you, Carly. Mom's always hovering around, and I can't do anything. You're never here. Luke's never here either. Every time I try to go to Eddie's house, Mom's in my face."

"Just tell her you need your space. She probably thinks Eddie's your boyfriend." In the back of my mind, I wondered if this little anti-Eddie move by Mom was a result of the Derrick situation. There was no way Mom or Dad had told her. And I highly doubt Luke had mentioned the rest of my confession to anyone. He was more of the hide-reality-in-the-closet kind of guy.

Miranda let go of me and stepped back. "I wouldn't mind if he was."

If my little sister was good at anything, it was making me laugh. "I'll talk to Mom tomorrow, okay?"

"Thanks." She ran out the door, but stuck her head back into my room. "If you want, I'll tell Gracin what I think."

"Thanks, Miranda. But I'll be fine."

I couldn't help but wonder if that was true.

∞ ∞ ∞

The show started at seven, so I arrived at the theater at six and made a few phone calls from Dad's office. It was quieter in there, and there was little to no chance I'd run into my brother. His avoidance skills were at an all-time high, and I wondered if he doubted what I'd told him. I also wondered if he'd talked to Derrick. Dad had demanded Luke cut all ties with Derrick, but Luke sometimes has a mind of his own. This might've been one of the times he chose to actually use the brain God gave him.

I kept a close eye on the clock and on the excessive amount of text messages from Gracin wanting to know exactly where I was. After the fifth one, I responded.

I'm at the theater, Mr. Ford. That was it. Simple and to the point.

Where? he responded immediately.

I'm in the main office scheduling your mani-pedi and massage for tomorrow afternoon between rehearsal and the show.

I stared at the phone, waiting for a response. It took him several minutes before my phone beeped.

We need to talk.

About what? I typed. If there was a barometer for my anger, it would've exploded as soon as I read his last text.

You know what.

Mr. Ford, we are not in high school. You were perfectly clear earlier in the day. It will not affect my abilities to do my job nor to ensure that you have everything you need for each performance. The formality in my text made me laugh. I loved going all fancy pants on occasion. This was one that deserved it.

After ten minutes of no response, I headed toward his dressing room to prepare for the show. Backstage was hectic, but in an organized way. Grips and stagehands fixed last minute problems. The band strolled toward the entrance to the stage without a care in the world. Gloria swished her skirts around the lead guitarist. He didn't seem to mind. With less than thirty minutes until showtime, Gracin should've been making his way toward the stage too. He liked to get a look at the crowd before he went on.

I'd timed it so I could avoid him as much as possible. Apparently, that wasn't part of his plan. When I opened the door to his dressing room, he stood in the middle of the rug with nothing but his jeans on.

"What the hell?" I stood there with my hand frozen on the doorknob.

He stormed toward me, getting close enough we could repeat our earlier performance of tongue hockey. "We need to talk."

"There isn't anything to talk about, Mr. Ford." I stressed his name as I pushed past him. Was I being childish? Yep, but he deserved it.

"Carly," he whispered, but I didn't turn around.

Heading straight to his wardrobe, I yanked out his usual costumes for the first half of the show. I moved back toward the door, holding his leather jacket in my right hand. Gracin hadn't moved from the doorway, so I had to push by him again, slamming the jacket against his chest.

"I'll be at my station," I said without glancing behind me.

Once I hit the steps, tears welled in my eyes. Did I regret kissing him? Maybe a little. Because I couldn't look at him without wanting to do it again. Rejection sucked on so many levels.

The show felt off. The band sounded great, but the energy wasn't there. Gracin wouldn't even meet my eyes during the costume changes. I watched him perform a karaoke version of some new hit song. He wasn't having fun at all. The crowd didn't notice. They swooned in the right places, screamed in the perfect moments. They loved him, but he didn't seem to love them back.

After the final encore, I followed him up to the dressing room like I'd done after every show. Gracin sat in his chair with his elbows on his knees. He knew the show had sucked more than usual. I could tell he was beating himself up over it.

"How long is this going to last?" he asked without looking up.

"What're you talking about?" My heart hitched in my chest, but I pretended not to be affected by him. Work would keep me sane. I started hanging his jackets, smelling each one to see what needed to go to the cleaners the next day. Gross, but effective.

"The cold shoulder? The silent treatment? Whatever it is you're doing. How long?"

I dropped three shirts and one jacket on the floor. Biting my upper lip, I debated on an answer. "Give me a few days," I whispered. I gathered the offending garments and rushed from the room.

No reason for him to see me cry.

CHAPTER TWELVE

I slept in the next morning. Well, if you consider eight o'clock sleeping in, which I did at this point. It felt glorious, until I remembered why. Gracin didn't text or call asking why I wasn't there for our morning run. That bothered me more than it should've. He was giving me the time I'd asked for. I wished I didn't need it.

Mom sat in the kitchen in a pale pink robe Dad had given her for Valentine's Day this year. She'd smiled when she first saw it, but the underlying sneer wasn't hard to miss. Still, she used it so it wasn't a complete fail of a gift. Her gaze focused on something outside, and the sun haloed her face like an angel. I tripped over my own feet, drawing her attention.

"Carly, sweetie, how are you?" Mom pulled out the chair beside, and I slid into it without bothering to get coffee. Her arms wrapped around me, squeezing me against her. "I never see you anymore with that job of yours. We haven't talked since …"

I didn't need her to elaborate. "I'm fine, Mom. I'm just glad it's over."

"I wished you would've come to me sooner," she whispered into my hair. Her tears dampening my hair. "To think, you've dealt with such a trauma for so long all alone."

Here we go. I rolled my eyes.

"Am I such a terrible mother you couldn't tell me what happened?" Her quiet tears turned into heavy sobs.

I loved my mother, but her reaction was exactly why I hadn't told her about Derrick. Everything became about her. If I'd told her, she would've wondered what she could've done to prevent it. Because, yeah, it was her fault Derrick had raped me.

So I did what I always did. I told her the truth, with the parental twist. "I was terrified, Mom. I thought I'd done something wrong."

"But you didn't, baby," she said.

"I know that now, but I was just a kid. I thought … I deserved it." The tears filled my eyes as I admitted it to my mom. "That's what he'd told me. I teased him, so I was asking for it, so I wanted it. Even though I begged him to stop."

"Oh, baby." Mom tugged me tightly enough suffocation was a possibility. "I'm so sorry."

"Me, too."

I let Mom comfort me until my stomach grumbled. She heard it and went into comfort food mode. She made bacon, scrambled eggs, toast, and even broke out the juicer for fresh orange juice. It didn't make everything go away like she always thought food did, but it was nice to spend some time with Mom. In a few short months, I'd be at U of N and she'd still be in Branson. It bothered me, so I let her make chocolate chip pancakes.

And I wondered what Gracin would think of the crap I shoveled into my mouth.

My heartache grew the size of a humanity-ending asteroid.

I ate two stacks of pancakes, letting the food fill the big hole inside me. Each time I talked about what happened with Derrick, which totaled three times, the hole grew bigger instead of smaller. Maybe I'd been fooling myself about being over what had happened, but I needed to keep moving forward, to keep talking about it with those who love me. That was the only way I'd heal.

∞ ∞ ∞

Gracin didn't push anything over the next two days. Actually, I was bored out of my mind. Denny and I texted every day, but I didn't see it happening. Our schedules didn't mesh, and quite frankly, getting rejected by Gracin stung more each day instead of less.

Sleeping in for three days rocked, but I missed my morning runs. The rush they gave me suited my daily needs. No need to find the nearest zipline or bungee cord if I ran every day. I woke up early and slipped on my shoes. Even if I ran alone, I wanted to get back into the groove. My heart lurched when I remembered each run with Gracin. I shook my head to dislodge the memories as my phone vibrated off my nightstand.

Will you run with me today? Gracin texted.

I smiled and glanced down at my running clothes. *Sure.*

His response was just as fast. *How long will it take you to get ready?*

Actually, I already am.

Good. I'm in the driveway.

I forced myself not to run out the door and jump in his arms. The situation didn't call for something so drastic, and it's not like I hadn't seen him over the last few days. But I really hadn't seen *him*. I'd been around Gracin the performer, not Gracin the person. I missed the person.

He leaned against his truck with his head down and one heel propped against the tire. Put him in jeans and a cowboy hat, and he looked like the cover a country album. The image cemented in my mind, and it was way too hot to ignore. When his hazel eyes glanced up and met mine, I knew I'd suffer the rest of the summer. He pushed off the truck and crossed his arms, shuffling from foot to foot.

Was he nervous?

I strolled toward him, stretching my arms above my head. Gracin bent over, stretching his legs. Just like that, we fell into our usual routine. Halfway into the run, the sweat dripped off my nose and chin. The summer had barely started but an early heat wave had the humidity at record levels. If I didn't have to work, I'd jump in the lake and not come out until September.

We sprinted the last two blocks, Gracin beating me easily. I fell on the concrete and reached my arms over my head.

"Get up, Carly, or you'll start cramping." How he

managed to form words amazed me.

"Fine," I huffed, rolling onto my side and forcing myself to stretch. "You trying to kill me or something?"

Gracin laughed. "Or something."

"Would that something be a sick form of revenge?" I stood and put my hands on my lower back, leaning back to tug the muscles of my abs. Stretching felt better than running.

He cocked his head to the right. "Revenge for what?"

"Losing in a game of tonsil hockey?" This was good. Making a joke out of the incident was better than admitting how much it still hurt.

"Don't be stupid." His eyebrows started their epic battle.

"Oh, Gracin, haven't you learned anything by now? Stupid is my middle name," I said, still trying to keep it lighthearted.

He closed the gap between us and stared into my eyes. "Carly, you're anything but stupid."

The fire ignited between us, well at least on my side of the kindling anyway. Just like the other night, I wanted to press my lips against his skin, tasting every inch of him. He tilted his head, leaning in enough a girl could get second thoughts.

And I opened my big mouth. "Then what am I?"

That seemed to break his focus and he stepped back. He cleared his throat and moved toward his truck, stopping before opening the door.

"You're a lot of things, Carly, but definitely not stupid."

He hopped in the truck, leaving me more breathless than after the run.

I went back inside after watching his truck disappear around the corner. Before the kiss, I would've been at his cabin for breakfast. Things were on the mend but not quite there yet. Maybe by the end of summer we'd have our usual banter back. If only he'd stop throwing me mixed signals.

"Hey, Carly," Dad said as I strolled into the kitchen. "Was that Gracin?"

"Yeah." I'd learned a long time ago not to elaborate on simple questions. I took the orange juice out of the fridge and drank straight from the container.

Dad never took his nose out of his tablet. He'd finally gone green and ditched the morning paper for the digital version. "I've noticed things have been tense between you two the last several days. Is there a problem I need to be aware of?"

I almost choked on the pulp. "No. We had a disagreement, but it's better."

"Remember," Dad said, looking at me over his half-moon glasses, "make him happy. This season's going well so far. It might be possible to extend his appearance here."

Rolling my eyes, I tried not to snort. Gracin wasn't going to stay in Branson. This was a stepping-stone for him to get his life back on track.

"Don't roll your eyes at me, bug." Dad smirked. He wiped it off his face rather quickly as he set his tablet down and put his hands in his lap. "We haven't talked since the ... incident with Derrick." His nose wrinkled when he said that name. "I ... I made you an appointment to see Dr. Winchester."

I didn't have a clue who Dr. Winchester was, so I stared at him waiting for further explanation.

"You don't know who I'm talking about?" My father was so rarely unsure of himself, and this would've been fun if I had any clue what was going on. "Let me rephrase then. I made you an appointment at the Hopewell Clinic."

The lightbulb exploded over my head. I'd called Hopewell several times over the last few weeks for Gracin's appointments. He saw a therapist weekly to talk about his issues and to stay sober. Why in the world would my father do this? I didn't need to see anyone.

Dad held out a hand before I opened my mouth to protest. "Just listen. You say you're fine. I actually believe you might be, but it would make … it wouldn't hurt to talk to someone outside of the family about what happened to you."

I did. Gracin knows everything. But I couldn't tell my father that. He'd already indicated his discomfort about my friendship with Gracin when he thought we were doing the sheeted tango.

"Please? Just one session. That's all I'm asking here." My father never said "please" to anyone. Even when he asked Mom to do something, it was always more of a command than anything else.

"Okay," I said. Dad sat back in his chair with wide eyes and an opened mouth. He'd been prepared for a battle. "If it means that much to you, I'll go once, but that's all."

Dad's eyes betrayed his doubt. It made me smile. "The appointment is at two."

"Perfect. Gracin's in rehearsal then. He won't even notice I'm gone." This was like a moment or something. I wasn't sure what to do, but a hug seemed to be in order. Dad was just as uncomfortable as I was when I wrapped my arms around his neck. "I really am okay, Dad."

"I know you are, bug, but I appreciate you going anyway." He let go and looked me in the eyes for the first time in recent memory. "I just wished this had never happened to you."

A sad smile quirked my cheek. "Me too, but I can't change what he did to me."

Dad hugged me again, harder and longer. If I didn't know better, I would've thought I heard a sob. But my father doesn't cry, he yells and screams. Never has he cried. His head rested on my shoulder, and it became colder with a damp sheen that could only be sweat from my run. Because my father doesn't cry.

∞ ∞ ∞

Dr. Winchester didn't smile. Not once. Not even when I cracked a joke. He was not my type of therapist. Honestly, I didn't know what type of therapist was "mine," but I knew it wasn't someone like Winchester. Keeping my word to Dad, I told the Doc everything, excluding the miscarriage. Only three other people in this world knew about it, and I intended to keep it that way. When we finished, he let me leave without making another appointment. Nice to know I was as well-adjusted as I believed. Or he knew I wasn't going to make another appointment.

I arrived at the theater at three-thirty to get the dressing room ready for the show. Gracin paced inside, wearing the carpet thinner each day. His black t-shirt was wet with sweat.

"Good rehearsal?" I closed the door behind me and strolled toward the wardrobe. Gracin's hand grabbed my arm, spinning me around. "What the hell?"

"Where've you been?" His eyes danced manically around my face.

"I had an appointment. Why?"

He closed his eyes and let go. "Sorry, I just … I was worried, and you didn't answer my text messages."

I pulled my phone from my pocket. Sure enough, there were six messages. I'd silenced the stupid thing when I went in to see Winchester instead of putting it on vibrate, because I knew I'd have to check it if I felt it moving in my pocket. The tiny red light flashed at the top, indicating the battery life was minimal. I turned the volume back up, grabbed the charger I'd left here, and plugged it in.

"Yeah, sorry." I shrugged. One thing I made sure not to talk to the good doctor about was Gracin, although my mind kept drifting there during the appointment. Lord only knew what would come out of that. Probably therapy sessions for the rest of the summer with a referral to a shrink in Nashville this fall. "I was busy."

"Just …" His voice strained over the word. "Do me a favor, and tell me when you aren't available, so I don't freak out."

I took my hand off the ugly blue sparkly shirt he wore for his Saturday shows and turned around. This guy was getting on my nerves. One minute he cared, the next he was hanging with Gloria. "Why would you freak out?"

He stared at me before answering. I didn't divert my eyes from his, searching for the answer I wanted, but the one he wouldn't give. Finally, he dropped his hands from his hips and sighed. "Because you're my friend." He paused and shuffled his feet. "Right?"

"Friends. Right." I turned around and yanked the ugly shirt off the hanger.

"Carly —"

Fortunately, my latest ringtone cut him off. I answered without looking at the caller ID.

"Carly?" Dad asked even though he had to know my voice by now. "Come to my office for a minute? This won't take long."

"Yeah, sure." I checked the battery on my phone and opted to leave it in the room. Facing Gracin, I said, "My father summoned me. Is it okay if I go? Do I need your permission?"

Gracin deflated and shook his head as he stared at the floor.

"Good. I'll be back in a bit." I hurried out of the room. As the door closed behind me, I thought I heard my phone chirp a text message. It could wait. Dad couldn't.

The smile on my face must've been enough to light up the stage. Dad asked me about the appointment, and then he let me out of my debt. Everything I made for the rest of the summer was mine and mine alone. That was enough to celebrate. Ten minutes later, I strolled back into the dressing room.

I opened my mouth to share my good fortune and closed it when I saw the grim expression on Gracin's face. He sat in his chair with his hands on his tight abs. The blue contacts hid his beautiful eyes. I hated those things.

"What's wrong?" I wanted to rush up and wrap my arms around him if only to make him smile. All that would do was piss him off even more.

"Whatever plans you have tonight, cancel them. I've been invited to a cocktail party at Andy River's house after the show." This should've made him happy. He'd been invited into the elite circle of Branson. "I need you to go to the cabin and get my black suit out of my closet."

"Sure, but what does that have to do with my plans tonight?" I crossed my arms and tapped my foot on the carpet.

"You're going with me." He stood and handed me the key card to his cabin and my phone. "And someone named Denny called. You might want to call him back."

I stared at him as he towered over me. "You answered my phone?"

Gracin cocked his eyebrow and deepened his frown. I waited for an answer, but he didn't say a single syllable. He broke our stare-down, moving away from me and out the door.

My fingers flew across the touch screen as I got to my call log. Denny's number. Beside it an eight-minute conversation. What in the hell did they have to talk about for eight minutes? A tiny war waged inside me. Call Denny back or text him? As if reading my mind, my phone chirped and vibrated at the same time.

Sorry, Carly. I didn't realize you weren't available. Let me know if that changes, Denny texted.

My thumbs typed faster than my fingers on a regular keyboard. *What're you talking about?*

But I didn't hit send. The curser blinked after the question mark, waiting for a command. My thumb hovered over send, then moved down and started to hit the backspace key. I erased each letter with a light tab that got harder until the final letter was gone. Despite the fact that I had no intention of seeing Denny, I was pissed. Questions swirled in my head, but the one I kept focusing on was the hardest one to answer. Why?

CHAPTER THIRTEEN

My to-do list for the evening grew with the cocktail party invite. There wasn't a lot of time to get myself ready and get all of Gracin's stuff done. It required help, and I hated asking for help. If he wanted me there, I was going to be there. Besides, doing something he wanted would require a little tit for tat on his part. He was going to explain in great detail why he'd answered my phone and scared Denny off. He just didn't know it yet.

Gracin hardly spoke to me once I got back to the theater two hours later. He may have had a suit at his disposal, but my wardrobe contained nothing suitable for a party at Andy River's house. The only shoes I owned were my Doc Martens, my running shoes, and a wide assortment of flip-flops. I hadn't even worn heels to prom. Much to my mother's delight, I raided her closet. She had more cocktail dresses than a Hollywood starlet. Every time Dad had a party to go to, Mom bought a new dress. I ended up taking a black halter dress with a form fitting bodice and a skirt that flared just right around the hips. I also grabbed a pair of low-heeled slingbacks.

After hanging the clothes in the closet, I sent Miranda and Luke a text. Less than five minutes later, Luke stood in the door to Gracin's dressing room.

"Are you serious? You can't do your job because you have a date tonight?" He shook his head slowly back and forth, a move he learned from Dad. "Unbelievable. Does Gracin know you're doing this?"

"Doing what?" Gracin asked as he pushed by Luke and headed straight toward his chair.

"Yes, he does. This is his fault." I crossed my arms, waiting for Gracin to come to my aid.

"Hey, Gracin," Miranda said as she stuck her head under Luke's arm. "How's it going?"

Gracin glanced at each of us in turn, finally settling back on me. "Are we having a Reynolds party or something?"

I rolled my eyes. "Only if you want the show to go off without a hitch tonight."

"Carly has a hot date after the show, and she wants Miranda to help her tonight." Luke crossed his arms in an effort to fill the entire door. Miranda ducked under his elbow and gave him her best dirty look. "I, however, don't think it's such a good idea."

Gracin glanced around again before settling his gaze on mine. I thought I saw a twinkle in there before his eyes went blank. "Hot date, huh? Do I know him?"

My face burned, and I hoped it didn't show. "Nope. You've never met Denny."

Luke said something, but I didn't hear a word. Gracin and I were locked in a silent battle. My anger dissipated as I willed him to see the real me again. If he would only face the truth, we'd be great together. Even if it was only for a few months, it would be everything.

"Carly!" Luke shouted, breaking the stalemate. "I asked if that's the same Denny –"

"The one and the same," I said, crossing my arms. Gracin turned around and faced his vanity, but his eyes found mine in the mirror. "He's taking me to some fancy cocktail party after the show."

"What happened to Jonathan?" Luke asked out of nowhere. It didn't matter that he hadn't seen "Jonathan" at the theater or even heard his name since the barbecue. Sometimes my brother was as bad as the worst blonde joke.

Gracin fought the smile and lost as half of the grin broke through. The twinkle I'd thought I'd seen earlier was definitely there as we stared at one another in the mirror.

Our little secret. The idea threw me. Ours. Mine and Gracin's. The ache in my heart grew. I wanted more from him. More than one moment when we pretended to be something or, at least, let people believe we were anyway. It wasn't enough. I wouldn't smile with him. It wasn't slightly amusing.

"Jonathan left," I whispered. The pain overwhelmed me, and a small tear slipped from the corner of my eye. "He didn't want … He couldn't handle …" I shook it off. There was no reason to finish what I wanted to say. The smile left Gracin's face, and I mouthed the last word anyway. "Me."

"That's too bad. He seemed like a nice guy," Luke said.

I tore my eyes away from Gracin and turned toward my

brother. "Don't you have something better to do? We've got a show to get ready for."

Luke looked like I'd slapped him in the face. "As long as Mr. Ford is okay with your ... alterations for the evening."

"It's fine," Gracin said through gritted teeth. He focused on cracking his knuckles.

"Come on, Miranda. I'll show you what I need you to do." I took Miranda by the arm and led her past Luke into the hallway.

"Bye, Gracin," she called over her shoulder. Once we were free from the prying ears of Luke, she whispered, "Who's Jonathan?"

I grimaced, but answered her honestly. "He's this guy I really liked, but he didn't want to hang out with me."

Miranda snorted. "Geez, Carly, how many guys can you fall for in one summer?"

Just one.

∞ ∞ ∞

Miranda did better than I expected. While I managed everything from Gracin's dressing room, she ran back and forth to grab costume changes from me and whatever else Gracin suddenly needed. I had the set list memorized down to the last crash of the cymbals, so I knew the second-to-last song before a brief intermission was four and a half minutes long. Just the right amount of time to shower.

Grandfather Reynolds had renovated the theater with the intention of having Broadway shows perform. Some actors' guild required that all theaters performing with dancers had to have showers, so Grandfather had put them in. Unfortunately, the cost to produce a show of Broadway caliber was too much, and he'd abandoned the idea after the first full season. Even with sellout crowds, the theater had lost money that year.

The hot water drained the tension from my body. I was downright schizophrenic lately. Part of me wanted to show Gracin what he was missing out on; the other part wanted to beg him to give me a chance to make him happy. One minute, I was pissed at his attitude, the next I was googly-eyed over him. I needed to get myself together.

I raced back to the dressing room a moment before Miranda burst in.

"He wants something … God, I forgot what it is!" Her face reddened as her eyes darted around the dressing room. She started toward the pile of clothes on the floor by the wardrobe.

"Meerkat, stop!" I snapped before she ruined my organized chaos. "Think. What did he say?"

Her eyes screwed up, and she stuck her lower lip out in a pout. "I don't …"

"Okay, here," I shoved the next costume change into her hands. "Was he freaking out? Calm? Angry?"

"Freaking out, I think. Why?"

I rushed to the fridge and grabbed his spritzer bottle filled with water and lavender oil Gracin sniffed to calm down. Even though it was a crock, he believed it worked, and it was all that mattered. I put the bottle in her outstretched hand. "Shake this on your way down. Don't spray him yourself.

He hates that. And if this isn't what he wanted, tell him I said it was better. He won't yell at you then."

"Okay," she said as she ran out the door.

The rest of the night went smooth. By the time the show ended, I was ready for the party. I stood in front of the full-length mirror in the corner of the room. This wasn't my style, but I kind of liked the way I looked. Mom wasn't getting this dress back any time soon.

I twirled and watched the skirt billow perfectly.

"Wow."

I almost spun myself to the floor at the sound of his voice. Gracin stood in the doorway with Miranda peeking around his arm.

"Oh my God, Carly!" Miranda squealed. She pushed Gracin out of the way and rushed over to me. "You look amazing. Denny's gonna flip. Don't you think so, Gracin?"

I didn't want to meet his gaze since I could feel it burning its way to my soul, but I did. Like earlier, our eyes locked and a silent battle began. My side pleaded for a chance, while his side said no. I needed to let this go.

"He's a lucky guy," Gracin said quietly. He moved toward the dressing table and grabbed his stuff for the shower. "Clean up later, Carly. Thanks for helping, Miranda. You can head out. Luke's supposed to meet you by the security door in five."

Gracin left the room without giving me another glance. Maybe this dress was a mistake. Hell, this whole experience was a mistake.

For the first time in my life, I regretted doing something

stupid. If only I'd realized how drunk Ivy was when she got behind the wheel of Dad's Mercedes, I wouldn't be in this position.

I roamed the theater for twenty minutes, wondering what to do. A couple of the grips gave me catcalls. While it made me smile, it didn't make me feel any better. I'd never been this gaga over a guy before, and quite frankly, it scared me. Weighing the pros and cons didn't help either. If Gracin and I hooked up, it wouldn't survive my move to Nashville for school or his move back to L.A. The long-distance thing wouldn't work for either one of us. Where would that leave us at the end of summer? Right where we already were. What if we went for it and he decided we totally sucked together? Could I keep doing my job for the rest of the summer without making myself miserable? What if we went for it and I decided we sucked together? After being the pursuer, could I tell him it wasn't working? Everything screamed "this won't work, so don't even try."

Then there was the fact that he'd rejected me.

Why do you keep doing this to yourself, Carly? The guy said no. Accept that he doesn't want you and move on. It's the only way to get over it. Call Denny tomorrow.

I went back to Gracin's dressing room determined to be his friend and nothing more. When I opened the door that thought almost shot out the heating vents. Gracin stood in front of the mirror with his jacket opened and the top three buttons of his shirt undone. He looked like he belonged in a spy movie, not in Branson.

"Wow," I whispered to myself.

He turned around, and I realized this was almost the exact same scenario from earlier.

"Hey." He shoved his hands into his pockets. Forget spy movie, he belonged on the cover of a magazine. "Tie or no tie?"

"No tie." I tore my eyes away from him and walked over to the vanity where I'd left the black sparkly clutch I'd liberated from Mom's collection. She'd never miss that either. "We should go."

Gracin nodded but turned back toward the mirror. He took his hands out of his pockets and smoothed the lapel. "I … Thank you for coming tonight." He closed his eyes and inhaled deeply. After an exhale to the ten count, he opened them and faced me. "I've been under a lot of stress lately, and I'm not going to lie to you."

The anxiety rolled off of him and onto me. I stepped closer to him and put my hand on his arm. "Whatever's going on, you can tell me."

He smiled sadly, and I wondered if I was the problem. I realized then that my unwanted advances as well as the pressures of his father among Lord only knew how many other things might push him over the edge. "Are you worried about falling off the wagon?" I whispered.

Gracin closed his eyes and nodded. "Sometimes I wish I could feel that lack of control again and forget it the next day. It's almost worth the hangover."

My hand slid down his arm, and my fingers entangled with his. I squeezed gently. "Don't worry, Jonathan. I've got your back."

Gracin smiled and squeezed my hand back. "Thank you, Carly."

"That's what friends do." I tried to smile, but even I knew it didn't look genuine. "We're friends, right?"

"Friends." His smile faded. "Right."

∞ ∞ ∞

We didn't talk or even sing along with Johnny Cash on the way to Andy River's house. Gracin let the GPS guide him to the luxurious home on the side of a mountain south of town. Everyone in Branson knew where Andy River lived, but we respected his privacy and didn't trespass. Unless it was a wild high school dare involving alcohol, but I'd only done it once my sophomore year. Dad wasn't too happy about it either. Stupid security cameras. At least, Andy hadn't pressed charges.

The sounds of a piano and laughter floated through the door. Gracin's tension tightened his shoulders, pulling them almost to his ears. I reached out and put my hand in his. Seeing him this nervous bothered me. Gracin was proud, confident, and cocky when he was in performer mode. When he was just being himself, he was sweet and lovable. Nervous Gracin was totally out of character. I had to remind myself there was a reason, and a damned good one.

Gracin slid his hand out of mine. My heart leapt into my throat, making it hard to breathe. This was just another rejection. He clenched his fist tight before ringing the doorbell. It opened before the melody, Andy River's number one hit song "Born to the Stars," ended. Standing before us was the towering butler-slash-bodyguard who hopefully didn't remember me. He stared at me for a moment and lifted an eyebrow.

"Ringing the doorbell this time and staying, Miss Reynolds? That's not your style." His voice rolled down my spine, leaving chills in its wake.

I cocked my head to the right. "Come on, Jeeves, that was three years ago. Can't a girl grow?"

Much to my surprise, he smiled before turning his attention to Gracin. "Mr. Ford, welcome. I hope you're keeping a tight leash on this one here. She's a wildcat."

Instead of relaxing, Gracin's shoulders tightened more. "That she is."

Jeeves stepped back to let us in. He leaned down and whispered. "Despite growing, I will be keeping a close eye on you this evening. Have no doubt about that. And my name isn't Jeeves."

I smirked and glanced at Jeeves. His serious expression made snakes coil in my stomach. One thing I planned on leaving behind in Branson was my "stellar" reputation.

Gracin made his way into the main parlor where Andy River sat at the piano beside a stunning blonde. Her fingers danced across the keys as a concerto filled the room. Andy beamed at the woman, his smile giving Liberace's a run for the money. His silver hair sparkled beneath the large chandelier. The one thing that stood out about him, and always had, was the color white. He wore nothing but white, and his house reflected the same. The only other colors accenting the room were silver and gold. Must be a bitch to clean.

The who's who of Branson strolled in and out of the room. I spotted at least three performers from the horse show down the road from our theater. A waiter stopped before us with flutes of champagne. Gracin took one automatically. I shook my head at the waiter and he moved on. The tension just grew around Gracin. I knew he wasn't thinking when he took the flute. That's why I was here, really. To stop this from happening. The minute any alcohol hit his lips, he would fall. At least, that's what he believed.

I put my hand around his on the delicate stem. His eyes snapped down and widened when he realized what was in his hand. He lessened his grip, letting me take it from him.

"Thanks," he whispered.

I set the glass on a nearby table, almost wishing I could take a sip to calm my nerves. "I'll go to the bar and get some club soda for you. The waiters will leave you alone if you've got a glass in your hands."

He nodded and faced the room. Someone came up to him with his hand out, ready to introduce himself. Frank Eaton, one-time manager of has-been country star Cody Clark, talked my father to sleep once. Gracin would be occupied for at least twenty minutes. Frank had to take a breath by then.

I kept Gracin in my sights while I stood at the bar, waiting patiently for the bartender to turn around. Frank seemed to be listening to Gracin, which was odd, but nice. The tension eased from Gracin's shoulder the longer the conversation went on.

"Hey, Carly. Funny seeing you here," a sweet tenor voice

said. I turned to face Sam Wilbright. "How's it going?"

"Great, Sam. How've you been?" If my eyes betrayed my shock, Sam didn't show it. Back in high school, he'd been awkwardly thin with thick glasses and bad hair. He'd gained some weight, making him appear more athletic than gangly, and his thick dark hair was styled in a faux hawk. The glasses were gone, revealing bright green eyes. It was kind of hot. Four years out of high school could change a person for the better.

"Doing well. How's the family?" Sam wiped down the counter while he talked.

"The family's great. Luke's running the theater this summer under Dad's watchful eye." Even though Luke and Sam weren't besties, they'd been somewhat friendly in high school. "What's up with you?"

"Oh, you know. Same old, same old. Just working for the summer before heading back to school." Sam caught someone's attention over my shoulder. "Your boyfriend's giving us the stink eye."

I turned around to meet Gracin's glare. He was still talking with Frank Eaton, but his eyes never left me. I nodded and faced Sam again. "He's not my boyfriend. Can I get a club soda with lots of ice?"

"Sure." Sam grabbed a thick glass and tossed the ice in. As he reached for the club soda, he asked, "So, if he's not your boyfriend, who is he?"

I laughed. That was a great question. "That's Gracin Ford. I'm his personal assistant for the summer."

Sam smiled at me. "You? A personal assistant? I thought

Carly Reynolds did what she wanted when she wanted."

I knew when a guy was flirting with me, and Sam was definitely flirting. I raised my eyebrows and smirked, taking the glass he'd set on the bar and walking away with a little more swing in my hips. When I glanced back at him, Sam was totally staring. His grin widened as our eyes met.

"– at least, that's what I'm seeing," Frank Eaton finished as I stopped beside Gracin. "Ah, Carly Reynolds, correct? Your father's talked quite a bit about you."

My first question was why, but I skipped saying it. Whatever Dad needed to do to schmooze wasn't any of my concern. I turned on the charm. "All good I hope."

Frank laughed. I glanced up at Gracin who stared at me like he'd never seen me before. "What?" I mouthed.

He shook his head and sipped the club soda I'd handed him.

"Yes, all good. If you don't mind, I'd like to steal Gracin from you for a few minutes. There are some people I'd like him to meet." Frank's smile never left his face, but there was something predatory about it. He was up to something.

"Be my guest," I responded. After all, there was a cute guy at the bar who was more than willing to chat with me.

I turned back toward Sam, but the bar was packed. Jeeves caught my attention by the front door. He was true to his word. His eyes locked with mine, and I smiled. Maybe I could cause a little trouble to keep him on his toes. I slowly made my way through the crowd, searching for something that would freak Jeeves out a bit. Without paying much attention, I'd found myself in a dining room larger than the lobby at the theater. Twenty people could sit at the table and there'd still be room for twenty more.

Gracin stood in the corner with Frank and two gorgeous blonde women, including the one who'd been playing the piano when I walked in. I stayed out of his line of sight and watched. The tension he'd carried with him early had left his body. But it moved into mine when blondie number two put her hand on Gracin's arm for longer than necessary. Polite touching was one thing, but this chick wasn't just being polite. And the glow in Gracin's cheeks told me he liked it.

I needed to get over this shit fast. Gracin had tried to ruin any chance I had with Denny, not like it wasn't reparable, but Sam was here and I was pretty sure willing. Taking a deep breath, I moved back toward the bar, giving up on my quest to make Jeeves miserable. Two waiters stood at the bar while Sam filled their trays with champagne flutes.

"I thought you'd left," Sam said after finishing putting one last flute on the waiter's tray. He leaned against the counter.

"Nah, you were busy so I cruised the dining room." Leaning close enough to give a tiny cleavage shot, I whispered, "This party kinda sucks."

Sam laughed. "They usually do." He paused and glanced over my shoulder. "I go on break in a few. Want to hang outside with me?"

I tapped my chin, pretending to think about it. "Let me see, decent conversation with a good looking guy or stay inside by myself with a bunch of old fogeys. That's a hard decision."

"Good looking guy, huh?" Sam laughed. "I doubt anybody's ever used those words to describe me."

"Then they haven't seen you lately," I replied.

Sam stared at me for a moment before leaning close enough I could smell the sweet aftershave on his chin. "Meet me on the side of the driveway. The guests won't see us there."

"I'll be there." I turned around and caught Gracin's gaze as he stood in the doorway. His face turned red, but he didn't make a move toward me. Instead, he turned and strode out of the room. My father always told me to trust my gut, and my gut said Gracin was pissed about me flirting with Sam. It didn't matter. He wasn't anything other than my friend, and therefore, he had no say in whom I flirted with or whom I made out with. Quite frankly, I wanted to know what Sam's lips felt like against mine, if only to forget how soft Gracin's were. I slipped out the front door when Jeeves turned his back for a moment. Little bonus.

The hot summer air stuck to my bare arms. A breeze from the lake below rustled the trees, catching the scent of roses and lilies. Andy River had the prettiest rose garden in the county. I should know. On my escapade a few years ago, I'd hidden between the bushes as Jeeves hunted me down. There were worse places to hide.

"Carly," Sam said from the side of the house. I strolled over to where he leaned against the garage with his hands in his pockets. He turned so his shoulder was the only thing touching the wall. "You graduated this year, right?"

"Yep." I matched his stance. The siding cooled my hot

skin. Maybe that would keep me from sweating.

"Going to school next year?" Sam inched closer.

"U of N." I didn't move.

He moved a little closer again. "Nashville, huh? That's only about three hours from Memphis."

Wait, what? Who cares how far Nashville is from Memphis? "Yeah, I guess. Why?"

He pointed to his chest. "University of Memphis."

Ah. Maybe I'd dyed my hair too much over the years to not see where this was going.

"Not far at all." He leaned closer, and I caught a whiff of pepper and leatherwood on the breeze. Sam smelled like Gracin.

"Carly?"

I froze at the sound of Gracin's voice behind me. Turning away from Sam, I glanced over my shoulder. Gracin's arms were crossed over his chest, and he was pissed.

"Yeah?" I asked with as much attitude as I could. It wasn't like Gracin had any say in whom I kissed.

He didn't answer.

Sam cleared his throat after a few minutes of our silent standoff. "I need to get back inside. I'll … Yeah, I need to go."

No "I'll call you later" or "Give me your number" from Sam, just a quick disappearing act.

I waited until he was out of earshot when I strode up to Gracin. Jabbing my finger into his chest as hard as I could, I snapped. "You had no right to run him off."

Gracin grabbed my hand and held it against his chest. "Seriously?"

"Yeah, seriously. You made your choice, Gracin. That doesn't mean I stop living my life. That doesn't mean I can't see someone else just because you don't want me. You can't tell me not to go out with other people. You have no right to do that!"

Gracin bent his head down so we were eye to eye. "You think he wanted more than a quick roll in the hay, Carly? You really want to be used, go ahead. Don't let me stop you."

He let go of my hand, and I used it to slap him. The tears I'd hidden from him rolled down my cheeks faster than the flooded Mississippi. "Fuck you, Gracin. You don't want me, but nobody else can have me. Is that the deal?"

"We're leaving. Now." Gracin turned his back on me.

I followed him, because it was either that or call a cab. Quite frankly, the cabs in Branson usually smelled of vomit this late at night. And I wanted answers. This time I was going to get them.

∞ ∞ ∞

The ride back to his cabin was worse than the ride to Andy River's house. Gracin gripped the steering wheel hard enough veins popped on the back of his hands. I tapped my foot against the floor, wishing like hell I had called the cab. The more I relived his interruption, the angrier I got. By the time he parked by my scooter, my temper was ready to blow.

Gracin didn't say a word as he climbed out of the truck and slammed the door behind him. He never slammed his door. The truck was his baby. He stalked to the door of his cabin and flashed the keycard, leaving the door open as he went inside. I took it as an invitation to finish our yelling match. Fuck the silent battles we kept having, this one was going to be epic.

I threw the door closed behind me, rattling the windows. Gracin paced the hallway between the living room and his bedroom.

"Why does it matter?" I asked, remaining calm despite my desire to scream at him from the top of my lungs. "Why do you care if something happened between me and Sam? You made your feelings clear, Gracin. So explain it to me, because I can't figure it out."

He stopped and stared at me like I'd just won the stupidest person in the world contest.

"That's not an answer. Just tell me what's so repulsive about me?" Damn it. I started crying again. "Is it because I'm not like the models you've dated? Or I'm not smart enough? Or because … because of what Derrick did? Is that it? Because Derrick raped me, I'm not good enough for you."

Gracin's eyes widened and he closed the distance between us. "This has nothing to do with Derrick, Carly." His hands shook as he put them on my shoulders. A slow heat rolled from his touch down to my toes. "You're beautiful, smart, funny, and everything a guy could want in a girl."

"Just not you," I whispered.

He leaned down, resting his forehead against mine so I couldn't see his face. "It's not that I don't want you, Carly. Please don't think that. I do … More than I should, but …

you'll be gone soon. I won't do the long-distance thing again. I can't."

"Again?" Hope swelled in my chest. He did want me. Maybe this could work after all.

He backed away and leaned against the small kitchen table, shoving his hands into his pockets. His head dropped for a moment before he lifted it to meet my stare. "You read my story. My girlfriend moved to New York a few months after we started dating, and I spent most of my time in L.A." He shook his head as the memories overtook him. "She ended it by getting photographed with some director in a more than friendly embrace. I … I lost it and ended up having my well-publicized breakdown. Mom took me to rehab. I was washed-up, a has-been before I turned eighteen." He met my eyes, tears rimming his. "She destroyed me, and I didn't feel a third for her what I feel for you, Carly."

Everything I wanted was within reach, but it wasn't either. We'd been doing this dance all summer. I'd known it when I'd kissed him the first time, but he kept ignoring it. I wasn't going to let him anymore. "These feelings aren't going to disappear." I stepped closer to him. "So what're we going to do?"

"I don't know," he whispered.

I took another step toward him, stopping as our knees touched. "Gracin, what do you really want?" Reaching out, I put my hand on his thigh. "Do you want to be happy for the rest of the summer? Or do you want to pretend there isn't anything between us and forget this ever happened?"

Gracin swallowed, not taking his eyes off of mine. "Forget what ever happened?"

I bent my head and leaned toward him slowly, waiting for him to stop me, but he didn't. My lips brushed over his. I broke the chaste kiss, still expecting him to push me away. Gracin leaned forward, letting his lips touch mine in the same way. Every nerve in my body reached out to him, needing more than tiny kisses. His hands found my waist and pulled me against him. When Gracin kissed me again, it was unrestrained. Thank God he supported me against him, because my legs turned to molasses. I wrapped my arms around his neck, digging my fingers into his hair.

Gracin pulled away, resting his forehead against mine again. "What happens when you leave, Carly? When I leave?"

I leaned back, smiling sadly because I didn't want to think about either one of us leaving. I just wanted to let myself be with someone I cared about. I wanted to let him love me, even if it wasn't love but very strong like. I'd never felt like this before, and I wanted to revel in it. I wanted to live in the moment. "I don't know, Gracin. No matter what happens. No regrets."

Gracin nodded and pulled me against him. "Never."

I fell into his kisses as my hands took on a life of their own. They moved up his arms and slid beneath his jackets, shoving it off his shoulders. Gracin's lips never left mine as he let me undress him. My fingers worked each button on his shirt until that was gone too. His fingers found the zipper of my dress, but he didn't unzip it.

"Yes," I whispered my permission against his lips.

The zipper came down, followed shortly by the dress. Gracin tightened his arms around my waist, lifting me off the floor. I wrapped my legs around him as he carried me to the bedroom, closing the door behind him.

CHAPTER FOURTEEN

I knocked on Gracin's door at six the next morning. It'd only been four hours since I left the cabin. I could still feel his lips, his silky skin against mine.

Gracin opened the door, in his boxers from the night before. I smiled, shyness sweeping over me. Normally, I was bold and brutally honest. With Gracin, it was different.

"Good morning, sunshine," I said through a slight strain in my voice. "We running this morning?"

Gracin's sly grin filled his face. "Kind of ran a marathon last night." He stepped back from the door to let me in. "Best marathon of my life."

My knees wobbled as I tried to walk with confidence into his cabin. "The best, huh?"

The door closed with a quiet click and Gracin pressed his body against my back. His arms snaked around my waist as his lips found that spot just beneath my ear. I leaned into him, wrapping my arm around his neck.

"Oh, yeah. I'm not sure it's over either." His fingers grazed the bare skin on my stomach. Holy hell, this was not what I'd expected this morning. "If you're up for it."

I was up for it, but I wanted to make him work this time. "After our run"—I turned around and captured his lips with mine—"maybe we can hit the showers."

Gracin moaned against my mouth. My entire body turned into a boneless pile of goo. Maybe running wasn't a good idea.

"Deal," he said and kissed me again.

He let me go, and I sunk into the couch. My legs finally regained some form of muscle mass when he came back in his usual running attire. That outfit made me have more doubts about running.

We stretched without pawing at one another and started our run in silence. It wasn't the uncomfortable quiet we'd experienced in the last week, but the peaceful kind we'd had before the first kiss. Gracin set a slow pace, and we made it a mile before the inevitable conversation began. We needed to talk before anything else happened. The fact we would both leave at the end of summer still hung between us. I didn't want it to spoil what time we had together.

"We should probably lay all our cards on the table," I said as our breaths hit the same rhythm.

Gracin tensed beside me, almost stumbling on a crack in the sidewalk. "Go ahead."

"You already said you can't and won't do a long-distance relationship." I hated saying this, but it had to be out there. We needed to agree this relationship had a time limit, even if that's not what I wanted. It was all Gracin could give me. The sooner he knew I accepted the situation the better. "So, we agree we are just for this summer. When I leave for school, we …" I gulped the lump forming in my throat. "We agree to mutually stop. No phone calls. No texts. No emails. No contact. We go our separate ways."

Gracin stopped in the middle of the sidewalk. I made it three steps before realizing he wasn't beside me. I turned around to the eyebrow battle.

"You said … I don't want to walk away from us with any regrets or hard feelings," I said as I cautiously walked back to him. "Let's make the most of what time we have together without ruining it for something we both know we can't have."

"You mean that?" His shoulders fell. "We don't try if we want to?"

"You said you couldn't, so I think this is what's best." I lied through my teeth. It left a welling of bile in my stomach. "Don't you agree?"

Gracin shifted from foot to foot before looking me in the eye. "If that's what you want."

I rose onto my tiptoes and planted a quick kiss on his dry lips. "We've got plenty of time to make a whole assload of memories." *Ones I will cherish.*

Slowly he nodded in agreement. "Okay."

I should've been elated, but my heart sunk to my heels. We started running again, not bringing up anything other than work until we got back to his cabin. The cool air from the vents made me shiver as soon as I stepped inside. Gracin let the door close with a thud. He stood in front of me with a slight scowl.

He wasn't going to push me away after last night or because of our conversation. I moved toward him, sliding my arms around his waist. Gracin's hands moved to my hips as he rested his forehead against mine. God, I loved that. It was intimate and loving at the same time. I shook the word "loving" out of my head. It was one emotion neither one of us could afford.

I bent my neck and seized his lips. Gracin kissed me with a slow, burning passion. It was ten times more intense than anything last night. I melted against him, forgetting everything we'd talked about to just experience being with Gracin Ford. We needed to leave emotion out of it, but it was too late for me. I already cared for him more than I should. He didn't need to know that, though. I had to keep myself in check so I didn't slip farther into the danger zone. He'd already had his heart broken once, no reason for me to be the one to do it again.

∞ ∞ ∞

Bliss, that was the only word to describe the next several days. June was coming to an end, which meant Gracin and I had about eight more weeks together. I planned on making each day the best it could possibly be. Wednesday after the concert, I held out a pair of tickets to the final showing of the latest action movie. Guns and explosions sounded like a great prequel to the fireworks that would happen afterwards.

"A movie?" Gracin eyed the tickets in my hand. "You sure you want to be seen with me in public?"

I threw my head back and laughed. "You sure you want

to be seen with me? I'm the bad girl here."

Gracin slid his hand around my waist and pressed his body against mine. "So bad, you're good."

I actually giggled before kissing his nose. "You know it, baby. Now get your ass in gear so we don't miss the previews."

The door to Gracin's dressing room opened without warning. We jumped away from each other before the culprit could catch us. We hadn't come right out and said we needed to keep our relationship secret, but it seemed logical. First of all, it wasn't anyone's business. Second, I didn't want to be part of unwanted gossip, even if I'd experienced it most of my life. Thirdly, when this ended, I didn't want to be the pity of everyone.

"Nice show tonight, son," Albert Ford said as he stepped into the room. He glanced between us before settling his glare on me. "Hello, Miss Reynolds. I didn't realize you'd still be here this late."

I'd had the foresight to shove the tickets into my back pocket when I realized who was interrupting us. "I'm always here this late, Mr. Ford. Gracin and I usually spend some time planning for the next day after each show. I like to stay on top of things."

"I'm sure you do," he said, narrowing his eyes. "If you'll excuse us for a moment, I need to have a word with my son. Whatever you need to discuss with him can wait until tomorrow. Goodnight, Miss Reynolds."

I stared at him, trying to comprehend the ease at which he dismissed me. I didn't like it and wasn't going to keep my mouth shut until Gracin cleared his throat. I tore my gaze off Albert and met Gracin's.

"I'll see you later, Carly." The defeat in his voice tore through my heart. Gracin wouldn't look at me as I stood there completely dumfounded.

I wanted to rush up to Albert and kick him in the shin. I wanted to pull out the rest of his comb-over. Instead, I walked out the door, slamming it behind me.

Then I leaned my ear against it so I wouldn't miss a single word between them.

"What do you want, Dad?"

"You're not sleeping with her, are you?" Disgust laced through Albert's words.

"Jesus, Dad. That's none of your business." I heard the chair move and imagined Gracin collapsing into it.

"She's a fucking redneck. You've been with runway models." Something tapped against the door. "But I'm sure she's a good enough distraction while you're here. Anyway, I didn't show up to talk about your sex life. I heard from your old bandmate Jay Edison. He's trying to get Accentuate together for a reunion tour. Naturally, I told him you're in."

"I don't want to –"

"Grow some balls, son. Just because things didn't end well doesn't mean you can't suck it up and go on tour. Think of the money. Plus you wouldn't have to come back to this hellhole again." Something slapped against something else. "This is a good thing."

Gracin sighed. "If you already agreed, why'd you bother to tell me?"

"Courtesy."

"Whatever, Dad."

"Glad to see we're on the same page, son." There was a pause. "And don't get too attached to the redneck. There's better fish in the sea."

I took off running down the hall and steps until I was outside. The fresh air filled my lungs, swelling against the growing anger inside. I didn't expect Gracin to stand up for me, but to take that shit from his father was incomprehensible. But what did I know. I was just another redneck and a notch in Gracin's bedpost according to his father. Maybe I needed to show that jerk that I was so much more, that I was better than all of those bimbo models put together. It wouldn't be hard. My anger deflated a little at one simple realization: It wouldn't be hard, but it wouldn't be necessary either. The clock had been counting down my relationship with Gracin from the beginning. It wasn't about to change just because I wanted to prove to Albert Ford I wasn't some redneck hussy.

Albert walked out of the theater and saw me leaning against the truck. He had no clue Gracin and I came to the theater together every day, even before we were friends with benefits.

"Did you need something else, Miss Reynolds?" He strolled up to me as if he was taking a walk along the beach.

I gave him my best smile. "Why, no sirree Bob, I's good right where I is," I said with the worst country twang this side of the Mississippi.

He stopped and lost all his swagger. "I take it you

overheard my conversation with my son. What would your father think?"

"What would he think of you calling his daughter a redneck slut? Or what would he think of how you referred to his theater as a hellhole? Knowing my father, you wouldn't even be able to set foot into a karaoke bar if he heard what you said." I didn't let my smile waver one bit as I steered the conversation away from Dad. "Now, if you must know why I'm here, I left my scooter at the cabin and rode to the theater with Gracin, as we've done since his truck arrived. Without any, oh how would a redneck say it, without any hanky panky going on."

"You've got a smart mouth, little girl." There was the Albert Ford I'd seen with Gracin. All malice and threats, but not a single bite.

"You wouldn't want me to run to Daddy, would you? Lose all the money you're raking in from Gracin's performances?" He flinched and I kept on attacking. "What would you do if Gracin decided to quit singing, Al? My best guess is you'd be broke and living in a box on the side of the road."

"Don't threaten me. My son would never let that happen. And I won't let white trash like you corrupt his mind." He pointed at me, almost sticking his finger where I could bite it off. "You keep your panties on around him. If I find out you're fucking my son, I'll ruin you."

I leaned in so he wouldn't miss a single word. "Try it, Al. I'm not the one who'll be ruined."

Albert stared at me for several seconds before stepping

back with his fake smile plastered across his face. "Very well, Miss Reynolds. I see we won't come to any kind of agreement. Just remember what I said tonight when you're spreading your legs. A little redneck bitch like you won't change the course I've set for my son."

He turned on his heel and sauntered to the rented BMW parked at the other end of the lot. I watched the bastard drive away until the taillights become nothing but a fading red dot in my vision.

"Hey, you waited." Gracin walked toward me with exhaustion covering his features. A conversation with Albert Ford would do that to anyone.

I smiled, fake at first, turning genuine when I looked in Gracin's eyes. The idea of the tour must've been haunting him. Hopefully, he could get out of it. But that was a problem for later. "Of course. I wasn't about to let your father run me off, Gracin. Now," I pulled the tickets out of my back pocket, "how about that movie?"

Gracin put his arm around my shoulders and pulled me in for a quick kiss. "That sounds like a great idea."

CHAPTER FIFTEEN

The alarm went off on my phone, jolting me awake. My eyes didn't want to adjust to the dark room, until it hit me like an anvil where exactly I'd woken up. Gracin's arm tightened over my waist as I sat up. Crap, I hadn't meant to fall asleep. Reaching for my phone while trying to free myself from the tangled sheets didn't work out so well. I fell off the bed with a loud thunk and grabbed my phone at the same time. Unfortunately, I hit answer, because it wasn't my alarm at all.

"Carly?" Dad's voice drifted out of the tiny speaker. My eyes widened as I stared at the screen with Dad's avatar, a photo of Stalin. I'd changed it the day after my sentencing for wrecking the Mercedes. Panic filled his voice. "Are you there? Carly?"

"Yeah, I'm here." I scraped my foot as I pulled it out of the bed. "What's up?"

Gracin leaned up, the sheet falling off his bare chest. He ran his hand down his face and opened his mouth. I yanked at the sheet to get his attention and put my finger over my lips.

"Are you even listening to me?" Dad's voice snapped me back to attention.

"Um … Sorry, Dad, I'm half asleep." I yawned into the phone. How in the hell was I going to explain this?

"Where exactly did you fall asleep?" Each word clipped like a shod horse on pavement.

My brain froze. I wanted to lie, but nothing popped into my head. "Um …"

"Carly," he said, dragging my name out into five syllables, one for each letter.

"Fine, but you have to promise you won't be mad." I sighed into the phone. Maybe if I acted put out, he'd back off.

"No, I don't."

"Then I don't have to tell you where I'm at." Matching his tone, getting defensive: all ploys to make him feel more like the bad guy than the good parent. It'd worked for three years—no reason why it wouldn't keep working.

"Don't try to tell me you're at Nena's or Ivy's. I already called."

Shit. Time for some truth. "I wasn't going to, Dad." I rolled my eyes even though he couldn't see me. Glancing at Gracin, I mouthed "I'm sorry" before throwing him under the bus. He reached out to stop me, but it was too late. "I'm at Gracin's." Gracin slapped his hand to his forehead and fell back on the bed. I rushed through the rest of my partial truth as fast as possible. "He started going all diva after the show, thinking one of the dancers tried to sabotage a routine because she didn't like it. I needed to calm him down before he went off the deep end."

Dad didn't say anything, so he either mulled it over or wanted to call me out for lying. I didn't dare say a word.

Gracin rolled to his side, propping himself with his elbow. He wiggled his eyebrows. Great, now he wanted to get flirty.

"Where is Gracin now?" Dad's tone softened a bit, but the tension seeped through the phone anyway.

"Standing in front of me." I reached out and playfully smacked his leg. "I'm sure he's wondering why I'm here as much as you are."

Gracin licked his lips, leaning toward me. I tried to scoot away, but my back hit the wall. There wasn't anywhere to go, and Gracin knew it. He slid his hand up my bare arm, over my shoulder and behind my neck.

"And where exactly are you?" Dad's voice sounded far away as Gracin bent his head, grazing his lips over the tender skin of my neck.

"Um … living room." I spit the words out, biting back the moan Gracin generated by kissing me this way.

"So, he just let you fall asleep on his couch?"

"Mmm … He kinda didn't know." I pushed Gracin away to think, to focus. "I wasn't going to leave until he fell asleep, Dad. Once he did, I sat on the couch to relax and must've dozed off."

Gracin leaned back in, but I pushed him away with all my strength.

"Carly, I want you to be honest with me. Is there something going on between you and Gracin Ford?"

I closed my eyes, wishing for a time machine to unhear the question. I'd lied by omission over the years. I'd lied by telling partial truths. It was how I kept my integrity when it came to my father. I hated lying, but sometimes it was the only way to keep the peace. Little white lies about where Gracin was, or where I was, those didn't count. And I'd never outright lied to Dad, outright lied about something that shouldn't be lied about. Until now. "No."

Dad might've been nodding in agreement or he might've been shaking his head. Either way, the guilt stone grew heavier in my chest.

"I'll be home in twenty," I said when he didn't respond. The silence pushed that stone farther down. "Okay?"

"Yeah, okay."

The difference between Dad silence and hang-up silence is that I could hear Dad breathing when he was still on the line. He'd never hung up on me without saying goodbye.

The phone fell from my hand, and I started crying. Gracin didn't say a word. He pulled me onto the bed and wrapped his arms around me until the tears wouldn't come.

"I'm sorry, Carly. This is my fault." Gracin squeezed me against him and kissed the top of my head. "If I hadn't totally exhausted you, you would've been home by now."

I snort-laughed and turned my head to stare into his face. "Yes, you did." I touched his cheek. "And I would do it again if I could."

Gracin's smile lit up the dark room. "Oh, you can."

It may have been meant for a laugh, but I didn't think it was funny. It only took seven minutes to get to my house.

That left thirteen for me to show Gracin just how right he was.

∞ ∞ ∞

Going to Golf-A-Round sounded like a good idea. It was one of my favorite places in Branson. Nena, Ivy, and I were expert mini-golfers, and Golf-A-Round was our course of choice. Most of the mini-golf courses kept getting bigger and "better," which I considered false advertising. Still, fine by me. Golf-A-Round wasn't as crowded as the touristy courses on Highway 76.

Besides showing Gracin what fun was really like, I wanted to see my friends. Nena and Ivy had taken a major backseat over the last two weeks. It never should be like that, but I had limited time with Gracin. Of course I had limited time with Nena and Ivy too. At least, I'd known them forever. When I looked back on my life at ninety, I'd have a ton of memories of my friends, but only this summer with Gracin. I wanted to make it as memorable as possible.

"Hey, chica, comp a girl a round of golf?" I asked the back at the window.

Nena spun around with a crooked smile that turned into a clown-like evil grin when she saw Gracin standing behind me. "Well, hello, Jonathan. You must be the reason Carly's been too busy to hang out with her best friends."

Ivy leaned over Nena's shoulder. "Not that we blame her."

"So, the evil boss let you get off for the afternoon? Or did he have to head over to Hopewell for another round of rehab?" Nena smiled, but her eyes reflected her annoyance.

Wow, talk about hitting below the belt. Gracin tensed behind me, but I laughed it off. Nena's thinly veiled anger didn't need to be directed at him anyway. She might be pissed at me, but she needed to keep it between us. There'd be time later to hash it out.

"Well, there wasn't much to do." I smiled as if her words weren't daggers. "He's slaving over the lighting again, like he does every day. Even the band's getting tired of showing up at two for sound checks."

"If he had boobs, he'd be a diva," Gracin said. How he kept a straight face, I had no idea, but I certainly couldn't. Gracin's hands slid around my waist, and he pulled me back against him. "Didn't realize I was that funny, Carly," he said into my ear loud enough for Nena and Ivy to hear.

"You have no idea, G … onathan." I pursed my lips, hoping neither one of the girls caught my almost slip. Gracin's fingers dug into my stomach. "Can you guys take a break and play a round?"

Nena shook her head as Ivy said, "Sure thing." Ivy glanced at Nena and rolled her eyes. "I'm up for it. I can only play a few holes."

"You're not coming, Nena?" In all our years, we'd never fought or even raised our voices. Nena's sudden chill toward me left me baffled.

She raised her eyebrows. "Sorry if I disappoint you, Carlsbad, but I took my break already."

Ivy came through the door by the ticket window. She held three putters and three different color golf balls. "Not that Chuck would care," Ivy said to me, "but she did just come off break."

I nodded, taking the red ball and a putter. Ivy smiled graciously at Gracin as she handed him a set of his own. We walked toward the first hole, a simple straight shot or so it seemed. The subtle inclines in the green took me four years to master. Ivy went first, wiggling her butt as she took aim. I glanced back at the ticket window, but Nena wasn't visible. A family of four stood in front of the window, blocking the view.

Ivy's hand fell on my shoulder. "Don't worry about it, Carly. She thought you were working your ass off, not getting your ass waxed by hotness."

I laughed and turned around in time to see Gracin's gentle putt not quite doing the job. "Yeah, he's pretty great."

Ivy didn't say anything as she pushed me forward. I placed my ball on the dot and angled my body to the left just a fraction of an inch. The easiest hole on the course was misleading. I tapped the ball harder than seemed necessary. The golf ball bounced off the wood railing on the left across the entire green to slam into the rail on the right. It then careened toward the back wall, hitting the sweet spot marked by years of people figuring out how to win before gliding toward the hole and circling the edge like a penny in one of those whirly coin donation things at the grocery store. It clinked into the tin cup.

"Seriously?" Gracin's mouth formed a perfect oval. He pointed toward the end of the green. "Seriously?"

I stepped up to him and smacked his ass. "Seriously."

Ivy laughed as she moved toward her ball and tapped it in. Gracin took two more putts before he managed to complete the hole, much to the chagrin of the family behind us. Ivy led the way to the next hole with Gracin trailing back beside me.

"You never cease to amaze me, Carly Reynolds," he said as he wrapped his arm around my waist.

"I try." Smiling up at him, the world felt right. The stars aligned perfectly. The poles balanced. Peace draped over Branson. Nothing could make what I had with Gracin wrong.

He leaned down and kissed my cheek. "Don't ever stop."

The words were meant to be sweet, loving even, but they stabbed at my heart. I had to stop when I left for school. If I'd learned anything over the last few weeks with Gracin, it was the simple fact I didn't want to stop. Ever.

And I could never tell him.

Each hole, my playing skill disappeared. I watched Gracin's every move. Listened to his every word with Ivy. They flirted playfully, but it was just for fun. Would he do that with another girl the minute I was out of his life? The thought tore through my heart. At the Windmill hole, Gracin's smooth putt slid through the tiny building with expert timing. Talk about a metaphor for our relationship.

God, melodramatic much, Carly. Get your head out of your butt. This is supposed to be a fun summer fling. Nothing more. Scolding myself didn't help.

"You okay?" Ivy asked.

I jumped, having forgotten where she was. If I could be

totally honest with anybody on this planet, it was Ivy. Well, and Nena, but she was pissed at me. The tear hovering on the edge of my eye slipped. I wiped it away quickly, but not fast enough.

"Carly, what's going on?" Ivy asked. The only time she ever sounded so concerned was when I was physically hurt.

"I don't want him to go," I whispered, hating the truth. Hating how I felt. This wasn't part of the deal. This wasn't the plan.

"Oh my God. I never thought I'd see the day." Ivy forced me to look at her. "You're in love with Jonathan."

"What?" I pulled away from her. "No. I just ... I like hanging out with him. That's all."

"If that was all, honey, you wouldn't be acting like this." Ivy crossed her arms and stared toward the windmill. Gracin walked around it, taking a wide berth to avoid the wooden blades. "If he was just a notch in your bedpost, you wouldn't shed a single tear over him."

Gracin raised his shoulders and held out his hands in the universal sign asking "What's taking you so long?"

Ivy moved to the starting point and set her ball down. Before she took her putt, she glanced over her shoulder. "Ask yourself something, Carly. What if you weren't going to Nashville? What if he wasn't going back to wherever he came from? What would happen then?"

Without looking, Ivy took her shot. Right through the center of the building. By the sound of Gracin's "woohoo," I knew it was a hole in one. Lucky girl.

Gracin leaned around the building, waving me on. The

smile on his face, the glow in his cheeks, and just the general way he stared at me were all I needed to know I was the lucky one here, not Ivy.

What would happen if we were both staying in Branson? It didn't matter, because it wasn't going to happen. There wasn't any reason to fantasize about anything after August twenty-seventh. It would only lead to heartbreak. And that wasn't part of the deal either.

CHAPTER SIXTEEN

The show was a well-oiled machine. Gracin cut back on the rehearsals, much to the band's joy, to hang with me. His diva-hectic schedule toned down to normal celebrity upkeep, which made my job so much easier. Instead of scheduling appointments on a whim, I had the rest of the summer planned up until the last show. The only things to worry about were last minute nitpicks, and those had become rare.

So far, the heat had waved in and out, but the beginning of July usually meant a solid two-month walk on the sun heat. I hated living here this time of year. If the heat didn't kill me, the humidity would. I'd avoided Dad at all costs. My instincts told me he was doing the same. If we both pretended my sleepover at Gracin's had never happened, we might be able to meet each other's eyes before I left for Nashville.

"Hey," Gracin said, dragging me out of my thoughts. I smiled and turned around. He'd just finished a sound check and walked toward me from the stage. "What's on your mind?"

I sighed and tossed my hands to my sides, evoking the diva I teased him to be. Well with a Southern accent added in. "This weather is gonna kill me one day, Mr. Ford." I raised my right arm dramatically, resting the wrist over my forehead. "I just can't take so much heat."

Gracin's fingers laced through mine, and he tugged my arm away from my face. "You really talking about the weather, or some other heat that's got you all bothered?"

Leaning away, I gave him my best offended glare. "Sir, you cannot mean what I think you mean. A true gentleman never speaks of such things in the presence of a lady."

Gracin raised his eyebrows and bent to kiss the back of my hand. "Forgive me, Miss Reynolds, for being so bold. I had no idea I was in the presence of a lady."

The laughter built in my chest and rolled up my throat. Gracin pulled me against him and pressed his lips against my ear, silencing my giggles. "Oh," I breathed.

"I like that you're not a lady, Carly." He moved his lips along my jaw. "I like that you're a smartass." His lips trailed around my chin and up the other side of my jaw line. "I like that you don't put up with my shit." He nibbled my earlobe, causing a moan to build deep in my chest. "I like the way you make me ... I'm a real person to you and not some dressed up shell dancing on a stage."

Gracin pulled away and stared into my eyes. I grabbed his face and yanked it down to meet mine, showing him with my lips how much his words meant to me. God, if only what he said would be enough for us to try. I let go and stepped back. These thoughts of more, of being together after I left, needed to go. I couldn't handle falling for this guy.

The same fear reflected in his eyes.

"Gracin … I …" *lo*—. No, I couldn't say that. I couldn't *feel* that. It wasn't going to work between us, so dragging the L word into the equation would only make the shit splatter farther once it hit the fan. I opted to do the next best thing, deflect away from love and to sex. "We should probably finish this conversation somewhere else."

"Oh, don't let me stop you." Gloria stepped out from behind a curtain. By the smirk on her face, she'd been there the entire time. She sashayed the two steps, using more swing in her hips than a metronome. "After all, I doubt the star of the show and the theater owner's daughter *could* be stopped by little old me."

I had never liked Gloria to begin with, but the sheer joy in her glitter-covered eyes made me want to show her the meaning of the phrase "chick fight."

"What do you want, Gloria?" Gracin asked calmly.

"Nothing you have to offer." Her eyes trailed up and down his body. Gloria spun on her heel and sashayed down the hall.

"Well, that kinda killed the mood," Gracin said. He turned and walked briskly toward his dressing room.

"Ya think?" I had to practically run to keep up with his pace. "What's she playing at?"

"Probably nothing, Carly." He stopped outside his dressing room, and I slammed into his back. Without facing me, he said, "Either way, I don't trust her."

We went into his dressing room and began our usual

routine. Gracin closed his eyes and began his pre-show meditation. I gathered his first wardrobe change as quietly as possible. My brain shifted into overdrive. I couldn't stop thinking about how careless we'd been. It was stupid, really, to even keep our relationship so quiet, but it was also easier. Even if Gloria ratted us out, it wasn't that big of a deal. We'd survive. Until I left for Nashville anyway.

∞ ∞ ∞

I left backstage during Gracin's encores. All this time I'd only seen the back of his performance and the front of the crowd. He fed off the energy of the people in the seats. Especially the screaming girls. What warm-blooded American guy wouldn't love hundreds of girls screaming his name night after night? One of the security peeps let me sneak into an aisle by the wall. Gracin returned to the stage and scanned the crowd. The chances he'd see me were a gazillion to one, but his gaze lingered toward my general direction. My heart played hopscotch on my ribs.

If I'd thought his magnetism was intense backstage, it was ten times that strength in the crowd. I couldn't take my eyes off him. Each sway of his hips hypnotized me. Every note in a song I usually thought sucked made my knees weak. And every time his eyes swept over my section in the crowd, it was as if he was staring at me and me alone. No wonder Gracin had been so successful. He was like a fire and the crowd his moths. Touch him and we'd burn.

I slipped backstage before the second encore ended and waited for him in my usual spot. He gave me an odd look when he ran offstage, but he didn't say anything. We strode to his dressing room like every other night. As soon as I closed the door, I grabbed his arm and whipped him around to face me.

"Wha —"

I crushed my lips to his, smothering his questions and relieving a bit of the tension built from watching him perform. Not like Gracin fought it. He pushed me against the door, lifting me off the floor until my legs wrapped around his waist.

"I don't know what that was for, but I liked it," Gracin said once we came up for air.

"Just keeping you on your toes." I nipped at his lower lip.

He set me back on my feet and backed toward his normal perch. "Uh-huh. Sure, it was."

I raised my eyebrows, pausing longer than initially intended. "Okay, fine. I went into the audience for the encores."

He nodded and rolled his hand in a circle for me to keep going.

"It was … not full of suck." Admitting that was not the worst thing I'd ever done, but it wasn't the easiest either. Especially since I'd bashed the show before.

Gracin's mouth tightened into a thin line as he nodded. A slight flush warmed my cheeks. Not my proudest moment.

"'Not full of suck.' That's the nicest thing you've ever said about my show, Carly." He rested his head on his hand, a finger pointing north over his chin and through those perfect lips. "Are you running a fever?"

"Bite me, Gracin."

He crooked that same finger, motioning me forward. "I'd love to."

My feet moved without my consent. Why was it whenever I was around Gracin Ford my body belonged to his mind? Whatever he wished for, I reacted on command. As soon as I was in grabbing distance, Gracin wrapped his arm around me and pulled me onto his lap.

"Now, explain," he ordered. "Or I'm not putting out tonight."

"Not likely. You're easier than a childproof bottle."

Gracin's hand slid up my thigh, squeezing gently. "I can also torture you until you break. That might be fun."

I opened my mouth then shut it. Some things were better left to the imagination. Or the experience. I wasn't entirely sure which one sounded better at that point.

"Well?" he prodded.

"Fine." I gathered my thoughts, trying to make this as minimally ego boosting as possible. "Even though I still don't like the songs, the energy of the crowd was amazing. I saw how you fed off it. And how they fed off you." I shook my head to unscramble the thoughts again. "You're like a magician up there, hypnotizing the crowd and making each one of them feel like you're singing to them and only them. Even though you couldn't see me, I … it was like you sang directly to me." The last words came out on the rush of the end of my breath.

"Carly," Gracin leaned back and stared into my eyes. "Every night I sing directly to you."

My entire body swelled with the emotion filling me, like I weighed nothing and everything all at once. Gracin lifted a hand to my face, brushing the tips of his fingers along my cheek. His eyes darted over my face as if he was memorizing every detail. At least that's what I wanted to believe he was doing, because it was exactly what I was doing to him. I never wanted to forget this moment.

I leaned toward him, slowly. Gracin's hand slid behind my head and his fingers tangled with my hair. Gently he pushed me closer. When our lips melded together, it wasn't the simple explosion of the moment. There was so much more going on. A savoring, a connection, a bond, and a commitment. That was all in one sweet kiss. I needed all of it and more. I needed him to love me. No matter how many times I told myself I couldn't fall for Gracin, with that one kiss, I knew beyond a shadow of doubt I had. Admitting it was one thing, dealing with it another. Adding to the knowledge was the inkling Gracin felt the same way about me.

We'd totally screwed the pooch.

But I wouldn't change any of it, even though the clock ticked away.

∞ ∞ ∞

"Sit." Gracin pointed at a specific chair at his table.

I sat in a different chair just because. Gracin shook his head and turned toward the fridge. He pulled the door open, sticking his head inside. I waited while he rummaged through the contents, most of which I'd bought and stored in there. My organizational skills were the stuff of legend. I knew exactly what and where everything was in his fridge. Something told me I'd be reorganizing it before the night was through.

"What're you doing?" I asked when curiosity got the best of me. It only took three-point-two seconds. Pretty long time for me.

Gracin's head popped up over the door that barely hid his grin. "You really want to know?"

"Duh." I rolled my eyes as dramatically as possible. "I wouldn't have asked if I didn't."

"Uh-huh." He ducked back behind the door without answering.

Half a second later, he backed up and closed the door with his foot. His arms were loaded with lettuce, tomatoes, cucumbers, onions, and a few other things I couldn't quite see. A green plastic bag hung from his mouth. Gracin smiled with a mischievous glint flashing gold in his eyes. I laughed as I stood. He opened his mouth and let the bag fall on top of the rest of his bounty.

"Sit," he ordered with a nod toward the chair.

"Seriously? You're making me a salad?" My brain said this deserved another eye roll while my heart turned into a pinball inside my chest.

"Yes, seriously." He strode two steps to the counter. Everything tumbled from his arms, a tomato almost making a successful escape to the sink. Gracin pulled the cutting board from the cabinets and a knife from the block. "Is it a bad thing to make you dinner?"

His voice strained even though he tried to keep the mood light. Something about this entire thing was significant. No way I'd take it away. Besides, it'd be nice for someone to do something for me. Other than Nena and Ivy, I was pretty much left to my own devices. None of the guys I'd dated ever made me dinner or held my door or just let me cry when I needed to.

I leaned back in my chair and put my hands behind head. "A bad thing? Not even close. I think it's a very good thing. Now," —I made a whip-cracking noise— "get to work."

Gracin glanced over his shoulder and cocked an eyebrow. "Didn't your mother ever tell you not to mess with a man with a knife?"

"Nah, Mom's advice was more encompassing. 'Don't mess with men.'" I bit my lip to keep from laughing. "Funny she ever got married."

Shaking his head, Gracin turned back to his veggies. I couldn't see what he was doing exactly, but it didn't take a PhD in physics to figure it out. The knife smacked against the plastic cutting board with expert precision. Through his thin t-shirt, I watched his shoulders tense and relax with each movement. It was intoxicating.

"I ..." My throat went dry without warning. God, the effect Gracin had on me. I cleared my throat and tried again. "I didn't know you liked to cook."

Gracin didn't turn around as he shrugged and kept cutting. "It's one of those things I enjoy but don't do enough. Back in L.A., it was always grab food when you can and wherever you can. Dad always had me on the go to one audition or another recording or an appearance. Once I went into rehab, things changed. I had to slow down." A quiet sigh slipped out. "I started to do things for myself while I was in there. Sometimes …" His voice softened and his shoulders fell. The knife clanked against the marble counter as Gracin dropped it to press his hands into the counter. "Sometimes I wish I'd never left."

I didn't think as I stood and walked around the table. He stiffened as my arms slid around his waist and my cheek pressed into back. I held him until he relaxed and put his hands over mine. We stood together for several minutes, neither one saying a word. There wasn't anything to say. Even though I'd never been in the same position as he was, I understood what he meant. Living in darkness was hard. Knowing there was an escape even harder when you didn't know how to get out. Gracin captured a bit of freedom in rehab he'd never had before.

"It was hard at first. I'd been going non-stop since I was ten." He rubbed his hands over mine. "It only got worse after I joined the band. Even after Jay left, Dad tried to hold the rest of us together, but nobody was interested in Accentuate without Jay." He shook his head. "Anyway, that's in the past where it needs to stay."

"What was it like?" I didn't really want to prod or open old wounds, but I didn't want to miss this chance to know him a little better. "Touring stadiums when you were only twelve?"

Gracin snorted. "It was exhilarating, exhausting, and sometimes I hated it as much as I loved it. I spent the second half of our world tour drunk. That's when I started drinking. It was a wonder I got through the shows at all. By the time I was fourteen, I was already an alcoholic. I can't get those years back." He tensed again for a few minutes, controlling his breathing until his muscles relaxed. "Sorry, it's not something I like talking about these days."

I cringed as the next words came out of my mouth. "If they got Accentuate back together, would you join them?"

"No." He tensed again but didn't wait to calm down before elaborating. "I never want to be in that poisonous environment again."

Which was exactly what his father had planned. Gracin didn't need Accentuate.

I kissed his shoulder and squeezed him tighter. The price of fame wasn't worth what Gracin had gone through. I wanted to ask him what he'd do if he hit it big on his own. Would he succumb to the pressures then? Fall off the wagon? I wanted to believe he wouldn't. We stood together long enough for the lettuce to reach room temperature.

"Anyway, whenever I get the time, I make salads. It's all I can really 'cook,' but I enjoy it." He patted my hands and I let go.

Moving back to my chair, I asked, "Why not learn how to cook more?"

"Besides the raw food diet that keeps this body finely tuned?" Playful Gracin reemerged and tore the lettuce into tiny bites.

"You never told me why the raw food diet, either." I pulled my knee up to my chest. This bothered me more than

I cared to admit. Food should be cooked. Preferably in butter with lots of cheese. I'd eat anything with butter and cheese. And bacon.

"My counselor introduced me to the idea. He'd actually prescribed it for me as a way to detox." Gracin turned with two salads sans dressing. He slid one in front of me and set the other on the table before turning back toward the fridge. "I stuck with it once I left. I feel better when I don't eat processed foods." He sat down with two bottles of water. "I have more energy."

I shoved a forkful of lettuce into my mouth with a small cherry tomato. The juices exploded on my tongue. Who needed salad dressing when tomatoes were in season?

"Haven't you had more energy?" he asked before shoving a cucumber into his mouth.

Guilt weighed me down, but only a little. I never agreed to go vegan or raw food. "Um … I guess."

Gracin's fork stopped midway to his mouth.

"I don't stick to your diet." My voice raised half an octave as each defense wall raised around me.

"I didn't think you did." His mouth quirked into a half grin. "But for the most part you have."

I popped another cherry tomato into my mouth instead of answering. He was right. Without thinking about it, I ate the same crap he did when we were together. Honestly, it didn't bother me. It was easier to go with the flow and whatnot.

"You never had to do that." Gracin let his fork drop against the bowl. The metal on ceramic rang in my ears. His hand touched the bare skin on my knee. "But I appreciate it."

The salad, the conversation was forgotten the minute he touched my knee. I set my fork down without the annoying sound and slid onto his lap.

"Maybe we should test your energy reserves," I whispered against his lips.

Gracin kissed me. That was all the answer I needed.

CHAPTER SEVENTEEN

The Fourth of July loomed in front of us. The weekend would be packed with the usual weekend crowds, plus the additional tourists who came just to see the fireworks over the water. It was pretty spectacular. Unfortunately, the holiday also brought Albert Ford back to Branson. Gracin went from relaxed to twenty-four-hour tense. Our time slipped away from us.

It helped that Gloria was gone. She hadn't bothered to call Dad or Luke; she just disappeared. Mita, the other dancer, said Gloria had often talked about going to Vegas. Maybe that's where she went. Whatever, she was gone and I was not one bit upset about it.

The afternoon before the holiday, Gracin and I finally had a minute to ourselves. Rehearsals had started again to get the newest dancer up with the routine of the show. I felt bad for her, until I saw her dance. She picked up on each move and took over Gloria's role seamlessly. Gracin stepped backstage during a brief break to grab the bottle of water I had for him. Nobody else was within earshot or eyesight of us. Just to be safe, Gracin tugged me closer to the curtain and didn't wait another second before covering my lips with his.

"God, I've missed you," he whispered once he came up for air. "Things can get back to normal Monday, I promise."

"I know." I reached up and ran my hand along his jaw and down his throat. *But how normal is normal for two people hiding their relationship?*

Someone shouted his name, and Gracin groaned. He kissed me quickly one more time. "I promise."

I watched him retreat back onstage. The weight inside me grew. These last few days had been an audition of my own, in a way. I'd practiced not being with him. And I hated it. Every time I saw him, I wanted to hug him or simply touch him. How was I going to handle not seeing him? Or only seeing him on TV or in the news or, God forbid, the tabloids. As my heart cracked over what I would lose, reality broke in like a dose of ice-cold water.

"Carly, please tell me I didn't just see that," Luke said.

I tore my eyes off the stage to where my brother stood halfway down the corridor. Obviously, Gracin and I hadn't learned our lesson about sucking face backstage. Luke stared at me with a mixture of disappointment and horror, the perfect combination of Dad and Mom.

"Please tell me you weren't just making out with Gracin Ford." He walked toward me with each word. His fists clenched at his sides. "Are you trying to ruin this family?"

"What?" The shock of his question forced me back against an electrical panel. It dug into my back.

"Did you even think about how getting involved with him would affect this family, the theater? Or were you too busy thinking about nailing a pop star?" Anger oozed from every pore in his skin. His eyes flashed red, and he really reminded me of our father. Dad didn't need to yell or scream to get his point across. Neither did Luke.

I collapsed against the wall, moving to the left to avoid the panel. Tears filled my eyes as the burden of my relationship with Gracin slipped a little. Luke didn't need the details, but he could at least see this wasn't just a conquest for me. "It's not like that," I whispered. "We're not like that."

His features softened, but the anger still simmered beneath the surface. "What do you mean, Carly?"

I'm in love with him. But I couldn't say it. "We … agreed to this summer only." I stared Luke in the eyes, hoping he would see how much this hurt to admit, how much I wished my words weren't true. "When we started this, we decided it would end when I left for school. And Gracin wouldn't hold anything against the family or the theater if things go bad between us. He's not like that, Luke."

Luke scoffed. "These Hollywood types *are* like that." He threw his hands in the air and spun in a circle. "God, I can't believe you of all people fell for his load of shit."

I slammed my palm against his shoulder, shoving him across the narrow corridor. "Fuck you, Luke. You don't know anything about him or about me. So keep your judgmental attitude to yourself."

"Really, Carly, I'm –"

"You're not the best judge of character. If you were, your best friend wouldn't have been a fucking rapist." I bit my tongue. That was totally uncalled for. It wasn't Luke's fault Derrick did what he did.

Luke sighed and dropped his holier-than-thou attitude. "Yeah, you've got a point there. I never thought .... You're sure this thing with Gracin won't backfire. We won't get a bad reputation out there?"

"Trust me for once." I let my head fall back and stared at the dirty ceiling. "Gracin is nothing like that."

I counted the rungs in the catwalk, waiting for Luke to say anything.

"Trust you? That's almost funny."

The lump forming in my throat choked back my breath. I might've been a lot of things, but untrustworthy wasn't one of them

"I'm going to have to tell Dad, Carly," he added. "This isn't something we can keep quiet from him."

The belly laugh that filled me was so unexpected it surprised even me. "Oh, Luke, there are so many things I've kept from Dad that he'd flip his shit over."

Luke snorted. "Yeah, I guess that's probably true."

I let my head fall to my chest, then raised it to meet Luke's eyes. "Please, don't tell him. I don't want Dad to ruin this for me."

Luke cocked his head to the side, looking more like Mom. "You care about this guy, don't you?"

More than you know. "It's just a fling," I said, ripping a gorge through my chest. "Nothing more."

Luke nodded and back stepped down the hall. "Okay. Between us. Just … be careful, sis."

"Don't worry. I will." *As careful as someone who knows how much this is going to kill her in a few months.*

No regrets, Carly. Never regret or take for granted every second you have with Gracin. They're far too few and far too special.

A sad smile crept onto my face. It was easier said than done.

∞ ∞ ∞

The show took more out of Gracin than usual. He was downright surly afterwards. Fortunately, his dad had left shortly before it had ended to catch a plane to catch another plane to L.A. Gracin collapsed in his chair and leaned back, covering his eyes with his arms.

I gave him ten seconds of rest before yanking him to his feet.

"What the –"

"Come on." I tugged him toward the door. Dragging a guy half a foot taller than me shouldn't have been so hard in theory. I had inertia on my side, at least until Gracin dug his heels into the outdated shag carpeting to slow his momentum. It only made me try harder. "Seriously, we have to go."

"Carly, I'm tired." The normal energy Gracin had even after a show wasn't there. He sounded eighty and ready to keel over. "Can't this wait."

"Nope. Now get moving, Grandpa, or we're going to

miss it." I tugged his arm one more time for good measure, moving him a fraction of an inch. "Trust me."

Gracin stopped fighting me. That was the first step. The next was to get him to walk a little faster. I didn't let go of his arm as I rushed toward the stairs leading to the roof.

"Carly –"

"Trust me,"I reiterated as I pulled him behind me. Seriously, I thought he'd get the picture by now. It was the Fourth of July after all.

The loud boom echoed into the stairwell. I had to let go of Gracin and use both hands to pull open the access door to the roof. The metal creaked open, sending shudders down my skin in a creepy horror movie way. I reached back for Gracin's hand and led him to the edge of the roof. It wasn't ideal, but there wasn't enough time to get from the theater to the water for the full view.

Another boom, followed by a burst of colorful lights exploding in a circle. Several small bangs with minuscule fireworks shot off in rapid fire, filling the air with the smell of gunpowder and the colors of the world. Gracin's arms slid around my waist, pulling me flush against his chest. My eyes focused on the display exploding over the lake. We stood together, heads tilted skyward, bodies pressed into one until the grand finale.

I turned my head slightly to watch Gracin as the finale blasted a massive amount of fireworks in rapid succession. The colors reflected in his contacts, but there wasn't anything fake about the wonder in his expression. His mouth opened in a silent "awe" as his cheeks lifted slightly.

I knew Gracin had seen fireworks before, but I'd never been with him. It was like watching a little boy. When the last of the lights faded, Gracin met my stare. He leaned down and brushed his lips over mine, squeezing me closer against him.

"Thanks, Carly." He kissed the tip of my nose. "I'm glad we didn't miss it."

"Me, too. I just wish I could've taken you down to the lake for a better view."

He smiled and glanced around the night sky before settling his gaze back on me. "This is the best view in Branson."

I spun around and pulled his face to mine. He was totally right. This was the best view in Branson. At least for this night.

After one of the best kisses of my life, with each one from Gracin fighting for the top spot, he pulled away. Exhaustion covered his face again. The exhilaration of the fireworks display had only delayed the inevitable. Gracin needed to get some rest. I led him back to his dressing room, where he changed and I straightened a few scattered items with bated patience. We managed to leave without any crowd waiting outside the stage door. Usually one or two fans would wait him out to get pictures or an autograph or both. Gracin always complied with a smile and a nice word. Everyone must've rushed to the lake for the fireworks. Gracin leaned against me more than the normal boyfriend leaning against his girlfriend. It was pure fatigue.

"Gracin, why're you so tired tonight?" I asked when I put the truck in drive. I still couldn't believe he let me drive this beautiful monster.

His head rolled toward me against the headrest. "I haven't slept much the last few nights."

"I didn't think you slept much at all," I pointed out.

Gracin chuckled. "True, but when I do, it's solid sleep. The last few nights … it hasn't been solid."

My fingers reached for him, caressing his hand. "What can I do?"

He didn't say anything until I parked the truck in the spot by the cabin. I turned to face him as he stared at me. "Stay?" he asked.

I nodded.

His smile was spectacular as usual, but all too brief. He opened the door and climbed out. I followed behind him, texting Ivy for a cover and Dad that I wouldn't be home. By the time I had everything arranged, Gracin had collapsed on the bed with his clothes on. I pulled off his shoes and jeans, pushing his legs to the left side. His eyelids twitched and his teeth ground against each other. Each breath huffed from his lips as if he ran a marathon. Whatever had been bothering him in his sleep wasn't gone. I grabbed one of his t-shirts from his dresser and changed. The coolness of the sheets comforted me as I slipped in beside him. Gracin's arm fell across my waist. He pulled me against him. I snuggled into his shoulder, letting his presence lull me toward sleep. Before I lost all consciousness, I noticed Gracin's breathing had evened out. A smile broke across my face, and I allowed sleep to overtake me.

CHAPTER EIGHTEEN

We only managed a week without the illustrious Albert Ford. Whatever urgent business he had in L.A. didn't last long enough in my opinion. Every time I saw Gracin's father, it was one time too many. That was a lot of one time too many's. The guy's sleaziness multiplied by twelve every day. When I'd first met him, I thought we shared a common thread: the dislike of Gracin's antics. Since I'd gotten to know the real Gracin, I realized how wrong I'd been and, therefore, so was his father.

Unfortunately, this brief weekend visit also meant I'd have less time with Gracin. That added another checkmark to the I-Hate-Albert-Ford checklist. Toss another one into the mix: Albert would be staying in Gracin's cabin. The sad thing was Dad would've gladly comped Gracin's father a room if the hotel wasn't full. On top of that, Albert thought he deserved to sleep in the master bed. Gracin, who worked his ass off every night, was relegated to the single in the loft.

Gracin's shoulders fell when his father knocked on the cabin door Friday morning. He stepped back to let him inside. Albert stopped when he saw me at the table where we'd just finished our after-run breakfast.

"What're you doing here, Miss Reynolds? I doubt my son has need for your *services* at this hour." He sneered as he emphasized "services." What a dick.

I kept my carefully calculated professional façade. "Actually, he does. We were just discussing today's agenda."

"At seven in the morning?" Albert dropped his bags by the door. No doubt he expected Gracin to take care of them. Like I said, what a dick.

"Carly runs with me, Dad," Gracin said. Exhaustion filled his voice, weighing down the words until they fell on Albert's deaf ears.

"Well?" Albert directed his question to me.

"As Gracin just told you, we run together every morning and have breakfast afterward." I kept up the increasingly tight smile. "And like I said, we discuss each day's agenda. For example, Gracin had an interview with a journalism student at two today. I had to reschedule it after the new dancer requested time with Gracin to work on the show, since she missed two of her marks last night." I paused, waiting for a tell from Albert and getting none. "Do you have any further questions, or shall I clean up from breakfast before I head home?"

If I learned anything in that moment, it was never to play poker with Albert.

"I'll get the dishes, Carly," Gracin said.

"No, son, let your assistant do it. I'm sure she's quite ..." Albert's eyes roamed down to my chest for a beat too long, "domestic."

I slammed my hands onto the tabletop and pushed myself to my feet. "Well, then. Let me get out of your hair." I left the dirty dishes on the table. Fuck Albert. He could lick the grapefruit juice off the plates for all I cared. "Gracin, I'll see you around noon."

Gracin nodded and wouldn't meet my stare. "At the theater."

I gritted my teeth. That wasn't the plan. We were supposed to go take a picnic lunch to one of the public beaches just north of town. "Of course."

"Make it one, Miss Reynolds. I'd like to have lunch with my son." His expressionless face made me want to shove my fist into it to see if it would bounce back.

I didn't say anything, instead turning to Gracin who still kept his head down. He didn't shrug, nod, or even bother to glance up with an apologetic look. Shaking my head, I strolled to the door, careful to stay far from Gracin. Not because I didn't want Albert to think there was anything going on between me and his son, but because I really didn't want to touch this Gracin. He was too much like a toddler around his father. Anger, and heartbreak, filled my gut as I left the cabin.

There was only one way to rid myself of these emotions. I needed a rush. After I climbed onto my scooter, I sent Nena and Ivy a text. Both had responded by the time I parked the scooter in the driveway. I smiled at their texts.

Time to do something stupid.

∞ ∞ ∞

"Are you sure you want to do this?" Nena asked as we parked on a bridge twenty minutes south of Branson.

"Yep." I climbed out, preparing my mind for the adrenaline.

Thompson Bridge used to be a railroad bridge over Thompson Valley deep in the Ozarks. Needless to say, the Thompson family owned a lot of the land. The railroad had appeased them by naming the now defunct bridge in their honor. If they'd known what the bridge was being utilized for in the twenty-first century, I doubt they'd approve. Then again, the only photos of the Thompson family showed them all frowning, so maybe they would.

"Carly Reynolds, what brings you down yonder, darling?" Jesse Simmons asked as soon as he saw me strolling toward him.

"Oh, you know me, Jess. Just looking for a good rush." I glanced at the harness in his hands and the parachute beside his feet. One of the best things about being an adrenaline junkie was the ease of access to the local businesses. Jesse and his brother, Mick, owned Simmon's Jumps, a base and bungee company Mick had started when he'd finished college six years ago. Jesse had bought in when he'd finished his master's in business last year. "Got time for me?"

"We've always got time for our best customer." He held out the harness and pointed to the parachute. "Pick your poison."

Bungee jumping would've been great, but I needed more control than that. Base jumping off a bridge into a valley definitely qualified as unsafe. Jesse and Mick had cleared the trees for a three-mile radius and built three large platforms, each with a giant X, on the ground. Each platform took in variants like wind and position of the jumper. They never let anyone jump who hadn't taken their course at headquarters, where Mick's wife ran the business. I'd taken it as soon I'd gotten my driver's license, conning Mom into signing the permission form by telling her it was a science project. She'd never bothered to follow up on my excuse, but I had used it as an extra credit science report on how adrenaline affects the body at different altitudes.

I pointed to the parachute. "Who's at the bottom? Mick?"

"Nate." As if to prove his point, Jesse took his walkie from his belt. "Heya, Nate. Carly's gonna be down soon. Look for her around three."

Static filled the air for a second before Nate responded. "Roger that. I'll be at two."

I smiled. Nate was not the brightest star in the constellation, but he played his stupidity up. He'd heard Jesse.

Nena and Ivy stood off to the side, neither one saying a word as Jesse helped me into the parachute. Normally, I'd do something like this without them. They didn't mind my need for speed if they controlled it, like on the boat or driving while I surfed on the hood of the car, but when it came to bungee jumping, base jumping, skydiving, or even propelling, they didn't want to be around. Of course, they wanted to hear about it after the fact.

Jesse adjusted the straps, giving them hard tugs for good measure.

"Alright, Carly. Same drill. Stay on course. Get off course, get hurt." He shoved the helmet on my head and slapped it twice after securing it. "Got it?"

"Yeah, yeah, yeah. This ain't my first rodeo, cowboy." I smirked as Jesse rolled his eyes. He'd heard that from me too many times.

My heart sped up as soon as I moved to the edge of the bridge. I glanced down at the valley below, eyeing platform three. There was a slight breeze, but nothing I couldn't handle. Hell, it'd probably feel great on the way down. The insufferable summer heat made B.O. a daily issue. I climbed over the railing and turned, careful not to let my hands or feet slip. Jesse grabbed my waist to keep me secure.

"Okay, Carly. Hold up your right hand, and I'll put the chute in it." I did as instructed, my heart pounding to the rhythm of a salsa song on fast forward. Jesse held me tight against the railing as he put the chute into the palm of my hand. "When I let go, jump."

I nodded. An ocean filled my ears as the adrenaline rushed through my body. This was only the beginning. The fifteen-second jump would amplify everything. The wind would attack my skin instead of graze it. The trees would bend instead of sway. The clouds would race instead of drift. The entire world would speed to astronomical proportions in the time it took me to let go of the railing until my feet hit the platform.

It was the best rush in the world.

Jesse's hand disappeared, and I fell forward until I was prone to the earth. It was beautiful as it rushed toward me.

I let go of the chute, and it yanked me back toward the bridge. I closed my eyes for a second to savor my survival, then opened them to savor the view. My heart slowed as I neared the platform. The best part of the rush was the anticipation. Once I jumped and my chute stopped me from plummeting to my death, I relaxed. I let the morning disappear, my anger fade, my disappointment slip off like oil on water. The answer was clear. That type of clarity was everything and nothing at the same time. I needed to see Gracin for who he was completely, not just who he was when he was with me.

My feet hit the platform, twisting my left ankle at an odd angle. I groaned, but managed to keep myself from falling completely. Nate grabbed my upper arms as soon as he grasped something was wrong. The concern on his face matched the agony on mine.

"Ankle," I said, pointing to the previously injured area. Great, this wasn't what I needed.

"I gotcha." He held me up and pulled his walkie.

I didn't bother to listen as he relayed the injury to Jesse. It wasn't that bad. Yet. Once the sneaker came off, it would swell to the size of a softball.

"Alright, Carly. Lean on me and we'll take the four-wheeler up top." Nate's arm looped around my lower back, his fingers dangerously close to the bra line.

"Not a good time to cop a feel, Nate." His fingers shifted lower. "Besides, I'm seeing someone."

Nate snorted. "The famous commitment-phobe Carly Reynolds just admitted to having a boyfriend."

I slapped him on the back of the head.

"What? I'm marking this moment on my calendar and laminating it for eternity." He leaned toward me and whispered unnecessarily in my ear. "It does make me wonder what type of guy finally nailed you down."

"Way to turn a phrase, Nate." Even though I should've been totally offended by what he'd said, his smartass words brought a grin to my face.

"Thanks. I've been practicing." He glanced down at my ankle when we stopped beside the ATV. "So, what'd you do?"

"Hit the water wrong about a month or so ago." *And kicked the shit out of the guy who raped me.* "Guess it wasn't as healed as I thought."

"Sprains are a bitch. Ice it and keep it elevated." He paused as I slid into the cart behind the four-wheeler and strapped myself down. "To be honest, Carly, you should probably see a doctor if this is the second time you hurt it. Might be more going on than a sprain. You might've torn something."

No fault in his logic. In the last four years, I'd gone to the hospital once, when it was clear I'd broken my wrist. It wasn't a pleasant experience, and one I'd rather not repeat. Still, something could be seriously wrong with my ankle. It could totally screw up the rest of my summer either way. And I wouldn't mind some pain meds.

We rode in bumpy silence up to the bridge. Nate had to know the exact location of every boulder on the path, because he made sure to hit them at full speed. My lower lip bled by the time he hit the pavement.

Nate had barely stopped when Nena and Ivy ran over. Any animosity Nena had had disappeared. She hugged me tighter than my mother did most days. Ivy wasn't much better. My breathing ability disappeared, but it was nice. If all else failed in my life, I could always take comfort in having the best friends in the world. Distance wouldn't change how much they meant to me.

"Guys," I said through clenched teeth. "You're killing me here."

They both let go. The push of oxygen into my lungs was a whole other type of rush. They chattered around me, but I wasn't listening. I tried to put weight on my foot. Bad idea. Ivy caught me before I knocked her over.

"I'm taking you to the hospital, Carly. No arguing." Nena pointed at me like a teacher pointing at a bad student. She was going to be a great teacher one day.

"No arguing," I agreed. My heart had relocated into the ankle and pulsed like a balloon deflating only to get inflated a second later. I let them lead me to the car and help me in the backseat.

"God, when you let go of the railing, I wanted to jump after you," Ivy said as she buckled herself in. "Then when you hit the platform and crumbled, I thought you were dead."

"You scared us both," Nena said.

"That's why I never asked you guys to come with me on these adventures." I let my head roll against the back of the seat. The throbbing in my ankle fought to break through the leather.

"Probably a good idea," Ivy said. I could tell by the way she bounced in her seat she didn't really mean it. Ivy lived for excitement as much as I did, only she went for the sexual variety.

"Can I ask you something?" Nena still hadn't started the car. She turned around to face me. "Why jump off a bridge? I mean, I get wanting to have some fun and go a little crazy, but why risk your life?"

I stared at her, holding her gaze and taking my time to answer in a way she'd totally understand. After a few minutes, I settled on the best response. "It clears my head. Lets me think when things … when they get to be too much."

Ivy turned and cocked her head. Her concern radiated through her eyes. "What's too much?"

"I …" Tears started down my cheeks without my permission. I'd figured out so much when it came to Gracin, but there was still the simple fact we wouldn't get the chance at forever, or even spend a Christmas or a birthday together. Every single day, I wanted the chance with him. Or at least another day past August twenty-seventh. What could it hurt to tell them? They'd been my best friends most of my life and never judged my past stupidity. I dropped my head and decided to tell them everything. "You guys remember Jonathan?"

"Yeah," Ivy said. She already knew how I felt about him, but she didn't know the whole story.

"That's not his name." I waited for a beat before I met their wide eyes. "His real name is Jonathan Gracin Ford."

Nena's eyes grew so wide they looked like they'd intersected. Ivy's hands came to her mouth.

"And we've agreed this … thing between us, this beautiful thing, will end when I leave for school." The clusterfuck emotions entangled into a poorly rolled ball of yarn in my chest. As it unraveled, another snag appeared. "And I don't want it to end."

Ivy shot out of her door and opened mine. She stood behind me, hugging my shoulders as the tears washed away the relief from earlier.

"That's why you haven't been around," Nena's voice softened to a near whisper. "So you can spend every minute with him."

I nodded and wiped my nose on my arm.

"Why didn't you tell us?" Ivy asked. She squeezed me against her. "And for that matter, why in the hell didn't we recognize him? His face has been plastered all over town for months."

"You weren't looking for him," I answered as simply as possible. It wasn't far from the truth. If they'd seen us together at the theater, it probably would've clicked.

Ivy huffed a little. "It's not like we would've acted stupid around him or anything."

The bubble of laughter shot from my throat in record time. Ivy *had* acted stupid around him at the lake, but she didn't see it that way. She was simply flirting. If she'd known it was Gracin, I'm sure her flirt-o-meter would've exploded.

"Or was there another reason?" Nena always tuned into things I didn't say.

"He wanted to be a guy for a day. Not a pop star or celebrity. Just Gracin." I smiled as his face hovered on the edge of my internal vision. His hazel eyes that turned molten gold when we were together. His sharp chin covered in morning stubble that was softer than silk when I ran my hand over it. The way he listened to me, really listened and cared about what I said. "And just Gracin is pretty amazing."

Nena raised her perfectly waxed eyebrows and puckered her lips as she fought the losing battle with her smile. "You've found him."

Confusion settled into my stomach. "Huh?"

Ivy squeezed my shoulder one last time and let go. When Ivy settled back into the front seat, Nena still hadn't explained what she meant. So Ivy did it for her. "She means you've found The One. The metaphorical yin to your yang. Your perfect match." Ivy turned around, her eyes saddened deeper than I'd seen in a long time. "She means you've found the guy you're meant to be with."

A harsh chuckle came from the confusion in my gut. "Yeah, right. Because that's just my luck. Find The One, only to lose him after a short period of time." Bitterness coated my tongue as I spit out the rest of my words. "Find my perfect match, the guy who knows we aren't going to last because he'll be on the other side of the country. The guy who won't give a long-distance relationship a chance. The guy who …" My tears waterfalled down my cheeks. "The guy I can share anything with, who knows everything about me, who doesn't judge me for who I pretend to be, but knows who I really am. Yeah, I've found The One, all right.

The One who will destroy my heart in a month."

Nena smiled. "And you'll let him."

I turned away from her, because she was right.

Neither one of them mentioned it as they drove back to town. Instead of the hospital where the wait would surely have been longer than any dying person could endure, Nena drove to an urgent care center. The wait was almost as long as the emergency room would've been. I flipped through a seven-month-old magazine with a brief story about Gracin's stint in rehab. They had pictures of a heavier version of him going in, and photos of a slightly slimmer Gracin exiting the building. None of the photos resembled the man I knew.

Ivy played nurse, while Nena stayed in the waiting room. When they wanted to cut my shoe off, Ivy jumped in and removed it even though it hurt more than losing the shoe would've. I appreciated the gesture anyway and kept the scream of agony to myself. My cell rang, and I heard Ivy answer it as they wheeled me to x-ray. When I got back, Ivy wasn't there.

After a few minutes, the doctor finally came in with some crutches and an elastic brace. I had a gel brace at home that would work so much better. The diagnosis was a mild sprain, and I needed to stay off it for three days, but it would take longer to fully heal.

I took my prescription for pain meds, the only good thing ever to come out of a doctor's office, and hobbled to the waiting room.

Gracin stood when he saw me, and I stopped. That's who called. I glanced at the clock. It was almost five, and he had a show to do in a few hours. I crutched over to him like the pro I pretended to be and stopped before slamming the rubber tip into his toes.

"What're you doing here?" I asked in a hushed voice. The waiting room was packed, and a little gray-haired lady leaned closer to eavesdrop. She wasn't even attempting to be subtle.

He stared at me, and the emotions swirled behind the contacts. I moved toward him like the apple toward Newton. Gracin grabbed my face with a gentle roughness and pulled me toward him. Crushing his lips against mine, he dug his fingers into my skin, adding to the urgency.

When he finally broke free, he put his forehead against mine. "Don't ever scare me like that again."

I nodded, fear and hope coursing through me at the passion in his voice. I only had a few weeks to scare him, but he made it sound like we had longer. That terrified me and gave me hope at the same time. Was it possible he wanted more, or was it just wishful thinking on my part? I didn't know the answer. And I was afraid of it, too.

If he didn't want longer, more, that would hurt worse than saying goodbye. At least, I knew he wanted me for now. For now was all we could give one another.

"I promise," I whispered. *For now.*

CHAPTER NINETEEN

I found a way to stay on the job anyway. Like the night of the cocktail party, I had Miranda do the hard work. She became my legs. I hated to admit it, but it was nice not to be on the go all the time. I didn't skip out my morning runs with Gracin though. Instead of using my legs, I used my hands to keep a steady pace with my scooter. When I showed up the first morning, Gracin rolled his eyes and fought back his sexy smile.

By Sunday night, we'd gotten into a routine. Gracin came into his dressing room an hour before the show, and I shooed Miranda out. Once we were alone, I sat on Gracin's lap and wrapped my arms around his neck.

"I've missed you," I whispered. He squeezed me closer to his chest. "Tuesday, I should be back to normal."

His lips moved along my neck. "Give it a week, Carly. Don't push your ankle too hard. Let it heal." He pulled away from me and stared into my eyes. Wiggling his eyebrows, he added, "Besides, there's another Reynolds girl who likes hanging with me." I slapped his shoulder, and he grabbed my hand, pressing it against his chest over his slamming heart. "See what you do to me?"

My ribs squeezed the breath from my lungs. Lost in his eyes, I waited for the shoe to drop. He sucked his bottom lip between his teeth.

"Carly …" His hand slid up my arm, gliding over my shoulder as I leaned toward him. He tangled his fingers in my hair. "Kiss me."

I left my hand where it was and obeyed the simple command. I kissed him like it was the last chance I ever would have. We forgot where we were, so lost into each other. I couldn't get enough of him, and he had to have felt the same way. He moaned as our lips merged over and over, until it sounded like someone cleared their throat. It didn't stop us until it happened a second time. We weren't alone.

Gracin pulled away first and muttered, "Shit."

I closed my eyes, knowing without a doubt we were totally busted. God, I hoped like hell it wasn't my father. Slowly, I turned on Gracin's lap to face my end. Instead of my dad, I stared into the cold eyes of Albert Ford.

"So, I guess you are a whore after all." He smirked as his gaze went down my body and up it like he was licking the melting ice cream off a cone. "Gracin, I don't care where you get your jollies, but this girl is your employee. You run the risk of harassment charges, or worse, she'll write a tell-all about how shitty you were to her and make a mint off your reputation."

"Fuck off, Albert." I tried to leap off Gracin's lap, but his hands tightened around my hips. "Let me go, Gracin."

"Calm down, Carly." Albert laughed as he moved farther into the room, closing it behind him with an audible click. "We can resolve this ..." He waved his hand toward us. "Well, whatever this is, rather easily." He took in the dressing room for a moment before he settled back on us. "First, you'll stop seeing my son. Second, you'll quit working with Gracin. Third, you'll sign a non-disclosure agreement, along with your father of course, so you can't run to the tabloids and brag about fucking Gracin Ford."

"You sonna—" I didn't get to finish calling Albert exactly what he was.

"Not happening, Dad," Gracin said through gritted teeth. His fingers dug into my shorts, almost bruising the skin beneath. Not that I minded. I wanted to dig my fingernails into Albert's eyes. "Carly isn't going anywhere."

Albert feigned shock. "I didn't ask your opinion, boy." His gaze shifted toward me. "Can you believe this child, Carly? He thinks he has a say in the matter. You know better. You'll do whatever is necessary to save your father's theater and his reputation in this godforsaken town, so you'll agree. Won't you?"

The air was sucked out of the room. Albert knew me better than I expected. He was right, in a way. But he was so fucking wrong too. Thinking he could threaten me into agreeing to his terms, thinking he had the upper hand in this conversation. Oh, he had no clue what I was capable of.

"No." I said with a firm voice. I stood, my knees wobbly from the hot make-out session and my ankle still not strong enough to walk on. I used the pain to strengthen my resolve.

"I'm not going to quit seeing Gracin. And I'm not going to quit my job." I moved closer, the throbbing in my ankle shooting through my calf faster than a cheetah on steroids. "There's no way in hell I'm signing anything you come up with. So stuff it up your ass."

Albert's eyes flashed his carefully controlled fury. "You're so smart, aren't you? Well, let's just call your father and see what he has to say about this."

"Why don't we?" I smiled and pulled my cell from my back pocket. "In fact, I'll call him myself."

I leaned too hard on my bad ankle and winced, but I managed to send Luke a text before I called Dad. Gracin's hand touched my lower back as he stuck one of the crutches under my arm. I turned my head and smiled sadly at him. We weren't going to have the rest of summer after all. That hurt me more than anything Albert Ford would ever say to me.

I tore my gaze away and hit the green handset button next to Dad's smiling face.

"Carly, is something wrong?" Dad asked in a clipped formal voice. Great, he was not in the best of moods.

Everything. "I need you to come to Gracin's dressing room, Dad. There's something you need to hear from me in person."

He paused. I could almost see him in the office, staring at the phone with confusion and anger fighting a battle on his face. Anger always won in these situations. "I'm on my way."

Luke hurried in a minute later. He stopped inside the

door and observed the standoff. Instead of coming to my side, he took up neutral ground between Albert and me. That wasn't promising. He didn't open his mouth once. Miranda popped in a moment later and, after glancing at everyone, she popped back out. The silence weighed me down, but I stood straight and proud. There was no way Albert Ford would win this battle.

By the time Dad showed up, he needed a metaphorical axe to enter the room. Like Luke, he took neutral ground, but his gaze stayed a moment too long on where Gracin's hand rested on my hip.

"What's going on?" Dad asked. He stared at his watch. Less than five minutes before showtime. "Make it quick, or we'll have to announce a delayed start tonight." He glanced between us and Albert. "None of us wants that."

"Albert Ford wants us to sign an NDA, Dad. I told him where to shove it." I reached around to Gracin's fingers and clutched them. It was time to throw out the biggest lie of my life. I hated it, but it was the only way to protect all of us from whatever Albert had in mind. "He thinks he's uncovered something you weren't aware of and is threatening to damage your reputation and the theater's."

"Uncovered what?" Dad asked with a hint of incredulity.

"Your daughter and my son seem to have entered into a … relationship." Albert's voice dripped with controlled malice.

Dad stared at him like he's forgotten to gas up the lawnmower. "And?"

That one little word knocked Albert off his perch. He

took a physical step back from all of us.

Luke shoved his hands into his pockets and shrugged. "Guess Mr. Ford was the last to know, Dad."

Dad nodded slowly to Luke. He wouldn't look at me. "I see." He turned toward Albert completely, his back to me and Gracin. "I've been aware of this for some time, as has my son. I don't know why Gracin and Carly chose to leave you in the dark about their relationship, but that was their decision to make. Now, if I understand correctly, you want her to sign a non-disclosure agreement. Correct?"

Albert stared back at Dad and nodded once.

Over his shoulder, Dad asked, "Carly, do you promise not to write a tell-all book, go on any tabloid shows or to any tabloid newspapers or legitimate newspapers or online news sources about your relationship with Gracin?"

"Yes." I let out a long breath. Dad came through. I had hoped he would, but after everything … I just wasn't sure he'd back me up. Still, he wouldn't look at me. He was furious at the way he found out, but the truth was he never *would've* discovered my relationship if there'd been a choice. Why tell him something that would upset him? It wasn't worth the pain.

"There you have it, Albert. Now, if you don't mind, the show will be starting late enough as it is and I'm sure Gracin needs to finish getting ready." Dad moved toward Albert and put his arm around the man's shoulders, ushering him out of the door.

Luke let out a long breath and turned toward us. "Well, I'm glad that's out in the open. Carly, good luck with Dad."

He shook his head and headed toward the door. "You're gonna need it."

I closed my eyes, squeezing them tight and gritting my teeth against the outside forces ruining the little bit of happiness in my life. This wasn't happening. I mean, it had happened, but I wanted to turn back the clock and make it not happen. If I'd only used my brain, I never would've let myself get caught in such a compromising position.

"Are you okay?" Gracin asked. He hadn't moved since everyone left. Neither had I.

"I don't know," I whispered. My shoulders fell, and exhaustion took root in every inch of my body. "I just don't know anything anymore."

Gracin spun me around so fast that the crutch holding me up fell to the floor with a bang. He grabbed my shoulders and pressed his forehead to mine. I inhaled his musky sent.

"No regrets, Carly." His breath danced along my lips.

I didn't respond right away, and he squeezed my shoulders. Did I have regrets? Yes and no, but we'd made an agreement before my emotions had gotten involved to muck everything up. "No regrets," I whispered.

He relaxed against me as a knock sounded on the door. We moved away from each other. My phone vibrated in my pocket. The text was a request for my presence as soon as possible. I'd have to handle this situation no matter how much I wanted to put it off until the next day or, even better, until after I left for Nashville. There was one thing for me to do.

Miranda came in, and we went to work getting Gracin

ready for the show. He kissed my forehead and left for the stage. There wasn't any reason to keep our relationship quiet anymore.

"Miranda, you're on your own tonight." My face showed no emotion, or at least, I tried to keep it blank. "Can you handle Gracin?"

My little sister scoffed and rolled her eyes. "Can you handle Dad?"

The wave of sadness I'd held back broke the damn of calm. Of all the people in this world, Miranda was the one who always broke through to me. "I'm going to lose him, Meerkat."

She pulled me in for a quick hug. "Just tell Dad the truth, Carly. The real truth, and not the half-truth crap you've pulled over the years. Tell him how you really feel about Gracin."

I nodded, but how could I? I couldn't even tell Gracin.

Miranda kissed my cheek and ran out the door. She might as well get used to doing this on her own. My gut warned me I would be out of a job after tonight.

∞ ∞ ∞

He was on the phone when I entered his office on my crutches. Dad glanced up at me, and his anger rolled off him like a tsunami. I deserved it. Over the last few weeks, I'd done everything to keep him out of my life. But when I needed him, he was there for me. Whatever happened, it was of my own making. He hung up the phone.

"Sit."

I took the chair on the left. Most people moved to the right automatically, but I decided long ago to do the things people didn't expect me to do. Childish? Maybe, but I wasn't one to bow before convention. Even when I probably should've, like now.

"First, you're going to tell me what really happened with your ankle and not that story about falling down Ivy's stairs." He leaned forward, resting his elbows on the desk and lacing his fingers together. His jaw clenched, grinding his teeth. This was a man I didn't want to cross. Ever.

"I hurt it about a month ago on the lake. Then I kicked Derrick with the same foot. Three days ago, I landed wrong during a base jump off Thompson Bridge." I kept the emotion out of my voice, but I wanted him to forgive me so much I had no doubt he could see it in my eyes. If he'd only look there.

He closed his eyes and took a long breath. "How long have you been base jumping?"

"Couple of years."

"Don't you need parental permission to do something like that?" He kept his eyes closed.

"Mom signed it."

His eyes snapped open then. "Did she know what she was signing?"

I almost smiled at my cleverness but managed to keep myself in check. "It was research for biology. I wrote a paper about the effects of –"

"Enough." His lips pursed together, disappearing against themselves. "You conned your mother into signing a form and used school as an excuse. Admit it."

I crossed my arms over my stomach. It didn't help calm the rolling tide. "It's not like I didn't do –"

"Just admit it!" Dad screamed as he slammed his fists into the desk. He leaned back, shocked by his own outburst, but not deterred by it. "For years, I have listened to your half-truths and outright lies. I'm tired of it, Carly. It's time for you to grow up. This shit won't fly in the real world."

I stared at the scuffed hardwood floor, unable to face him. The theater's main office wasn't big, but it was bigger than Luke's makeshift one behind the stage. There was just enough room for Dad's desk, a filing cabinet, and the two uncomfortable chairs in front of the desk. Dad kept most of the paperwork at home and transported it between his home office, the theater's office, and the resort's office. He liked having everything with him all the time. His tablet rarely left his hand, even when he wasn't supposed to be working.

I opened my mouth, but the words wouldn't come out.

"How long have you been seeing Gracin?" His words were tight.

"A while." I closed my eyes for a moment to clear my head. Then I opened them to meet his gaze. "It's not what –"

"It's not what? What I think? Isn't that your go-to line, Carly? You do something I don't like. You tell me it's not what I think and come up with a carefully constructed story to pacify me. That's how you work, isn't it? Well, that's not good enough. I want the truth, so don't try to bullshit me. I will know."

I sat up in my chair, determination taking over. This was

a war between us. He didn't trust me, and I wanted him to more than anything in this moment. He needed to know I wasn't a liar. "I'm not going to bullshit you, Dad."

"Good. Now, how long have you been seeing Gracin?"

"We started seeing each other after he was invited to Andy River's cocktail party." I took a deep breath. "We … we tried not to get involved, but …"

Dad held up his hand. "I don't need details."

"It's really not what you think, Dad."

I'd never seen my father roll his eyes before, but he did now. "What exactly do I think, Carly?"

I stretched my shoulders while I debated how to say it. Finally, I realized the truth was going to hurt me as much as him, but it was all he wanted from me. So that's what he was going to get. As delicately as possible.

"Well?" he prodded.

"You think I'm doing him 'favors.'" I air quoted the word. "You think I'm taking your directive to give him anything he wants literally. You think I'm sleeping with him to make sure he's happy so it'll be good for business. Basically, you think I'm a hooker."

His eyes grew wider while I detailed his opinion. Well, my version of his opinion anyway.

"But that's not what's going on." I swallowed hard and said the one thing I'd never admitted to anyone out loud. Tears welled in my eyes, and the pain of losing Gracin too soon froze my limbs. "I'm in love with him, Daddy. And he doesn't even know it, because we agreed this thing between us would only last until I left for school. So I can't tell him. He doesn't want a long-distance relationship, and I didn't want to not be with him. When August twenty-seventh rolls around, I'll lose him." A small sob escaped, but I held myself together for a little longer. "I'll lose him, and it was all my idea."

We stared at each other until my phone buzzed in my pocket. I didn't want to break eye contact with Dad, but Miranda might've needed me. I pulled it from my pocket.

I'm sorry. ~ G

That sent me over the edge. Gracin blamed himself for this mess, when it was all my fault. I'd pushed him to get involved with me. I'd set the deadline. And then I'd fallen in love with him despite my best efforts not to. The fault was mine and mine alone.

"Carly, look at me," Dad said softly.

I did as he asked. Dad cocked his head and stared at me, the tension draining the longer we sat there. He didn't say anything for a while.

"This has been going on that long, huh?" he asked.

I nodded. Honestly, I couldn't form a coherent sentence at the moment.

"Then I don't see why you can't keep doing your job." He scratched his eyebrows. "I'll handle Gracin's father."

Time must've stopped or something, because there was no way Dad had just said that.

"As for your relationship, continue to keep it quiet, and don't lie to me about it anymore. There's no need to flaunt it around town. That's damage control I don't need to deal with, understood?" Dad reached for his tablet and started flipping through the screen.

"Yes." I stood, wobbly for reasons other than my crutches, and moved toward the door.

Before I opened it, he cleared his throat. I turned around and met his gaze. This was the most eye contact we'd had since before I hit puberty.

"I expect you to keep up this honesty thing. It suits you." A small smile blessed his features for less than ten seconds. I relished every second.

"I will, Dad."

He may not have realized it or even have believed me, but I meant it. He wanted the truth. He was going to get it, even if he didn't like it.

I stopped at the doors to the theater and peeked inside. Gracin's performance didn't miss a beat, but he wasn't bouncing around the stage as much. I slipped inside, leaning against the wall, and listened to the rest of the show until he was ready for the encores. His upbeat songs sounded more like fast power ballads, and his ballads resonated to my soul. I wished these people who had paid good money to hear him could actually hear the real Gracin without all the shitty electronics.

My progress to the dressing room was slow, but I made it there before the final encore. I sat in his chair, exhausted from the evening's events and from crutching all over the theater. I closed my eyes while I waited.

The door opened. Gracin pulled me into his arms and buried his face in my hair.

"I'm so sorry, Carly." He kissed my hair and squeezed me so tight I could barely breathe. "Please tell me you're not here to say goodbye."

"I'm not here to say goodbye, Gracin."

He loosened his grip and leaned back to meet my stare. "Seriously?"

"Seriously. I'm here to make sure Miranda doesn't take my job. I kinda like the guy I work with."

He tightened his grip and lifted me off my feet. "Thank God."

"No, thank my father." I kissed his nose as he laughed. "Now we need to talk about your show. It's time you do something new."

The joy seeped from him, and his entire body tensed. I slid out of his arms as his grip loosened and stared into his eyes, but they hid everything. Suddenly I was faced with the mask Gracin often wore and not the man I'd fallen for.

"I'm not changing the show just because you don't like the music, Carly." He stepped around me and headed toward his wardrobe. "There's no reason. It's a success."

"But it's not you." I hobbled over to him and put my hands on his bare shoulders. "If you would let them hear the real —"

He turned around and glared at me. "The real me? Who is that anyway? Something you've conjured in your mind because who I am isn't good enough for you."

It was my turn to step away from him.

He followed me. "You've got it in your head that who I am out onstage isn't me at all. Guess what, Carly? That's all I am. It's all I've been for six damn years, and you're not going to change that. You can't anymore than I can."

I stared at him, completely dumbfounded. "Is that what

you really believe? That I want to change you into someone else?"

"It's the truth, isn't it?" he snapped.

I'd cried enough when I had told my father about my relationship, so there weren't any tears left for this moment. And this moment demanded for them. He was calling me out for something I hadn't done. Yeah, I wanted the world to see the real Gracin Ford, but he didn't. Even if I'd never taken that into consideration, he didn't have to treat me like this. Like he hated me. Like he never wanted to see me in the same room again.

"No, it's not, because you're so much more than you realize." I was wrong; apparently, there were enough tears left for me to shed. Each word accompanied a sob, but Gracin didn't flinch at any of it. Maybe I'd imagined how he really felt, because the guy who cared about me wouldn't stare like I was a poison dart and he was the target. "But if you don't want to be anything more than that guy onstage, I won't … I won't stand in your way." My chest broke open, but I had to tell him the truth. "And I can't … I can't stand with you, either."

He glared at me, breathing heavy, but not saying anything to make me stay.

"So, I guess you were right." I reached for my crutches and hobbled toward the door. Without turning around because I couldn't look him in the eye, I choked out the words I'd been dreading for weeks: "This is goodbye."

CHAPTER TWENTY

For once in my life, I followed directions given by an adult. I stayed off my ankle for the next week and stayed away from the theater. Miranda managed fine without me. When I was ready to get back into the game the last few days of July, I knocked on Miranda's door.

"Come in," Miranda shouted over the music blaring in her room. Unlike me, my sister loved everything. Music was background noise for her, but for me it was the soundtrack to my life.

I opened the door. Miranda glanced up from the fashion magazine and glared at me. I yanked my eyes away from her and took in how much her room had changed. The walls were still the same pink from her princess era five years ago, but instead of tiaras and staffs, she had cowboy hats and posters of half-naked men tacked to her wall. Sometime in the not-so-distant past, my little sister had gone country.

"What?" she snapped, drawing my gaze off a shirtless cowboy with lickable abs and back to her. She didn't even give me a chance to answer. Throwing her legs over the side of her bed, she stood up and jammed her finger in my direction. "You suck, you know that."

Did everyone in my life have to verbally smack me these days?

"Just because you and Gracin had a fight doesn't mean you just tell him it's over!" She stalked toward me, her finger finding my solar plexus and tapping out a beat to her words. "God, Mom and Dad fight all the time and they're still happy. Why'd you do that to him? He's miserable, and judging by your clothes, so are you."

I glanced down at my running shorts and stained tee. So, I wasn't dressed to go clubbing, big deal. "Then why hasn't he called me?" I whispered.

"You're the one who dumped him." Miranda tilted her head. "Right?"

I collapsed on her bed and curled into a ball. "You weren't there. He acted like I was the worst person in the world. What was I supposed to do? Forgive him?"

Miranda sat beside me. "Yep. He's a guy. By design they're egomaniacs and you slapped him in the ego pretty hard from what I heard."

"He talked about me? To you?" I sat up, pulling my legs against my chest and resting my chin on my knees.

Miranda mirrored my pose. "Yeah, he's pretty miserable, Carly. He needed to talk to someone, and you're his best friend. When you left, he kinda lost everything in a way."

"I didn't want to leave, but ..." I started sobbing. God, I was so over crying this summer. I'd spent more time shedding tears over Gracin Ford than I had over anything else in my life. "But I didn't feel like I had a choice, Meerkat. The way he looked at me, it tore me up."

Miranda wrapped her arms around me.

"And it was easier to say goodbye to him if he hated me than …" I sobbed uncontrollably for several minutes. My little sister comforted me. This was wrong. The older sister was supposed to be the comforter, not the comfortee.

"This whole deadline thing's stupid." Miranda rubbed her hand up and down my arm. "You guys are so head over heels in love with each other, and you've put a time limit on your relationship. That's the dumbest thing I've ever heard of. Even dumber is that you guys both intend on honoring it."

I wanted to laugh, because I agreed with her. We sat in her room, letting the music fill the silence, until an hour before Miranda was supposed to leave for work.

"I'm going with you," I said, getting to my feet and hurrying out of her door. "Don't leave without me."

"Only if you promise to talk to him," she shouted as I ran down the hallway to get ready.

Regardless of what had happened, I still had a job to do and money to make for school. Talk to Gracin? Yeah, when he got his head out of his ass and admitted I was only trying to help, then we'd talk. Maybe even salvage the rest of the summer. It didn't matter if Miranda thought our deadline was stupid, because it was still there. It wasn't going to change.

∞ ∞ ∞

Mom dropped us off at the theater. Miranda insisted I ride with her so I wouldn't make a grand escape on my scooter. It was a fair assessment. If things got to be too much, I'd leave in half a heartbeat. Without the scooter, I'd have to find a way home or call a cab. Either way, Miranda theorized, I'd have time to doubt my decision to run with my tail between my legs. Why she thought I was the dog in this situation defied logic, but whatever.

A few of the guys smiled as I strolled backstage. I smiled at them as my nerves somersaulted in my stomach. Despite my apprehensions, it was nice to be back at the theater. I hadn't realized how much I loved it here. Maybe Luke could manage the resort and I could take over the theater one day. I shook my head. Dad wouldn't go for it, but that didn't mean I couldn't manage a different theater. Just the thought surprised me. I always hated this place, until I got to know it. Now I can't imagine being anywhere else.

Miranda knocked on Gracin's door and waited. I held my breath until Miranda elbowed me in the gut and it whooshed out.

Gracin pulled open the door with a smile for my sister that disappeared the minute he saw me. If I was totally honest with myself, which, face it, has been a problem my entire life, I'd hoped he would see me and pull me into his arms. Totally not what happened.

"What're you doing here?" he asked. Venom rolled through my veins.

"It's her job, Gracin," Miranda chided as she pushed her way inside. "I'm just filling in, remember?"

I followed Miranda without a word and stopped when the disaster hit me full force. Gracin's dressing room had been hit by a twister. That was the only excuse for the way it looked. His wardrobe was empty. The vanity where he kept his expensive and extensive hair care collection was so disorganized someone with OCD would've had a heart attack. I didn't even know where to start.

"What?" Miranda said, grabbing my arm to steady me. I hadn't realized I was swaying. "What's wrong?"

I pointed to the vanity, then toward the pile of costumes on the floor by the wardrobe and covering the loveseat. Gracin's dressing room wasn't big to begin with, but with all his shit everywhere it was downright claustrophobic.

"Geez, Carly, relax. The world isn't going to end just because a few things are out of place." Miranda shoved my arm playfully.

Facing her, I found my voice, and it was loud. "A few things? FEMA would recommend disaster relief. What the hell, Meer?"

"Not my job." She shrugged and moved toward the door. "And it's not yours either. I'm going to Luke's office and make a few phone calls."

Not one for quiet reflection, Miranda slammed the door shut and rattled the two pictures on the wall. I took a deep breath, unsure where to start. The clothes were a priority, but so was the mess on the vanity. I headed toward the mess on the loveseat first when the odor hit me.

"Oh my God, when were these last dry-cleaned?" I asked myself.

"The last time you took them."

I jumped. So focused on the disaster in front of me, I'd forgotten Gracin hadn't left the room. My toes curled in my boots, and my fingers tightened into my palms. I couldn't bring myself to face him.

"Miranda said it's not her job, and she was right." He sighed and I heard the slight creak in the dressing table chair. "You didn't have to do any of those things either, but you did without asking. So … thank you."

"You're welcome," I whispered.

We didn't say anything as we continued to not stare at one another, but the smell emanating from the toxic pile in front of me sent me into action. I pulled my cell out of my pocket and texted Miranda to get four or five bottles of fabric freshener to me as soon as possible, as in right now. It took me ten minutes, but I found the first costume change and hung it behind the door. Miranda walked in less than a minute later, raising her eyes at Gracin who hadn't moved from his chair. I wanted to pull the top of the bottles off and pour the liquid over his clothes, but that wouldn't do anything for tonight's show.

"Miranda, you keep Gracin clothed onstage while I get this nightmare cleaned up during the show." I hung up the hated denim vest, flinching from the added stench.

"Oh, you don't need that. Gracin's not wearing it anymore." Miranda took it from me, not batting an eye at the visible green fumes. "It's ugly. I told him to wear that pinstriped one over the white tee instead. It's much sexier."

Time slowed down as I turned toward him. My adorable

little sister could suggest a change in the show, but not me. What. The. Fuck.

"Miranda, could you leave, please." I bit each word, trying not to yell at her. She hadn't done anything at all, but Gracin, oh that was an entirely different problem and it needed to be addressed immediately if I was going to seriously work around him again.

"Um … okay." My overly confident sister sounded unsure of the idea, but she wasn't going to fight it.

Gracin cocked his manscaped eyebrows and stared at me through those perfect, but not real, blue eyes.

"If I'm going to finish working this summer, and I need the money for school, we have to clear the air." I crossed my arms and waited for him to respond. He just stared at me with no expression whatsoever. I wanted to smack some emotion into him. "We had this … amazing thing between us, and you threw it away because I wanted to suggest something for your show. Yet, Miranda tells you to ditch the horrible denim vest that belongs in 1992, and it's all fine and dandy? Explain that to me, Gracin, because I've been kicking myself for a week wishing I could take it back and knowing I can't. And knowing I don't want to."

Gracin stood and strode two steps, stopping before me. I wasn't going to back down from this fight, and if he really knew me, then he knew *that*.

"So, what's the difference?" I whispered. His presence raised my blood pressure to medication-required levels.

"I threw it away?" His teeth flashed as he ground them together. Damn if it wasn't sexy as all hell. "You're the one who walked out on me, Carly. You're the one who said goodbye. Don't blame me for your decision."

"Seriously?" I closed the gap between us to get a better look at his eyes. "You were the one who …" The turmoil in his eyes threw me off.

"Who what?" The intense anger was gone, leaving his voice husky. He lifted his hands and moved them toward my shoulders, but he dropped them back to his sides before touching me. Oh God, how I wanted him to touch me right now. "What did I do?"

"You accused me of trying to change you," I said after a long pause. "When all I wanted was to show the world the guy I see, the guy … the guy who writes beautiful music in his cabin. The guy who pours his heart into songs he doesn't share. The guy who holds the door open for me or holds his raincoat over my head when it drizzles. That's all I wanted to do. I just wanted them to see Jonathan Gracin Ford." I swallowed the cotton ball growing in my mouth.

He stared at me, his lips twitching. "What if he saves all of that for you?"

I gasped as his hands slid up my arms. His skin against mine created an electric current igniting every nerve in my body.

"What if he's afraid nobody else would like the guy you see?" He squeezed me tighter.

"How could they not?"

His lips brushed mine, tentative at first. Goosebumps trailed behind his fingers as they made their way to my hair. I put my hands on his hips, pulling him against me until we backed into the door. Gracin's mouth should be nominated for sainthood, because I found heaven there.

Someone pushed against the door, but I reached down and turned the lock. The damned show could start at seven-thirty for all I cared. For the moment, I had Gracin back. And I wanted, no, needed to relish every second, because we'd already wasted too much time.

CHAPTER TWENTY-ONE

Gracin and I fell back into our routine, but when the calendar turned from July to August, something shifted between us. Again. The guillotine inched closer to end us every day.

I spread out on his couch, resting my feet on his lap while he played his guitar. We only had two and a half weeks left together. Gracin played a melody and jotted down some chords on the paper hanging half off the arm of the couch. Quite frankly, as much as I loved listening to him sing and play, I was bored. There was so much I wanted to show him but not enough time to do it all. Plus, I wanted him to pay more attention to me than the six-strings preoccupying him.

"Gracin," I half-whined. My toes pressed into the guitar, shoving it away from him.

"Let's go do something. Head to the wax museum —"

"Later. I need to get this down." He pulled the guitar closer to him, and tapped my feet until I moved them.

I sat up quickly. "I'm only going to be here for seventeen more days, and this is how you want to spend our day off?

Glad to see I'm so important."

"Carly –"

It was too late, I'd already moved toward the door and had my hand on the doorknob. The door was lighter than I remembered, or I was angrier than I thought, because I threw it open and it bounced back so fast it hit me in the ass. I let out a harrumph but kept going to my scooter. If he didn't want to spend time with me, there were things I could do without him. Hit the zipline or find a bungee cord. I started the scooter and sat there. The engine hummed its little buzz.

But I didn't drive away. I couldn't.

When I glanced back at the cabin, Gracin leaned against the open door frame in nothing but his shorts. He crooked his finger at me. It was like a fishing hook reeling me toward him. I shut the engine off and stormed back toward the door, pushing past him and inside.

I didn't get very far before he scooped me against him, pressing his bare chest into my back and trapping my arms to my sides.

"I'm sorry." He kissed up my neck and nibbled on my ear. "You're right. I wasn't thinking. In fact, your leaving is the one thing I don't want to think about, Carly."

"Because we have to …" The word stuck in my throat. I didn't want to say it this time.

He nodded against my skin, but he didn't say it either. "The wax museum sounds like fun."

I swallowed back the lump and pressed against him. "We can take hundreds of stupid pictures we'll have for the rest of our lives."

"Then we should probably get cleaned up, don't you think?" He stepped forward, pushing my legs in front of me as he moved us toward the bathroom. I let him, because I wanted as much of Gracin Ford as I could get for the next seventeen days.

∞ ∞ ∞

It wasn't hard to get people to take our photos at the wax museum or on the Duck tour. Gracin had never ridden in the vehicular boats, and when the duck moved toward the lake, he grabbed my arm and bounced in his seat like the five-year-old in front of us. It was endearing, and heartbreaking. I loved that I was the one experiencing this with him, but it hurt too. I tried to shake it off and hide it as the day progressed, focusing on the fun we were having instead. If Gracin noticed, he didn't let on. If he felt the same, he didn't let it show either.

Maybe we should've been actors.

The sunset was magnificent, as usual, and I rested my head on his shoulder as we watched it.

"Aren't you supposed to wish on a sunset?" Gracin asked.

I sat up and stared at him. "What? I've never heard of that before."

"So?" He shrugged one shoulder and glanced at me from the corner of his eye. "Maybe it'll be our thing. Every time you see the sunset, you think of us and make a wish."

I put my head back on his shoulder, contemplating his idea. It wasn't a bad one really. It would be something for just us. "Can I tell you my wish?"

"Yes," he whispered.

"I wish this summer wouldn't end." A lone tear slipped free, and I let it fall.

Gracin didn't comment. He kissed my hair and wrapped his arm around my shoulder. I wanted him to agree, but that was too much to ask. Gracin made his feelings clear before we got too involved. Just because I'd fallen in love with him didn't change anything. After this perfect day, we'd only have sixteen left. Then fifteen. Fourteen. The countdown would continue until I drove off toward Nashville, leaving Gracin and Branson a memory in my rearview mirror. A few weeks after my departure, Gracin would make his own.

We'd only be memories to one another.

∞ ∞ ∞

Dad's presence at the theater increased as Luke prepared to return to school in Chicago. Everything ran smoother with Dad around. For one, Luke liked to negotiate too much whereas Dad's stance was more "do it or I'll find someone who will." I preferred my father's approach to theater management.

The only issue I had was personal. Sneaking around with Gracin was harder with Dad constantly taking my boyfriend away to talk about one thing or another. It seemed like every single day Dad would call Gracin into his office, and they'd be in there for hours.

After a week of this, I finally asked Gracin what was going on.

"What do you mean?" He tugged his hair up, gliding gel

through his tresses so they appeared perfectly messy. Kinda like bedhead, but not nearly as sexy as his real bedhead.

"I hardly see you when we're here anymore. It's like the principal keeps calling you to his office." I tossed the day planner I'd used all summer to keep Gracin's appointments organized onto the loveseat in the corner. It bounced off the soft cushion before falling to the floor. I plopped on the seat in full pout mode. "If he had a problem, he should've said something back in June."

Gracin picked up the day planner and sat beside me. "His daughter was coming home every night back in June."

My face must've looked like a bruised apple. Over the last few weeks, I spent less time at home and more time at Gracin's. Sometimes I didn't even bother coming home. Dad never said a word, and I never lied about it. I omitted details, but I never said I was staying at Nena's or Ivy's. I would simply say I wasn't coming home. It didn't take an Ivy-league education to figure out where I was.

"Please tell me you're kidding." My fingers curled into my palms, the stubby nails managing minor damage to my skin.

"Yeah, I'm kidding." Gracin draped his arm around my shoulders. "He just wants to make sure I've been happy here."

"Oh," I sighed, relief washing over me. Dad was being the owner, not my father, in his conversations with Gracin. Understandable. He didn't want to get a bad reputation among bigger name performers. Gracin's run had brought in mega-revenue, and he needed that to become the norm or he'd have to sell eventually. Then another thought hit me, and I had to ask him. "Have you? Been happy here?"

Gracin pulled me against him and kissed my hair. It was his standard move when he didn't want to answer a question. I let myself believe he meant this in a positive way, but I still needed an answer.

"Well?"

"You know I have, Carly."

His words rolled through me, and I felt the heaviness in them. Thirteen days and that weight would sink me to the bottom of Table Rock Lake.

The show flew by, and I waited in my usual spot for Gracin to come offstage. He'd just started his first encore when someone tapped my shoulder. I glanced back to where my father stood behind me, his eyes focused on the performance.

"Have you noticed how much he's changed?" Dad nodded toward Gracin's dancing form. I followed his gaze toward Gracin before he disappeared out of our view.

I shrugged, not sure what he was getting at.

"When he first got here, he was angry." Dad's hand fell heavy on my shoulder. "Honestly, I worried about you working with him, but it was good for him." He squeezed my shoulder, and I glanced back at him again. "And for you."

Turning on the balls of my feet, I wrapped my arms around Dad and hugged him for the first time in years. Oh, there'd been casual congratulatory hugs here and there, but it had been too long since I hugged him just to hug him. He reciprocated, holding me like I was still his little girl, when we both knew that wasn't the case anymore.

"You've been through so much, Carly. A lesser person would've wilted, but not you." He pushed me back but held my shoulders as he stared down at me. "I wish I could've been there for you more." A tear glistened on his lashes. "I wish …"

My father had never cried in my life. And, now, I'd seen him do it twice in the span of a summer. Even when his parents had passed away, Dad had been drier than the Sahara. The unprecedented nature of this entire scene made the world shift under my feet. I hugged him again, grateful he was my father and not somebody else's. Yeah, we'd had a rough time over the last few years, but that was the past and we had a future to discuss.

"Dad, I …" I pulled away from him, wiping my own tears from my eyes. Taking a deep breath, I finally let him in. "I want the theater."

The song ended on the stage, and Gracin ran toward us. I held out the water bottle without taking my eyes off my father.

"What's –" Gracin began, but I cut him off with my finger. He snatched the full bottle and gave it back to me three loud gulps later completely empty.

The music started again, and Gracin greeted the audience for his final encore.

Dad decided to open his mouth. "The theater?"

"Yes." I closed my eyes, pressing them down to remind myself this conversation was real and not the one I'd been practicing for the last month. "I love this place, Dad. And Luke's going to take over the resort one day, but he sucks at managing the theater. You've spent most of your time running between here and the resort all summer as it is. Imagine if Luke tried. Things would fall through the cracks –"

"You don't know—"

"Yes, I do." I tugged at my hair, trying to not get frustrated and failing miserably. "And you do, too. Luke doesn't even want to be here. And I … I don't want to leave." Desperate for him to understand, I pleaded with my eyes. How could he not see how much I wanted the theater? "This is where I belong, Dad. This theater is what I love, what I want to do."

"You're serious?" He crossed his arms, lifting his right hand to his chin to tap it.

"U of N has a theater program. And I'll double major, theater and business." I sighed and softened my tone. "I can do this. If you'll just let me have a chance."

Dad straightened his back, turning into the businessman I knew so well. This stance meant logic and a plan. I liked a good plan. "Okay. But you'll spend your summers working here, and you'll have to work your way up from the bottom. Just like your brother will at the resort. Once you graduate, we'll determine the best course of action. It may be better for you to go to New York or L.A. to work at a few venues before coming back home. You have two years to decide if this is really what you want. If you realize the theater isn't going to make you happy, you drop the theater major and stick with business. Okay?"

"Okay." For some reason, I hadn't expected this to go in my direction. Well, not for some reason, but for the Luke reason. My brother had been groomed since birth to take over the family businesses. I was not. Neither was Miranda. How would he feel when he learned about this deal with Dad?

The second encore ended. Gracin stopped beside us, half out of breath, and stared at me expectantly. During my conversation with my father, I'd totally forgotten to grab a bottle out of the cooler for Gracin. I smiled at him, barely able to contain my excitement. Gracin smiled back, but there was a question in there. One I couldn't wait to answer.

Dad clasped Gracin on the shoulder and congratulated him on another great show before disappearing in the mass of people crowding backstage. We made our way toward the small cluster of fans so Gracin could sign autographs and have photos taken. My patience was tested. I wanted to tell Gracin about my deal with Dad. When I'd first told Gracin about my desire to take over this part of the family business, he'd told me to let Dad in on the idea. Never did he pester me into talking to my father, but he always encouraged me to be honest about what I wanted.

Standing behind him as he smiled and signed his illegible scrawl on paper and, sadly, even some forty-year-old woman's breasts, I had an epiphany. One that wasn't necessarily of the woohoo variety.

As soon as the door closed to his dressing room, he turned on me. "What was going on with your father?"

I stepped back, shocked by the hardened tone in his

voice. Regaining my composure like a seasoned pro, which I was, I attacked back. "Why? Think it had something to do with you?"

Gracin pinched his nose, slowly exhaling. He dropped his hand and stared at me, exhaustion creeping through his body. "No. I'm sorry. That's not how I meant to ask. I just … Is everything okay?"

I dropped the defenses. "I told him I want the theater."

Gracin's head shot up. "Are you serious?"

The smile spread faster as I nodded.

"That's great." He closed the short distance between us and wrapped me in his arms. Once he pulled back, his eyebrows furrowed. "Wait. What did he say?"

"I have two years to decide if this is really what I want. If it is, he may even send me to New York or L.A. or somewhere to study before I come home. Then I'll have to work my way up from the bottom. So, basically, he's onboard with the idea."

"That's great, Carly." He kissed my forehead and repeated his words.

I inhaled his sweating stench and forced out my epiphany. "Can I ask you a question? Have you ever told your father what you want?"

Gracin stiffened.

I pushed onward even though my heart said stop. My brain had taken over. Stupid brain. "I know you don't want to perform the songs you do, Gracin. Don't tell me otherwise. If you really liked that music, you'd write it." I let my arms fall away from him and stepped back. "And I know why you do it, too. I know you love the stage. And the people love you on the stage. I just …" I took another deep breath, wishing his expression would change from cold anger to something less, well, cold and angry. "The music you write is the real you. And it's incredible. People should get a chance to hear those songs. Who you are up there now is good, but who you really are is amazing. And … I just want you to be happy."

He didn't say anything for a long time. He wouldn't even look at me, but I didn't move. I wasn't giving up so easily. The anger I waited for didn't come. Instead, Gracin's face softened and the exhaustion I'd seen earlier weighed heavier on his entire being. He didn't look like an eighteen-year-old pop star; he looked like an over-the-hill singer who just needed to rest. We didn't talk while we finished up for the night. We didn't talk on the way to his cabin. We didn't talk as I settled the place for the night, making sure Gracin was in bed before I left.

As I headed toward the door, Gracin's voice drifted across the room. He said only one word, but it was the word I needed to hear.

"Stay."

CHAPTER TWENTY-TWO

August twenty-sixth slapped me the minute I woke up. My last day in Branson. The next day I would be in the Mercedes that started everything and on my way to Nashville. Knowing I'd spend my last night with Gracin, I'd come home to wake up in my bed one last time before Thanksgiving break in three months. By some miracle, my stuff had been purchased and packed. I'd done so little, my mother had taken the time to manage everything in the last few weeks. She'd take photos of things she wasn't sure I'd like and text them to me. It made shopping so much easier.

My room was cleaner than it had been in years. The boxes in the corners stacked neatly on top of each other, labeled in my mother's neat script. Further evidence of my departure. It felt more like I was moving out for good than leaving for college.

I put on my jogging clothes and hopped on my scooter. As much as I hated the stupid thing, I realized how much I'd miss it, but Miranda was set to inherit it and Dad didn't want it stolen in Nashville. Freshmen weren't allowed cars on campus, and the scooter had been my only way to get around town all summer. With the exception of Gracin's truck. A small bubble expanded inside my chest.

Parking the scooter, I stared at the cabin and took in the wash of memories it held before heading toward the door. In a few weeks, Gracin wouldn't be here either and someone else would take over the cabin. It would stop being Gracin's place. The bubble grew again, lodging in my neck.

I didn't get a chance to knock before Gracin pulled the door open. He stared at me for several minutes. The silence pressed into me.

"Ready for our last run together?" I said, choking on the words.

Gracin grimaced and nodded. We stretched, the silence taking its toll on me. My mouth opened and rattled out how much my mother had done for me. I detailed the boxes and the location, and even the stupid color of marker she'd used.

"Carly, stop," Gracin said softly. I turned toward him. "Let's not talk about that, okay? I … Let's just run."

"Okay," I whispered.

We started out, taking our usual route. The pounding of our feet on the pavement soothed me for a moment. Our breathing filled the lack of conversation between us. It was one of the things I loved most about Gracin: he enjoyed the quiet. It killed me as we ran, but this was what he wanted. And I intended to give him anything he wanted on our last day together. I needed him to remember everything about me, because there was no way I'd forget a minute of our time together.

Halfway through the run, Gracin slowed to a jog and stopped. I made it half a block, lost in my own thoughts, before I realized he wasn't beside me.

"Carly," he said as I turned around. His pinched expression propelled my legs back to him.

"Are you okay?" My eyes took in every inch of him, searching for some physical injury that would've caused him to stop. "What hurts?"

"I'm fine. I just ..." He cupped my face between his hands and kissed me so softly I thought I might have been imagining the way his lips caressed mine. "Sorry, I just needed that."

My smile was genuine, if a little pained. "Never apologize for kissing me."

We ran slower back to his cabin. I didn't want this run to end anytime soon, but it had to. Just like so many other things that were ending in my life. We walked the trail back toward his place when we usually raced it. Our hands linked, his thumb tracing circles on the inside of my palm. Stopping at his front door, he turned toward me.

"I wish you didn't have to leave." He lifted his hand and ran a finger along my jaw. Hope welled in my chest. "But I understand how much you need to see your friends today."

I nodded, swallowing the deflated balloon before I choked on it. Why had I allowed myself to hope he meant anything else? Nena, Ivy, and I had planned this last day dinner since January. They'd graciously agreed to move it to a brunch so I could have the evening and night with Gracin. I couldn't bail on them, even though the only thing I wanted to do was follow Gracin inside and lock the door until we were old and gray.

He kissed me again, touching my face as if tracing it to memory. I melted against him like butter in a cast-iron skillet.

"I'll see you around noon?" He kissed my nose.

"Yeah, noon."

Nodding, he let go and stepped inside. His eyes never left mine as he closed the door. The quiet click shattered my heart.

∞ ∞ ∞

Nena and Ivy sat at our usual booth at Burger Haven in the corner by the window. We'd claimed it freshman year under the idea that we could people watch while not being obvious about it. At fourteen, it had been sound logic. I plastered a smile on my face, faking a joy I didn't think I'd ever feel again.

"Hey, Carlsbad," Ivy said. Her eyes darted over my face. "You okay?"

"Great. Why wouldn't I be?" I slid next to Nena, avoiding her penetrating gaze. "Can you guys believe we're all leaving this week?"

Ivy scrunched one eye, but didn't push me. She knew better. "No, I can't. This summer has been amazeballs."

I laughed at her choice of wording. "Amazeballs? Really?"

Nena elbowed me. "She's been hanging out with some guy who's going to be a sophomore at Southeast. Apparently, he graduated from St. Pius last year and uses that word all the time."

"St. Pius?" I raised an eyebrow at Nena. "Ivy's falling for a Catholic guy? That's so not her."

"I know. She's more of a Methodist kinda gal, right?" Nena's lips turned into a smirk, but she cocked her head, examining me.

"Guys, I'm right here. And just because I swore off Catholics after Jimmy Weaver grabbed my boob in ninth grade doesn't mean I haven't grown and matured." Her eyes glazed over as she stirred her ice tea. "Besides, Greg said he's a recovering Catholic."

"Yeah, and I slept with the football team last year." Nena tilted her cup toward Ivy to emphasize her point.

Ivy rolled her eyes then stared at me for minute. "So, are you guys all packed?"

Nena nodded. "My room's a mess though. My last night in Branson for three months will be spent cleaning."

I closed my eyes for a minute to regain the little bit of composure I'd just lost.

"What about you, Carly?" Nena prodded. "All packed?"

"I guess." I shrugged. "Mom did it all for me. I've been … busy."

Nena's arm fell across my shoulder, and she squeezed me into a hug. "We know."

My composure crumbled as the tears spilled down my cheeks. Better to cry now than later with Gracin. He didn't need to see me like this. I put my head on Nena's shoulder, letting the sobs rack my body. Ivy slipped into the booth beside me, making this a group hug.

"I'm sorry, guys," I said, pushing Ivy off me and wiping

my eyes. "I didn't want … I didn't mean to …"

Ivy slid back into her side of the booth, laughing. Nena joined in. I didn't get it, but seeing my friends happy made me smile a little.

"God, Carly, only you would fall in love with someone you couldn't have for more than a few weeks." Ivy reached out and took my hand. Her smile was both happy and sad. "I just wish you didn't have to go through the heartbreak."

"Me, too." Nena took my other hand. "But be glad you had him."

I smiled, the tears starting again. "I am. I just want more."

With my admittance, the mood in the room shifted along with the conversation. Boys were tossed aside to discuss memories, classes, and staying in contact. The food we ordered went untouched for long periods of time, but we eventually ate everything after it cooled. I didn't care. As much as I didn't want to leave Gracin behind, I didn't want to leave my friends either. We had barely seen each other this summer, and I regretted it.

Maybe life wasn't about having no regrets. Maybe life meant recognizing those things you wished you would've done and making sure you didn't repeat the same mistakes.

Or maybe life just sucked sometimes.

∞ ∞ ∞

I got to Gracin's a little after noon. He opened the door and yanked me inside without saying hello or well, anything for that matter. It was surprising and kind of sexy. He pressed me against him, kissing my neck like ice cream dripped along it.

He stepped back, and pulled me onto the couch. I slid off his leg as he wiggled away from me. He pointed to his acoustic guitar and waited for my nod of approval.

"I've been writing this morning," he said as if that was explanation enough as he tuned the strings. "I've never played this one for you, but I want you to hear it."

His fingers moved over the strings like a caress. The chords sounded familiar and I knew the song the minute he started singing.

No regrets, that's what she said
No promises, no goodbyes,
This is the time for us,
Every second we melted
Every moment we seized,
By morning, she disappeared.
No regrets, that's what we had
No chance for more,
Memories to live on,
Memories to love on,
Something to cherish
Even as it burns.
No regrets, that's what I said,
When regrets are all I have.

His fingers continued across the strings with an acoustic solo. Each note shredded inside me, tearing me down and bringing me back up again. This song was about us, about everything, we had and wouldn't have. But did he mean the last two lines? That he regretted this summer. That he wouldn't be able to look back on us without regretting everything we had together.

God, I was so sick of crying, but I didn't know how to take this song. I didn't want him to feel this way about me. All I wanted was for him to love me as much as I loved him.

He finished and set the guitar gently on the stand. My heart seized up when my eyes met his. I traced each part of his face with my gaze. His perfect eyebrows arching elegantly over those gorgeous hazel eyes. His smooth cheeks angling toward the sharp square chin. His unstyled hair, far sexier than his overly gelled show hair. I reached up and used my finger to gently follow the path my eyes had taken.

Gracin moaned, closing his eyes as I moved along his jaw line. "Carly, please."

I moved toward his mouth, tracing his lips with the tip of my finger. He blew out a small breath when his lips parted, and I leaned forward. I didn't kiss him though; instead, I let my own heated breath caress his skin. I needed to memorize everything about him. He may have had regrets about us, but I only had one. And I wasn't about to let him see how much his song hurt me. I needed to end this day, this night on a positive. If only for my own sanity.

His eyes opened, and the heat inside could melt a thousand igloos. Gracin closed the gap between us, devouring my mouth as he took possession of me. We fell back on the couch, letting the passion take over and control us. Even if he regretted the summer, there was no way he could deny the chemistry between us, the physical heat that led us to something resembling heaven.

And I needed to make sure he would never forget.

∞ ∞ ∞

"He's a little melancholy tonight, don't you think?" Luke asked behind me.

I didn't take my eyes off the stage where Gracin sang Accentuate's power ballad. The song sucked, but Gracin made it sound new and fresh with his anguish mixed in. Doubt filled me from the afternoon's private performance. For a short while, I'd believed Gracin loved me too. That obviously wasn't the case.

"He sounds normal to me," I finally said.

Luke's hand fell on my shoulder. "Ready for tomorrow? Dad's got the Mercedes packed already. He had me help him this afternoon while you were … well, doing whatever you were doing."

I glanced over my shoulder to catch the smirk leaving Luke's face.

"You okay, sis?" He stared down at me, taking his hand off my shoulder.

Nodding, I turned back toward the stage. Gracin sang about partying until midnight. Not my favorite song either. Grips, stagehands, performers, and even the janitors stopped me throughout the evening to wish me luck at school. As much as I appreciated the kind words, the reminders stabbed me like staples stuck in the carpet. Gracin had an unusual amount of fans waiting for him backstage, taking more time away from our remaining hours. Bitterness seeped into me as I watched him smile and sign every autograph.

The hands on the clock kept moving without my consent. It was nearing midnight when we finally made it to his dressing room after the show. I paced while he decompressed.

"What's wrong, Carly?" Gracin asked from his chair.

I shook my head. If I opened my mouth, things that didn't need to be said would be said. It was better to keep my mouth shut.

He reached for me, grabbing my arm and spinning me onto his lap. "Talk to me."

"We're running out of time," I whispered, pressing my forehead into his shoulder.

He didn't say anything to comfort me. "Come on. Let's go home."

A few stragglers waited in the parking lot. Tension boiled over as Gracin stopped to sign for them. It took another hour before we climbed into the truck. I was doing everything with him for the last time.

"You could've told them no," I said as I buckled my seatbelt.

"You know I couldn't." He put the truck in drive and headed straight to the cabin, the same route we'd taken for months.

He parked in the same spot. We walked in together, for once not talking about the show. In fact, we didn't talk at all. As soon as he closed the door behind him, I wrapped my arms around him and kissed him like he was coming in from a blizzard and needed to be heated up. My anger flowed through every action. I didn't even give him a chance to protest or tell me to take it slow. I pushed him against the wall and devoured him. He needed this as much as I did. Or so I told myself.

We ended up in the bedroom, more exhausted than after any run or show. The tension hadn't left my body, but I didn't need to break down in a mess of tears. My head rested on his shoulder, and I traced the definition of his arms. Gracin squeezed me against him, kissing my forehead. He rolled me off him and stood, tugging on his boxers. I reached for the t-shirt I always wore here and pulled it over my head before following him into the living room.

He sat on the couch, staring at a small box with a red bow on top sitting in the middle of the coffee table. Smiling sadly, I strode over to where I'd dumped my bag by the front door. I took the gift out of my bag, hoping he loved it as much as I did.

"What's that?" He pointed to the plaid-wrapped present.

I pointed to the box on the table. "What's that?"

"Fair enough. Same time?"

I shook my head. "No. I want to see your face."

"Okay." He took the small box off the table and turned, tucking one leg under the other. His hands rolled the box between them. He stared at it while he spoke. "I wanted to get you something special, Carly. Something you would look at and think only of me." He raised his head, meeting my gaze. "I …" He closed his eyes and shoved the box in my hand. "Just open it."

I pulled the ribbon free. The lid lifted with a small creak.

The world stopped spinning when I saw what sat on the velvet. A silver guitar pick pendant with the words "No Regrets" engraved in cursive script hung beside a crystal encrusted acoustic guitar like the one he treasured. I ran my finger over the words, over the guitar. Tears stung my eyes again. I quickly wiped them away.

"It's ... beautiful." Taking it out of the box, I held it up. "Would you?"

Gracin reached around me, clasping the necklace in place. He ran his fingers along my neck where the chain rested against my skin, lifted the pick and guitar in his hands.

"It suits you." He smiled, letting the silver fall from his fingers.

My hand landed on the suddenly inadequate gift I'd made for him. It wasn't enough. Gracin reached for it, tugging it out from my death grip. I heard the paper tear and faced him, watching as the gift emerged.

"It's not ... It's not enough," I said.

Gracin stared at the wooden photo album cover that read "Gracin & Carly ~ No Regrets ~ Branson, MO" in my own erratic scrawl. I'd taken a woodworking class my junior year for shits and giggles. When I'd decided to make this, my former teacher had been more than willing to help. He'd done most of the work, but I'd carved our names into the cover. He opened the book. The first page was a detailed description of how we'd met, and my true reactions were totally included. Gracin smiled as he read the page.

"Don't read them all," I said when he went to turn the page.

He glanced at me before turning to a page of photos from Ivy's barbecue. "There are more?"

I nodded even though he couldn't see me. "I didn't want to forget anything about this summer, so I wrote it all down."

"This is …" He ran his hand over the photo Ivy took when we played mini-golf. Neither one of us knew she took the photo. Gracin had his putter in front of him, leaning on it as he bent toward me with one of his million dollar smiles brightening the world. My pose was similar. We looked like two people lost in one another, which we were.

"It's not enough, but –" My fingers caressed the necklace.

"Not enough?" Gracin set the album on the coffee table and moved closer to me, taking my hand away from the pendant. He stared into my eyes, and I lost myself again. "Carly, nobody's ever given me something like this before. You … You have no idea how much it means to me." Gracin pulled me toward him. "Thank you. For everything."

We sat on the couch, listening to the clock tick away our time.

CHAPTER TWENTY-THREE

I woke up before dawn. Dad and I needed to leave by nine to get to campus before five. Nashville was just over seven hours away, and Dad wanted to stop at some famous diner in Sikeston, Missouri.

Gracin rolled into me, tightening his grip around my waist. I had to be home by seven-thirty to make sure everything was packed and to have breakfast with my family. I didn't want to leave Gracin, but I didn't want to stay any longer either. We agreed we'd say our goodbyes and the morning would be time with the family. I regretted that decision, but it was the right one. Our relationship had ended last night. This tiny bit of morning I got with him was nothing more than torture.

While I debated waking him or running out the door, his eyes fluttered open. A lazy smile filled his face and disappeared almost as fast. He closed his eyes and sighed.

"For a moment, I forgot," he whispered.

I opened my mouth, but shut it quickly. Forgetting was the easy way out.

"When?" He sat up, pulling me with him.

"Soon. Too soon."

He nodded. I glanced down at the shirt I'd slept in. It was Gracin's first marathon shirt. He'd let me wear it the first night I'd stayed, and I'd worn it every night after.

"You can keep it." Gracin nodded to the shirt.

"I shouldn't."

"Please. I'd sleep better at night if I knew you were wearing that." His face turned a light pink. He turned his head away so I couldn't see his expression.

"Okay. Thank you." My stomach rolled. Our conversation had never been so awkward or uncomfortable. I didn't know what to say. I took in the room one last time.

"Do you want breakfast? Or something?" Gracin turned his back to me and stood, already wearing running shorts.

"Having breakfast with the fam." The words, forced and unwanted, weighed on my tongue. "I should … I guess I should go."

"Can I walk you out?" Gracin stood by the door to his room and ran his hand through his hair. "Damn it, Carly. Why is this so fucking hard?"

I closed my eyes, not wanting to cry again. "I wish I knew. Do you … Do you want me to leave?"

"No." His head snapped to me. "But we can't …."

Nodding, I stood and made my way toward my bag. "But if things were different?"

"They aren't." Gracin slipped his arms around my waist. "As much as I wish they were, they aren't going to change. We can't …."

"The more you say it, the harder it hurts, Gracin." I pulled away from him and took my bag to the bathroom, locking the door behind me.

Thirty minutes later, I looked more human than I felt. Gracin sat on the couch with his head in his hands, the album open on the table. I glanced at the page. It was the details of the cocktail party, the night we agreed to have only this summer. I cleared my throat, and his head shot up.

"I should ...." I motioned toward the front door.

Gracin nodded and stood. I stared at him for a moment, memorizing everything about him. He wore a black t-shirt that defined every inch of his toned body, and a pair of jeans hung low on his hips. He didn't bother with shoes.

I pulled my eyes away from him and moved toward the door. Gracin stopped me with a hand on my shoulder. I turned around. His eyes betrayed everything and nothing. The turmoil roiling through them matched my own. This was for the best.

"If only things were different," he whispered.

"If only," I agreed.

He bent down and brushed his lips against mine. "Goodbye, Carly May Reynolds."

Here was my chance to come clean, to tell him how much I cared. But I couldn't do it. It wasn't fair to him. "Goodbye, Jonathan Gracin Ford."

I ran out the door and hopped on the scooter, not looking back. Once I was far enough away, I pulled over and let the tears fall. Had I known how hard this moment was going to be a few months ago, would I have spared myself the pain? This hurt more than I'd anticipated, more than I thought possible, more than I wanted. I never wanted to let a guy into my heart, and I'd done that with Gracin, knowing it wouldn't last past summer.

This was my own doing. As much as I wanted to not experience this agony, every moment we had together was worth it. He was worth it.

∞ ∞ ∞

Leaving Gracin had taken everything from me. I didn't have any fight left when it came to my parents. I simply agreed with whatever they said during breakfast without hearing a single thing.

Miranda leaned closer to me during a particularly heated debate about where my parents thought I should eat breakfast the next day. "I'll keep my eye on him for you."

"Who?"

"Gracin, of course. I'll let you know what he's up to." Miranda smiled like this was a good idea.

"Please don't." I stared at her, hoping she understood how much pain I was in. "We promised each other … I can't handle …" Dad said my name, and I faced him with a fake smile. "Yeah?"

"What do you think?" He raised an eyebrow.

"Honestly, Dad, I wasn't listening." I put my hands on the table and stood. "I'll figure this stuff out when I get to school, okay? The world won't end if I don't figure out where I'm eating breakfast until tomorrow morning." My hand went to the necklace, and I rubbed the pick. "I'm going to check my room one last time."

Their voices drifted down the hall, but I couldn't understand anything they said. My room was packed and everything I needed for college loaded into the Mercedes. I sat at the vanity I've had since my eighth birthday. Pictures of me and Nena and Ivy were tucked into the frame of the mirror. I wanted to bring them, but I didn't. They belonged to this part of my life, not the one I was heading toward. My eyes drifted over each one until they finally met my reflection. Had I seen this girl on the street, I would've thought she was strung out on something. My eyes were hollow and my skin pale. A pair of fake fangs and a swipe of too-red lipstick and I'd make a great vampire.

I stared at the necklace. A surge of pain lifted up my chest into my throat. It had only been a few hours, but it seemed like years since I'd seen him. My eyes may have looked hollow, but I was truly empty inside. A big piece of the Carly puzzle was missing, and I doubted if it would ever be found again.

"Come on, Carly. We need to get on the road," Dad yelled down the hall.

I stood and walked out of my room, closing it behind me. Dad waited by the front door. He stopped me before I made it outside.

"You okay, kiddo?" The etched concern around his eyes made me want to lie to him, but I'd made a promise.

"No, Daddy. I'm not."

He hugged me. "You'll be home for Thanksgiving."

"That's not it," I said.

"Gracin?" He held me away from him, staring into my eyes. I nodded. "Things have a way of working themselves out, bug."

I smiled at his poor attempt to make me feel better. "Maybe."

He nodded and held out his arm toward the door. I stepped outside. Mom and Miranda stood at the end of the driveway along with Luke, Nena, and Ivy. I ran to my friends and pulled them into my arms.

"I'm not leaving until tomorrow," Ivy said through a round of fresh tears. "Nena's not leaving until Monday. No way we were going to let you go without seeing you off."

"Thank you." I squeezed them again.

"Girls, dry your eyes. I want a picture of you three together." Mom moved us into the same pose we'd done for years.

I laughed and dried my tears on the hem of my shirt.

Miranda grabbed me next, promising to stay out of my closet, which was a total lie. Luke hugged me with one arm, because he was too cool to give his little sister a real hug. Typical. Mom snapped pictures of me with everyone and made Luke take several of me with both her and Dad. I didn't mind.

"Okay, guys. We need to go. We're running late as it is," Dad announced.

I looked at my phone. Five minutes until nine. Nena and Ivy pulled me aside for another hug, but my eyes drifted toward the street. He wasn't coming. I knew he wasn't, but hope springs eternal and all that jazz. I pulled away from my friends and moved toward the passenger door. Glancing one last time down the street, I waved to everyone and climbed into the Mercedes.

"You ready?" Dad asked as soon as his seatbelt clicked.

I nodded and pressed my forehead against the cool glass. Hopefully I'd fall asleep quickly so I wouldn't have to think about this anymore. Once I was in Nashville, I could really move on. The engine cut off.

"What's wrong?" I turned toward Dad.

His eyes focused on the rearview mirror. "Someone else came to say goodbye."

I turned around to see Gracin getting out of his truck. My fingers couldn't release the seatbelt fast enough. I pulled open the door and ran to him, jumping into his arms and crushing my mouth against his.

"I'm sorry. I couldn't let you leave without seeing you one more time. I know we agreed …" His lips found mine again. "I'm going to miss you so much, Carly. You have to know… You need to know …." He pressed his forehead to mine, and the dampness on his cheeks matched mine. "You need to know how much you mean to me, how much you've helped me. God, Carly, you've made me a better person just by being with me. I can't … Nobody will ever mean this much to me again."

I reached up and put my hands on each side of his face. Staring into his eyes, I said what I should've said a long time ago. "And you need to know how much I love you, Gracin."

His eyes widened and a sad smile spread across his face. "If only."

"No regrets, okay?" My thumbs wiped away his tears.

"Never." He pressed his lips against mine. "You better go. Your dad's going to have a heart attack if you don't get on the road."

I nodded. "You'll be okay, Gracin. Better than okay."

"And so will you."

I walked backward until my ass hit the passenger door. This time it really felt like goodbye.

CHAPTER TWENTY-FOUR

I'd hoped school would be enough of a distraction, but it wasn't. My roommate wasn't a party animal or a study animal. She wasn't a terrible person, but the illusion of her ever being my best college friend had disappeared after the first day when she said she'd never heard of Merle Haggard. We co-existed from that point on.

Two weeks went by, and I hadn't really talked to anyone other than the school's therapist. And that had only been one appointment so far. I was a shell walking around, checking my cell phone for a call that would never come. It was a good thing freshmen weren't allowed cars or I would've driven home the first weekend.

There wasn't a point now. Gracin had left two days ago. Miranda had sent me an email with that update. I'd cried myself to sleep. It was the final nail in the coffin.

Dr. Snyder was cool. She had listened as I'd blubbered on about Gracin and hadn't pushed me. I'd scheduled another appointment for the following week. As much as I wanted to believe I had my shit together, it was just another lie I told myself. I'd promised Dad I wouldn't lie to him anymore, so it was time I stopped lying to myself too.

I sat at my computer, staring at the blank screen. My first English comp essay was due in a week, and I had no idea what to write about. My email siren wailed, sending a shot of bile up my throat. Every sound made me hope Gracin was the one contacting me, no matter how many times I told myself that wasn't going to happen. I swallowed hard and clicked open the browser. Miranda. The weight on my heart returned ten-fold. She probably wanted to rehash her day, and I wasn't in the mood. Then again, I didn't have anything else on my plate besides a nonexistent essay and three chapters of history to read. Miranda's email couldn't be half as bad as all that.

Hey Carly,

Okay, now that he's gone, I have to tell you something. Remember when you and G got into a fight about his show? Of course you do! Anyway, you know his last show was Monday night. He did three encores that night. For his final song, he performed something he'd written himself. It was AMAZING. The audience cried! Well, so did I. It was beautiful, sad, and haunting. Even weirder, but in a good way, it was COUNTRY. Seriously, he sounded better than most country guys on the radio. Anyway, I thought you should know that. I mean, you encouraged him to go out there with his stuff and he did.

*By the way, high school is awesome. Why didn't
you tell me how much fun it would be?*
Love ya!
Meerkat

Instead of being happy, it tore me up. He'd finally let the real Gracin out and I hadn't been there to see it. The walls closed around me. I had to get out of this room. After grabbing my tablet and messenger bag, I ran from my dorm room and down three flights of stairs until I was outside Peabody House. The weather was gorgeous, perfect for reading boring history chapters and researching an essay I didn't want to write.

I found an empty table in front of Kensington Library. The red umbrella opened to shade my books as I spread them out on the surface. Checking the time on my phone and making sure I didn't miss any texts or calls like a fool, I settled into the American Revolution. Nothing had changed since US History my freshman year.

The sun dipped behind the gothic buildings. The late summer air held a chill of fall in its breeze. I crossed my arms and kept reading.

"Aren't you in my Comp class?" a voice said.

I glanced up and, sure enough, a girl I barely recognized stood on the other side of the table. Her blonde hair swirled around her face as the wind kicked up. With the practiced hand of someone used to such hair issues, she pulled it back into a ponytail and tied it as she sat.

"Do you have any idea what you're writing about?" she

asked as she took out her laptop and a notebook. "I was thinking about doing the whole how-I-spent-my-summer personal essay gig, but Dr. Ranston might find that blasé. I mean, I spent the summer at a camp for kids suffering from AIDS, so she might not." Frustration filled her face. "What do you think?"

"I think any prof who hates kids with AIDS should retire to the Appalachians with a banjo." I kept my voice from cracking. Who the hell was this girl anyway? I didn't invite her to sit with me.

She laughed and held out her hand. "I'm Chloe, by the way. What's your name?"

"Carly." I touched the tips of her fingers and pulled away quickly.

"Major?"

Apparently, she was not to be deterred. "Theater and Business. You?"

Her eyes widened. "Interesting mix of a double major there. Mechanical Engineering here." Her shoulders fell a bit as if she just realized something. "I'm sorry. My mother's always telling me not to be so … forward, but I recognized you from class and you're always alone –"

"It's fine." I didn't want to make her suffer for being herself. My thoughts flicked to Gracin, and I cringed. "Don't worry about it."

She stared at me, a sad smile flashed on her face. "This is a lot harder than I expected, you know? I thought college would be work but a lot of fun. So far, it hasn't."

"I miss home," I blurted.

"Where's home?"

"Branson, Missouri. You?"

"Memphis. I wanted to go away for school, but not too far." She shrugged and stared past me toward the library. "So, do you mind if I study with you?"

I smiled.

Chloe and I studied until she declared herself famished, then we headed toward Peabody, where she lived a floor above me, and raided her mini-fridge. By the end of the night, I'd inadvertently made a friend. When I got back to my room, I realized I hadn't checked my phone for hours. I wasn't sure if that made me happy or sad. I glanced at it, disappointed again that Gracin hadn't tried. I'd hoped telling him how I felt would make our deal null and void.

Wasn't going to be the last time I was wrong in my life.

∞ ∞ ∞

By the end of the week, Chloe decided we needed some real college fun. To her, that meant a frat party and lots of booze. The more I got to know her, the more she reminded me of Ivy. Her energy infected mine, and I found myself seeing more of the campus than just the buildings where my classes were held.

I wasn't interested in the alcohol, but doing something other than sitting in my room on a Saturday night seemed like the best cure for a broken heart. If I stayed in my dorm, my thoughts were sure to stray toward Gracin.

We walked across campus to Greek row.

"What's with the necklace?" Chloe asked.

My hand dropped. I hadn't realized I'd been playing with it. Funny how something so new in my life had become so important.

Chloe stopped and lifted the sterling silver pick and guitar. "No regrets? Sister, we aren't going to regret anything tonight. Except maybe a hangover in the morning." She laughed at her own joke. "But seriously, what's with the necklace?"

I smiled and stepped back. The necklace landed with a thud against my sternum. "It was a gift."

Her eyes widened. "Boyfriend?"

Shaking my head, I moved around her and restarted the trek.

"Ex-boyfriend?" Chloe caught up with me.

This time I nodded.

"Let me guess, you left for school and the jackass dumped you? What a jerk." Chloe put her hand on my arm, stopping my forward progression. "I'm sorry, Carly."

A small sigh escaped. It would be easier to let Chloe believe her own story, but it wasn't the truth. My anti-lying policy was still in place. "It wasn't like that. We … It was nothing but a summer fling. We both knew it would be over when I left." I shrugged like it didn't matter anymore, because it really didn't. Gracin was in my not-so-distant past, but my past nonetheless. "It just hurt more than I expected. That's all."

"Then it was more than a fling."

Again, I shrugged and started walking again.

"Does he know? Have you talked to him since you got

here?" Chloe's short legs had to run-walk to keep up with my increasing pace.

"We agreed it would end when I left, Chloe. No texts, no emails, no calls. Nothing. Once I drove away, it was over."

"And you're okay with that?" Her voice hitched, which meant shock beyond normal human shock. If she was mildly shocked, her voice would hiccup. It was her predominant emotion.

I shoved my hands in the pockets of my jeans, fingering the fake ID I'd had since my sixteenth birthday. "I have to be."

Thankfully, we didn't discuss Gracin the last two blocks. Not that I would've heard her anyway. The music blared from each house, filling the streets with pop and country, alternative and jazz. It was a musical mess. Chloe seemed to have a good idea where we were going and led the way through the bodies cruising along Gillete. I grabbed her arm before losing her in the growing crowd. She led me up three steps and into a house where the music almost blew me out of the water.

Before I figured out what was actually going on, Chloe had shoved a bottle of microbrew in my hand. She chugged half of her own, swaying her hips to the kind of crappy music I'd endured all summer. To say it dampened my mood was an understatement.

"Hey!" She waved her arm at someone across the room. "I'll be right back, Carly. There's the guy who invited us."

I leaned against the wall, feeling more like a fool than I

ever had. After all the things I'd done in my life, a frat party was not what I thought would bring me down. I could jump off a bridge with nothing but a parachute and hope, but I couldn't stand to be in a house full of drunken co-eds.

What had happened to me?

Oh, right. Gracin Ford.

I caught sight of Chloe grinding against some guy, presumably the one she'd mentioned. My fingers found their way to the necklace. Just the memory of Gracin putting it around my neck made me shiver. I missed him more each day.

Abandoning Chloe wasn't an option, but I couldn't take the heat inside. I pushed my way through the mass of bodies and found a back door to a small yard. It was just as crowded outside with plenty of thrashing and grinding there, too. I kept moving until I discovered a relatively quiet piece of retaining wall near the house. The breeze took the scent of stale beer away. I sat, leaning against the siding.

The microbrew in my hand weighed like an anvil until I finally took a swig. I didn't owe Gracin any more sobriety. The warm beer slid down my throat. It tasted terrible, probably wouldn't have been better cold either. The song inside changed and a few girls screamed. It took me a few minutes until I recognized it. "Surrender 2 Me" by Accentuate. God, I'd hated this song until I'd heard Gracin sing it with nothing but his guitar. I lifted the bottle, draining the nasty tang of stale hops and wishing someone would break the fucking stereo.

"Not your type of music?"

I glanced up at a fairly nerdy looking guy with tortoise shell frames. In two seconds, I pegged him as someone who took his nerdiness to the level of popularity. I could respect that. His dark brown hair fell across his forehead in a happy-go-lucky way. He wore a red plaid shirt buttoned to the neck and baggy cargo shorts. Two bottles of the shitty microbrew hung from one hand.

"Or not your type of party?" he asked.

I pointed to the bottles. "Either you were planning on coming over here or you've been carrying two bottles around for a while until any unsuspecting girl needed a drink. Which is it?"

"Answer my question first and I'll answer yours." His eyebrows disappeared under his hair.

"I hate this fucking song. And if you'd asked me four months ago, this would've been exactly my type of party. Now, not so much." I waved my hand at him. "Your turn. Be honest. I'll know if you're lying."

He moved toward where my feet rested on the wall and sat down, offering me one of the bottles. "Okay, I'll play. I saw you here, grabbed two of what you were drinking, and came over."

The bottle was cold, so he wasn't lying. "Why?"

He sipped the beer, his face cringing. "God, this shit sucks. How can you drink it?"

"Don't change the subject." I took my own sip, and my grimace had to have matched his. The beer was not better cold. "But you're right, this shit does suck. Don't lie to me. Why me?"

"Wow, you shoot straight from the hip, don't you?" This time he didn't cringe when he took a gulp. He held the bottle up and stared at the label. "Maybe you need to chug it to avoid the taste and get the buzz."

I sat up and pointed at him. "One, no clichés. Two, you're avoiding my question."

"Okay, fine." He tilted his head and stared at me for a minute longer than polite company required. "One, you're beautiful. Two, beautiful girls should never be left alone at a party. Three, you looked sad. How's that? Honest and to the point."

It was my turn to stare at him.

"Or should I disappear into the crowd because your massive boyfriend is three seconds from pummeling me into the ground?"

My laughter took me off guard. "No pummeling. Not tonight."

He held out his hand. "Tagg."

"You're it?" I let my fingers grip his for the briefest of moments. Just enough to be polite without leading him on.

"No, Tagg is my name. Short for Taggert. My parents thought they were being unique, but didn't take into consideration years of torture I'd suffer at their creativity." He tilted his bottle and drained it. "God, this shit sucks."

"You said that already."

He pointed the neck of his bottle toward me. "You still haven't told me your name."

"Who said we were on a first-name basis?" Flirting with Tagg was fun, but it was wrong. I ignored the stone of guilt weighing heavier in my stomach the longer I talked to this guy.

"Ah." He nodded his head, pursing his lips. "I see how you are now. Get a guy all riled up with witty banter, let him think he might have a chance, and shoot him down like Dillinger in an alley."

Now he was just pissing me off. "First, you know nothing about me. Second, witty banter in no way means I'm giving you a chance. Third, it's not going to happen, Tagg. I'm not looking for a date or a one-night stand or anything else for that matter. Clear?"

"Crystal." He tilted his head again.

I waited for him to leave, but he didn't. He leaned back on the palms of his hands and stared at the night sky. My phone buzzed in my pocket. I pulled it out without taking my eyes off Tagg. He didn't move an inch. I glanced at the text from Chloe. Apparently, a one-night stand was exactly what she needed. For someone who'd seemed so shy a few days ago, she'd really come out of her shell. Regardless, it meant I could leave without an ounce of guilt.

"Well, Tagg, it's been real, but I gotta go." I stood up, stretching my arms toward the clear sky. Fuzziness filled my head. It'd been too long since I had alcohol, and I really didn't miss feeling slightly out of sorts.

"How're you getting back?" he asked, his gaze still on the stars.

I pointed to my boot-clad feet.

"What dorm?"

"Seriously?"

He finally dropped his head to meet my stare. "You're in one of the freshman dorms on the other side of the campus and planning on walking there. I, for one, do not intend on letting you walk alone."

"What makes you think I'm a freshman?"

"Not sharing all my secrets tonight." He smirked. "Now, what dorm?"

I almost laughed at him. "I'm a big girl, Tagg. I can take care of myself."

"Oh, it's not you I'm worried about. What if some innocent beggar comes up to you and you beat the life out of him for begging for a quarter? I couldn't live with myself if that happened." He stood and offered his arm. "If you don't let me walk you back, I'll just follow you."

I pushed his arm out of the way. "Look, you seem like a nice guy –"

Both hands clenched at his chest. "Not the nice guy line. Please. My heart can't take hearing that again."

A snicker snuck free from my lips.

He smiled and crossed his arms. "You like honesty, right?" I nodded and he continued without breaking his gaze. "Okay, here's honesty. I saw the pic on your phone. You either have a boyfriend who isn't here or you just broke up with some guy. Either way, you're not available and I'm cool with that." He leaned down like he had a secret only I could hear. "This has been the most stimulating conversation I've had with another person since I got here, so I'm not about to let this go. So I have a proposal."

That's what got me into this mess. I raised a single eyebrow.

Tagg held out his hand. "Friends?"

"That's it? Your big proposal is friends?" Something in his eyes told me not to believe him.

"Yes, friends. Can you do that? Or are you more of the loner type of girl who'd rather have the plastic recreation of a skeleton as her best friend?"

Regardless of his intentions, Tagg made me laugh. I hadn't done that in weeks, and I missed it.

I took his hand in a firm shake this time. "Friends."

"So, does this mean we're on a first-name basis now, friend?" His smile grew with each word.

"I suppose. You may call me Carly."

Tagg kissed the back of my hand, and despite everything else in my life, I kind of hoped a spark would erupt. It didn't. The relief I felt surprised me more than I expected. I wanted to move on with my life, but Gracin was fully imbedded in my heart. Nobody was bound to shove him away. No matter how much I wanted the pain to ease up, I wanted to hold on to it, too.

"It's my pleasure, Carly. Now, let's have more stimulating conversation on our trek across campus." Tagg offered his arm again. "I will be a perfect gentleman. You have my word."

"Good," I said, linking my arm through his. "Because these are steel-toed boots, Tagg. And I'm not afraid to use them."

"I have no doubt about that."

CHAPTER TWENTY-FIVE

Miranda's emails became more frequent over the next two weeks. Each subject line had one word: Gracin. At least until she realized I wasn't reading them, then she'd write "Urgent" or "Need Ur Help" instead. The minute I opened them, Gracin's name popped out at me. I didn't want to know. It wasn't like we agreed not to cyberstalk each other, but I couldn't stand the idea of him with someone else. In L.A., that was sure to happen. He had called them celebrogroupies, girls who didn't care how many stars you had as long as they got seen with you. Gracin's celebrity may have waned in Branson, but that didn't mean it didn't skyrocket the minute some paparazzi caught sight of him back in California.

Saturday, a month into my new life, Miranda called me at seven in the morning. She might have expected me to be sleeping, but she was wrong. I'd kept up my running schedule since getting to school.

"Hello?" I answered when the phone rang its old-school ring. All of my previous ringtones had been little recordings of Gracin playing in the cabin. A week after I'd checked into my dorm, I'd changed them to the default setting. His voice was too much to take every time someone called.

"Are you ever going to read my emails?" Miranda's voice broke on every other word, as she usually did when overly excited.

"If they concern a former pop star, no." I started to slide my finger over the screen when she yelled, "Wait." Putting the phone back up to my ear, I waited as requested.

"Fine, I won't talk about Gracin, but I do need to talk about something." She sighed, and I heard something else in her voice. Something sad.

"What's going on, Meerkat?" I sat on the bench outside my dorm. The sweat I'd worked up chilled quickly in the early morning breeze. Autumn was gaining momentum. Soon enough I'd have to run in sweats and a sweatshirt.

"Eddie likes someone else." She sniffled and barreled into the story. Apparently, Eddie had a crush on a new girl in school, and he'd asked her to homecoming. Much to Miranda's dismay, the new girl had said yes.

While Miranda poured her heart out, Tagg strolled toward me with his hands shoved deep in his pockets. He cocked his head when he saw me on the bench and smiled before sitting a little too close.

"I don't know what to do." A small sob echoed through the phone.

Several not-so-nice things popped into my head. A few months ago, they wouldn't have stayed there, but Miranda didn't need to hear them. She needed an honest opinion from someone who'd risked her heart and lost. God, I hated thinking of myself like that, but it was the truth.

"Meerkat, if you want Eddie, you need to go for it," I whispered. Tagg didn't need to overhear this conversation. I turned so my back was to him.

"What if he …" She didn't finish, but she didn't need to.

I sighed and gave her the advice she needed from me. It was the real reason she called. Sitting straight, I kept my voice steady although the pain seeped through me like a fresh wound. "If he doesn't want to be with you, it's going to hurt like hell, but then you'll know. And it's better to know than not know."

"What if he does, and it doesn't work out?" she squeaked.

"Then you gave it everything you had, Miranda. If you don't try, you won't know."

She breathed into the phone, heavy with the weight of her choice. Go for it with a boy she'd liked for three years or just be his friend. It wasn't easy nor a choice I ever wanted to face again. Especially because I'd lost.

"Carly, can I ask you something? But you have to promise not to get mad at me."

I inhaled sharply, knowing this wasn't a question I wanted to come from my little sister.

"Did you try? With … *him*, I mean. Did you really try?"

My eyes closed, and I had to tell her the truth. "There wasn't anything to try for, Miranda. He's on the other side of the country."

"What if he wasn't? Would you try then?"

"Yes," I said without a second's hesitation. "But he's not. So there's no point in dreaming about something that won't happen. Okay? Can we please not bring this up again?"

"If that's what you want." Her voice lifted, happier than when she first called.

"I *need*, Meerkat. I'm trying here ..." A hand touched my shoulder. I'd totally forgotten Tagg sitting next to me. "I really need to go, sis. Let me know how it goes with Eddie, okay?"

"Just check your email, and I'll keep it only about me."

I laughed as she hung up the phone.

"Sister, huh? I kinda pegged you for an only child." Tagg's hand was still on my shoulder and I shifted gently to let it fall off naturally.

"You pegged wrong. So, what're you doing here?" I scooted down the bench an inch and turned to face him. "It's a little early, don't ya think?"

"Only if you're not up for the best breakfast in Nashville." Tagg held up his hands in mock surrender. "What do you think? Can you suffer through a morning with me for the best pancakes this side of the Mississippi?"

"That's a tall order to fill, Taggert. You better be ready to deliver." I pointed as I stood and turned my back on him. "Give me twenty minutes, okay?"

"Mind if I wait in your room, or is your roommate still sleeping?" He held the door for me, forcing me to duck under his arm.

"She went home for the weekend. With any luck, she won't be back." I stopped in the middle of the stairwell, and Tagg slammed into my back. His hands gripped my hips, digging his fingers into my skin. Even though it was only to stop himself from falling, it didn't feel right. My only reaction to this smart boy was a shiver of get-your-hands-off-me. I moved up two steps to put some distance between us. "Sorry."

"No worries. So not digging the roomie, huh? Is she that big of a bitch or just that lame?"

"Neither, she's just not someone I'd choose to live with." I stopped again, remembering why I'd done it before. I glanced over my shoulder with a single eyebrow raised. "You have to promise me one thing. You won't snoop through my stuff."

"What about your roomie's?"

"Couldn't care less."

Tagg smiled wickedly and held up one hand while the other crossed his heart. "I promise to put everything back where I found it."

Shaking my head, I ran up the stairs, taking them two at a time. Tagg huffed behind me, trying to keep up. As I opened the door, my phone rang. This time I glanced at the caller ID before answering it. It wasn't a known number, but the ID flashed "California Call" across the screen. My heart froze. Could it be?

I swiped the screen and answered. "Hello?" A long pause, so long I thought he'd hung up. "Gracin?"

"Are you in debt? Consolidating your credit cards –" The computer-generated voice stabbed me with each icicle-like needle.

My phone took flight across the room, slamming into my bed and bouncing against the wall. Why the hell had I let my hopes soar? I blamed my conversation with Miranda. If Gracin lived closer or had stayed in Branson, I would've found a way to make it work. Even thinking about him gave me hope, and I didn't need that right now. I didn't need to miss him. I needed to let him go. But I didn't want to. I wanted to wrap my arms around him and tell him I loved him again. Wish in one hand, shit in the other.

"You okay? That seemed like a harsh reaction for a sales call."

I breathed deep. Damn it. I'd forgotten about Tagg again. Letting a fake laugh escape, I decided to do what I did best, crack a joke. "You should hear me when I get a real person."

"That would be … interesting." He reached for my phone and thumbed it awake. I stopped breathing entirely. "Screen's not broken." He held it up for me to see. The lock screen showed me with my arms wrapped around Gracin's neck. "Who's the bloke?"

"Nobody." I yanked the phone from his loose grip and shoved it in my waistband. Moving around the room like an errant rocket, I grabbed my shower kit and a change of clothes. "Just wait here. I'll be back in a few."

Once I was free of Tagg, I let the tears stream down my cheeks. Would this ever end? It'd been a month. I hadn't expected the pain to go away overnight, but I had thought it would lessen. A shower would help. I hurried down the hall toward the bathrooms, thankful most of my floor didn't get up before nine on the weekends.

The hot water eased the tightness in my muscles, and

washed away the tears. Would I ever stop crying over him? Even more, did I want to? Would that mean I was over him, when I didn't want to be? The answers were more elusive than a chupacabra.

When I got back to my room, Tagg sat on my bed with my photo album on his lap.

"Guess you forgot our deal?" I stood in the room, ready to kick his ass out when he glanced up at me.

"I didn't make a deal. I distracted you into thinking I did by throwing your roommate into the mix, but I never agreed to not snoop." His smug expression made me want to punch him. He pointed to the photo of me and Gracin at the cocktail party. "This the California guy?"

I nodded slowly, trying to figure out the best way to throttle him without smashing his pretty face. Even if I didn't get the warm and fuzzy for the guy didn't mean I should ruin it for any other girl.

"Can I ask you something?" He dropped his gaze back to the photo. "If he wasn't in the picture, would you give a guy like me a shot?"

Again, not the question I'd expected. Just the idea of it scrambled my brain. I'd tested the chemistry between us, and it was nonexistent. Maybe if I hadn't fallen for Gracin, I would've bagged Tagg, but I was so sick of the maybes in my life.

"Tagg, it's not that simple." I moved into the room and sat on the other bed. "I don't know what I'd be like if … It doesn't matter anyway. He's not in the picture. Not anymore."

"Because he's in California?"

"Yeah." The word came out on the wave of a sigh.

Tagg shut the album and put it on the bed beside him. "Well, then, there's only one solution to this problem." He raised his head, meeting my gaze. All the seriousness of our brief conversation was gone. Relief washed through me, and I relaxed a little.

"And what's that?"

"The solution to all the problems in the universe. Have I taught you nothing, grasshopper?" He stood with flourish and wiggled his fingers. I let him pull me to my feet, dropping his hand as soon as balance was achieved. "Pancakes. And lots of them. I promised you the best pancakes in Nashville, now I must keep said promise." He paused for a moment as if considering part of the equation that eluded him before. "Unless you don't want to."

"Friends eat breakfast together, right?" I needed to set the boundaries with absolute clear lines. Tagg needed to understand where he stood so he didn't waste his time on something that wasn't about to happen.

"Yes, they do." He headed toward the door and stopped with his hand on the knob. "And the best part? Friends don't worry about how many pancakes they eat either. And I totally plan on eating my height, if not my weight, in their fluffy goodness."

"As long as you don't need to unbutton those jeans, we'll be good." I pushed him out the door, glad to be back to our usual banter.

"You'd be surprised how many girls say that to me, Carly.

I just can't understand why." His sarcasm was a gift few people used with grace.

"That's a discussion for another day. Now, wow me with your pancakes."

Tagg shook his head. "That's too easy."

CHAPTER TWENTY-SIX

Three months, and nothing. No texts, no emails, no phone calls. I avoided typing his name into the computer. I avoided Hollywood blogs and news. If he was already seeing someone else or making waves with the paparazzi, I didn't want to know.

I stared at my roommate's empty bed. She hadn't made it past the middle of October before dropping out. I liked having a single room, but I felt bad for the girl. She'd moved out one Saturday and never said goodbye. Shaking my head, I shoved the rest of the laundry in the bag and checked my phone for the time. Luke would be here in twenty minutes or so to take me home for Thanksgiving. It'd be nice to see everyone, but I wasn't sure how I would handle the rush of memories being home would bring. That was the best part about living seven hours away. I was far enough away the memories wouldn't overload my brain every time I saw something that reminded me of Gracin. I had enough memories inside as it was.

The necklace was cool between my fingers. I let the silver

fall to my chest and closed the rucksack. Taking laundry home for the holidays was a rite of passage for college students. I imagined Mom's face when Luke and I showed up with overfilled bags of dirty clothes.

The rat-a-tat-tat on the door drew me from thoughts of home. I pulled it open, knowing Chloe would be on the other side. She liked drumming on my door.

"Can you believe it's already Thanksgiving?" Chloe rushed into the room and eyed the empty bed. "We are totally rooming together next semester. No way I'm stuck with the Shrew anymore. God, if I'm even on the phone with a guy, she's rolling her eyes and telling me I'm going to hell. I mean, hell's totally on my agenda but after college."

I chuckled as she fell onto the bed. "Too bad you have to suffer another night before heading home."

"Yeah, but it won't be long until I'm living the dream." Chloe rolled to her side and propped herself up on her elbow. "Speaking of dreams, I've been talking to Tagg."

"Not this again," I said, leaning against the door and sliding to the floor. "We've had this conversation, Chloe. It's not going to happen."

"Why not? He's a great guy. He's totally into you, and he knows why you're resistant." Chloe sighed and shook her head. Her voice softened. "It's been three months, Carly. He hasn't tried to contact you. Don't you think he would've despite your dumbass deal?"

Yeah, but the phone works both ways. Not that I'd tell her that. Not that she didn't already know.

"Look, I'm not saying you need to run off and marry

Tagg." I cringed, and she kept right on going. "Just give him a chance. Open up to him a little. You guys are great together. When he's not trying to get in your pants and you're not cock-blocking him, it's like you're already a couple. I'd give my right nipple for that kind of chance."

"No, you wouldn't." I smiled despite myself. Tagg's face crossed my mind. He wasn't unattractive, and we did get along great. Three months, and nothing. Chloe was right. I needed to move on, but with Tagg? I wasn't sure he was a one-and-done kind of guy. Hell, I wasn't sure I was that girl anymore. "It wouldn't be fair, Chloe. To Tagg, I mean. He'd only get hurt in the long run."

"Maybe he will, maybe he won't. But don't you think he knows that already?" Chloe slid off the bed and sat cross-legged in front of me. "He's willing to take the risk for you, Carly. You just need to be willing to take the risk for him." She glanced at her watch. "Oh, shit. You've got to get going. Your brother's probably waiting for you." She stood and pulled me to my feet, hugging me like we'd been best friends forever. "Just think about it, okay? Don't throw away a chance at something great for something you don't have anymore."

Chloe let herself out as I gathered my rucksack and a nearly empty pilot case. I'd be back on campus Sunday and still had clothes at home to bring back with me, so there wasn't a lot to pack. I locked my door, staring at a new message on my dry erase board. A few of the girls on my floor had wished me a great holiday weekend. A small message in the corner caught my attention.

He's the past, find your future. ~ C

Sometimes Chloe was less than subtle, but her concern made me smile. Maybe she was right, it was time to really let Gracin go. Even thinking about it made my stomach clench. I imagined what it would be like to kiss Tagg as I walked down the stairs. I'd lean into Tagg, but it would be Gracin when we broke apart. Could I really use Tagg like that? Could I intentionally hurt him just to get over Gracin?

I pushed open the door and saw Tagg sitting on the bench. He hadn't noticed me yet. I took a few minutes to observe him. His head bobbed to whatever played in his ear buds, flopping his hair against his forehead. It was probably the band we'd seen last weekend. He'd loved their sound and found their website, downloading all their songs. He lifted his hand, using a finger to adjust the oversize tortoise frames. His foot rolled to the beat in his vintage gray boat shoes. Everything about Tagg screamed "This is who I am, deal or leave." I liked that about him.

But could I love him?

Maybe someday. Maybe not.

As if he knew I was watching him, his head turned and he met my gaze. A smile slipped onto his face, spreading like a river out of its banks. I smiled back. He stood and strolled over to me, taking the rucksack and tossing it over his shoulder. Then he kissed my cheek. There was a tiny tingle. Just enough to make me think Chloe really was right.

"Hey, I thought you might need some help."

My face heated. Tagg was thoughtful. More importantly, Tagg was here. "Thanks."

We started walking toward the visitor lot where Luke had promised to meet me. The conversation was casual, just the usual chit-chat about family holidays, but the underlining tension wasn't dissipating like it normally did.

"So, did you talk to Chloe?" he asked, shifting the rucksack from one shoulder to the other.

I nodded, not knowing what to say to him. My gaze stayed on my boots. It was easier not to look at him as I decided. Why was this so damned hard? I'd never worried about hurting a guy's feelings before. Maybe that was because I knew where I stood with them from the beginning. Most of my previous relationships were nothing more than making out, and maybe more. At least until I'd met Gracin.

Was I going to compare every guy I met to Gracin for the rest of my life? Gracin didn't want me. If he did, he'd be here. Wouldn't he?

Tagg put a hand on my arm to stop me. "Just give me a chance. That's all I'm asking."

A chance. Was that really so much? I lifted my head to meet his eyes, but I couldn't. Not yet. I wasn't ready to hold my broken heart out to him. I glanced toward the parking lot, and the world stopped. A black Nissan Titan sat in the front row. My heart raced with the hope of seeing Gracin again. I glanced down to license plates. Tennessee, not California.

I closed my eyes, fighting the stream of tears that hope brought to my eyes. Even though it wasn't Gracin's truck, it answered all the questions swirling in my head. I faced Tagg, staring him straight in the eye. He needed to understand how I really felt, and that it wasn't going to change in three little months.

"Tagg, you're a great guy," I began. He rolled his eyes, but didn't interrupt me. "But I can't do this anymore. I … I love Gracin. Even if he's not here, even if he's in California with some other girl, I love him. That's not going away. And it's not fair to you. I can't … I can't hurt you." I reached up and wiped the tears from my eyes. "I don't want to hurt you, but I can't be anything other than your friend."

"I don't …" He broke eye contact and stared at something behind me. His shoulders slumped further. "You really love this guy that much?"

A sad smile broke on my face. I pointed toward the truck in the lot. "I know it's stupid to love someone who doesn't love you back, but I saw that truck and I thought it was him. I wanted it to be him so badly, Tagg. I needed it to be him. It was like I finally came alive after a three-month sleep." I turned back to my friend, hoping he wouldn't throw it all away. "I can't change how I feel. I love Gracin with every fiber of my being, and I doubt I'll ever stop loving him."

Tagg's eyes never came back to meet mine. He shook his head, still focused on something other than me.

"Do you mean that, Carly?"

That voice. It wasn't real. It couldn't be. Slowly, afraid of seeing an illusion, a ghost, I turned.

Gracin stood on the edge of the sidewalk. His hair was a little darker, and his eyes weren't obscured by the fake blue contacts. My body wanted to run into his arms, but my brain wasn't working.

"Carly?" Tagg put a hand on my arm.

I glanced over my shoulder, afraid Gracin would disappear if I took my eyes off him for too long. "I'm sorry."

Tagg nodded and set the rucksack at my feet. He backed away from me, his eyes void of his usual happiness. When he spun on his heel, I finally turned back toward Gracin.

"I … Carly, I've missed you so much," Gracin said as he cautiously closed the distance between us.

I poked his chest just to make sure he was real. I mean, I knew he was real, but I needed physical proof. Gracin pressed my hand against his chest. His heart beat in time with my own. I closed my eyes.

"I had to take care of a few things before …"

I opened my eyes, staring into his unobscured hazels. My hand slid out from his. I reached up, touching his cheek. His skin was as soft as I remembered it. God, it had only been three months but it seemed like a lifetime. I wanted to collapse against him. I needed his arms around me. But I didn't know why he was here. I didn't know how long he'd be here. I didn't know so many things.

Stepping away from him, I swallowed. "Like what?"

Gracin shoved his hands in his pockets. "Firing my manager. Hiring a new manager. Moving to Nashville. The usual."

His glib attitude didn't cut it for me. I needed more. Couldn't he see that? "Start over. Explain in detail."

"I flew to California once my run at the theater ended. Dad wanted me to do a reunion tour with Accentuate and had signed the contract for me. I couldn't let that happen so hired a lawyer and fired my father. It took longer than I expected, but it could've been a lot worse. Dad decided to go quietly instead of having his reputation ruined. If anyone found out he'd forged my signature on that contract, he'd never manage another act again." He glanced to his left before turning back toward me. "Your dad helped. Before I left, hell before you left, we started talking a lot. He helped me find the right lawyer. Remember Frank Eaton?"

I nodded. Frank had been one of the guys chatting Gracin up at Andy River's cocktail party. My mind spun like an out of control top with all this information. I still couldn't believe he was standing in front of me.

"He told me to call him when I needed a change. I called him the day you left." Gracin stepped closer. His fingers caressed my cheeks and kept me from looking away. "I wanted to get here sooner, Carly, but I needed to get my life in order first. You … you helped me see who I can be. I'm … I moved to Nashville last weekend. I've finished a demo of original songs. Frank thinks … he believes I can make it in country music."

"But why didn't you call? Text? Email?" God, I didn't want him to stop touching me.

"You told me not to." He sighed against my skin. "Miranda told me to get my head out of my ass."

I laughed. My sister never ceased to amaze me. "She's a pain."

"Yep. A good pain."

"What about us?" His answer scared me, but he was here. Did he want the same things I did?

"I don't know, but we've got forever to figure it out, don't we?" He smiled, but the fear wasn't gone from his eyes. "Don't we?"

I wanted to say yes. My eyes filled when I couldn't. Regardless of how much he wanted to wash away the last few months, it still hurt. "I ... I'm not sure." I shook my head, and his hands fell away. "You know ... You know how I feel about you, Gracin, but I don't know where I stand. I told you, and you ..."

Gracin reached for me again, clutching my waist and pulling me against him. "I need you in my life. Without you, I'm not ... I'm not complete." He pressed his forehead against mine. "These last few months have been hell on earth without your smartass remarks and beautiful face. I can't go through that again. I don't want to. Every day, I picked up my phone to call you, but I couldn't do it until I had my shit straight." He pulled his head back, meeting my eyes. "I love you, Carly Reynolds."

I grabbed his face and brought us together. His lips brushed mine, before devouring them like a starving man. Not that I was much better in the restraint department. After a very public display of affection, we finally came up for air.

"What happens now?" I asked when I caught my breath. My hands clenched his shoulders as if he might fly away.

"Well, we drive to Branson where I'll stay through Christmas." He leaned in for another quick kiss. "Your father's graciously asked me to perform during the Christmas season. And I'll be singing original songs. Frank's shopping the demo and thinks he'll get me a deal by the end of the year. If not, we're going to sell the songs. Well, except one."

"Which one?"

He tugged at the necklace, bringing the silver pick to his lips. "No Regrets."

"I've never regretted anything with you, Gracin."

"I have one," he confessed. His fingers brushed through my hair as that old familiar stone sank into my stomach. "I regret ever letting you walk out of my life without a fight. You can bet I'll never do that again, Carly. For as long as you'll have me, I'm yours."

Gracin leaned down and kissed me like we had all the time in the world. And maybe we did. I hoped so. Either way, we were going to find out.

Also by Lynn Stevens

Westland University Series
Full Count
Game On

About the Author

Lynn Stevens flunked out of college writing her first novel. Yes, she still has it and no, you can't read it. Surprisingly, she graduated with honors at her third school. A former farm girl turned city slicker, Lynn lives in the Midwest where she drinks coffee she can't pronounce and sips tea when she's out of coffee. When she's out of both, just stay away.

www.lstevensbooks.com

www.ingramcontent.com/pod-product-compliance
Lightning Source LLC
Chambersburg PA
CBHW031952120726
47898CB00002BA/347